A STUDY IN SECRETS

Also by Jeffrey Siger

The Chief Inspector Andreas Kaldis Mysteries

MURDER IN MYKONOS *
ASSASSINS OF ATHENS *
PREY ON PATMOS *
TARGET: TINOS *
MYKONOS AFTER MIDNIGHT *
SONS OF SPARTA *
DEVIL OF DELPHI *
SANTORINI CAESARS *
AN AEGEAN APRIL *
THE MYKONOS MOB *
A DEADLY TWIST *
ONE LAST CHANCE *
AT ANY COST *
NOT DEAD YET *

* *available from Severn House*

A STUDY IN SECRETS

Jeffrey Siger

SEVERN
HOUSE

First world edition published in Great Britain and the USA in 2026
by Severn House, an imprint of Canongate Books Ltd,
14 High Street, Edinburgh EH1 1TE.

severnhouse.com

Cover and jacket design by dholmesgraphic

British Library Cataloguing-in-Publication Data
A CIP catalogue record for this title is available from the British Library.

ISBN-13: 978-1-4483-1706-6 (cased)
ISBN-13: 978-1-4483-1894-0 (paper)
ISBN-13: 978-1-4483-1707-3 (e-book)

All Severn House titles are printed on acid-free paper.

Typeset by Palimpsest Book Production Ltd., Falkirk, Stirlingshire, Scotland.
Printed and bound in Great Britain by TJ Books, Padstow, Cornwall.

The manufacturer's authorised representative in the EU for product safety is Authorised Rep Compliance Ltd, 71 Lower Baggot Street, Dublin D02 P593 Ireland (arccompliance.com)

Praise for the Chief Inspector Andreas Kaldis Mysteries

"Highspeed action . . . Will keep readers engaged"
Booklist Starred Review of *At Any Cost*

"A timely mystery with an engaging cast"
Kirkus Reviews on *At Any Cost*

"Breakneck action"
Library Journal on *At Any Cost*

"Atmospheric and exciting"
Booklist Starred Review of *One Last Chance*

"Will appeal to fans of Donna Leon and Louise Penny"
Publishers Weekly on *One Last Chance*

"Engrossing"
Library Journal Starred Review of *A Deadly Twist*

"Ingenious plot twists"
Booklist on *A Deadly Twist*

About the author

Jeffrey Siger is an American living on the Aegean Greek island of Mykonos. A former Wall Street lawyer, he gave up his career as a name partner in his own New York City law firm to write the international bestselling, award-recognized Chief Inspector Andreas Kaldis series. *The New York Times* has named him as Greece's thriller novelist of record, and the Greek government selected him as the only American author writing novels that serve as a guide to Greece.

He's also served as Chair of the National Board of Bouchercon, America's largest mystery convention, and as Adjunct Professor of English at Washington & Jefferson College, teaching mystery writing. *A Study in Secrets* is the first in his brand-new Redacted Man mystery series.

jeffreysiger.com

To Barbara Zilly Siger. My best friend, honest critic, and love of my life.

Acknowledgments

Dimitris Auersperg-Breunner; Terrence, Karen, and Rachel McLaughlin; Jeffrey W. Moses, MD; Carol and Victor Raskin; Grand Master Mark Shuey (founder of Cane Masters); Alan and Patricia Siger; Barbara Zilly Siger; Jonathan, Azriel and Gavriella Siger; Rachel Slatter; and Ed Stackler.

ONE

Michael had grown quite fond of the anonymous souls who paused beneath his window. He wondered if they knew. No reason to think they did, for they never exchanged a smile, a nod of recognition, or even a word. He showed them no sign of existing in their world. That is how he wanted it to be. His time of faithful service on their behalf was long past. He had no duty to do more. He sought no more medals.

He watched them from his window through rough-barked limbs far older than anyone alive, across a well-worn road to a place just inside the entrance to a park. The park had a name, as did the tree and the road, but he simply called it the Park, ignored the road, and never thought to learn the name of the tree.

On either side of the entrance closely spaced, wrought-iron spears cordoned off the Park from an uneven flagstone walkway roughly edged up against a well-trodden grassy verge. Beyond the fence were glimpses of a neglected asphalt path rambling off into the Park and on to other entryways.

The path was wide below his window and ran straight away from him between pairs of matching cast-iron and wooden-slat benches. Every spring the slats were freshly painted green, but it was a false look and the color quickly faded, for no effort was ever made to scrape away the accumulated layers beneath. Beside each bench stood a wrought-iron lamppost topped by a pair of eagle-wing griffins gripping in their talons matching milky glass bulbs that glowed dimly through the night.

On those benches was where they gathered. The lives he watched. He didn't remember when he began watching. Probably when he stopped listening. He believed in his heart he still cared about people, but they besieged one another with such an endless rush of words, too many and too fast for him to possibly care what was true and what was not. He'd spent a career immersed in all of that, charged with culling truth from lies and misdirection. But now he chose to let the words flow past, unheard.

Besides, for conversation he had his housekeeper, Mrs. Baker.

There were so many faces he saw from his window with lives he'd never know. But for a few, he couldn't tell you their names. He wouldn't want to, for that would be a terrible distraction. Names triggered preconceived notions of their bearers and led to assumptions about their pasts that clouded the present and beyond. He couldn't bother with any of that. So, he gave them no names; he simply lived their lives.

Not their real lives, mind you, but what he envisioned them to be. He saw no harm in his simple choice to live their lives rather than his own. He only observed and imagined, sitting in his seat by the window, his cane close at hand. He changed no one. He knew he did not have that power. Nor did he know how different their actual lives were from what he invented or what meaning might lie within those differences. And, yes, he had wondered if those he watched would prefer his concocted lives for them over those they actually lived.

But that was something he couldn't imagine ever knowing.

Spring was almost here, and soon the benches would be freshly painted. Michael hoped the caramel-haired girl was careful.

For weeks now, almost every morning at dawn, she sat on the bench farthest up the path, facing east. The sunlight first struck her face, then slowly wiped the shadows from her hidden figure. He thought she was twenty or so. Hard to tell with so much of her face shrouded in hair draping on to her shoulders and running loosely braided down the back of her gray cloth coat. She wasn't tall, nor thin, it seemed. Her skin was lighter than her hair, but not by much. He thought she must be foreign. She sat quietly, waiting for the sun to clear a horizon she could not possibly see from her position. She must sense it, for she always hurried deeper into the Park after sunrise. Her patience in welcoming the sun must make her late for less serene commitments. He thought she was sad. Never talked to anyone. Just sat there. Always alone.

One morning, a week ago, a man stood outside the gate. He seemed to watch her. He was older than the girl but of the same color skin. He might be her father. But he never came in and she seemed not to notice. He simply stood and watched until she left.

Then he went off in a different direction. He'd not seen the man again or noticed anyone else show interest in the girl. If that *was* interest.

It was dawn. She was there. And it was time for Michael to return to her thoughts.

I remember watching the sun rise across the fields and the sharp scents of freshly turned, winter-hidden soil. I couldn't see my father's tractor through the deep morning mist but I'd hear it moving toward the house, then fading away as he turned his rows. He loved to say, "Take your bearings from the rising sun if you wish to plow through the haze." I'm sure he thought it profound. All fathers must say such things to their children, especially their little girls. I know he worried about me growing up in the middle of so much darkness.

She looked down at her hands. Then up and back at the sun.

I'd better go.

She hurried off, and out of Michael's thoughts.

The girl never minded sitting alone on a park bench waiting for sunrise. Some might think it dangerous, but not she. There were far more threatening things in her world. Always had been.

At least she had a coat to wear. The weather was colder here than where she'd been born. Damper too, especially on foggy mornings. Her boss had given her the coat and promised he'd get her a better one, but she doubted he would. She tugged the plain cloth coat snugly around her.

Most people she'd known didn't keep their promises. Her parents had. But they had died within sight of the freedom they'd promised her. She never knew why she survived and they hadn't. Perhaps God was testing her.

A test she'd surely failed.

Four years had passed since then. Now she's sixteen. How she managed to live this long and end up here was a mystery to her. But at least she had the coat. And a place to stay. As long as she kept her job. She pulled the coat tighter and stood.

Her work began each dawn at this very spot, with a morning stroll through the Park along always the same route. She never knew who'd be waiting for her or how many times she'd be met. No one ever said a word to her, just reached out, opened her coat, and slipped sealed envelopes into an inside pocket. That procedure had to be followed to the letter by anyone seeking to contact her boss. Attempts to hand her anything directly were refused. It was her boss's simple method of verifying that the envelopes came from sources who knew to abide by his rules.

Some mornings there'd be one encounter, other times more. There was no pattern, and unless her boss told otherwise, her instructions were always to finish walking her route no matter how many met her along the way. She'd never bothered to ask what to do if no one approached her, because her boss told her that would never happen.

But today it did.

She'd walked the route three times without a soul showing a sign of interest in her. Had she done something wrong? Would her boss blame her even if she hadn't? Lately, she'd not seen him checking on her from outside the Park as he sometimes did at random places along the route. That meant he wouldn't know she'd done everything she was supposed to do. She panicked and ran to the neighborhood diner close by the Park where she went every morning after completing her route.

Once inside, she hurried to the rear and hung her coat on a hook not visible from the front of the diner, same as she did every morning. Then she returned to the counter and sat on her usual stool, patiently waiting for whatever breakfast had been ordered for her by her boss. But no breakfast came.

She dared not speak. She was frightened. She went back for her coat, hoping to find a message in the inside pocket. But the pocket remained as empty as it was after every breakfast. She pulled on the coat and hurried out the front door.

Standing outside, she wondered what to do next. She'd entered with an empty pocket and left the same way. Her boss would be wrong to blame her, but she was certain he would. That's just the way things worked. When something goes wrong and a man's involved, she invariably takes the blame.

She only hoped he wouldn't hurt her.

She thought to run away but had nowhere to run. Returning to a life on the streets would certainly victimize her more. She tugged at her coat, fixed her eyes upon the pavement, and wondered whether she should go back to where she now stayed, the place he'd taken her to live. Without money or a protector, she had few options, all obvious, and none without risk. Prayer was not a choice. Besides, she'd given up on that long ago.

TWO

The slender, middle-aged man came into the Park only when it was busy. Michael knew this man. He knew his father well. His name was Gabriel and he sometimes seemed to sense that he was being watched. He was underdressed for the still wintry weather but did not seem to mind. Today was no exception. He must be chilly in just a pale blue shirt, Mister Rogers-style beige cardigan, and khakis. His hair was gray and never neatly combed, but he was clean-shaven and did not move as older men do.

He followed no discernible pattern, perching first on one bench before abruptly lighting on another, all the while darting his head and eyes in synch, snatching birdlike glimpses of his seated neighbors and passing faces.

He did not pause to absorb what he saw, and his glances continued until the number of passers-by dwindled to the point where he must decide it was time to move on. Michael saw him as addicted to the repetition, not unlike a player of a game of chance who sat for hours, unblinking and unaware of the world around him. They both sought the same thing—the mesmeric passing of time without the need for a single stray thought.

But Gabriel might think differently, imagined Michael.

Everyone is depending on me. I must make a decision. I am the responsible one. They are all my children. Look at them. Each face different. Each waiting for me to act. I can't let them down. But what if I'm wrong?

Gabriel leaned forward on the edge of his park bench, wondering why so many passers-by were in such a hurry. His eyes darted from one face to the next, searching for a common thread . . . some sort of explanation. To him, the Park was a blessing, a refuge from the tumult of daily life raging outside its gates.

He came to the Park every day, no matter the weather, and always first sat on the same bench. Yet rarely did anyone ever say a word to him, or even return a glance. It was as if he did not exist, and in that he found the strength he needed to persevere.

Being unnoticed was like being invisible, which meant he couldn't be blamed. It hadn't always been that way. As a child, he did whatever he could to attract his mother's attention. Making her laugh was his greatest joy.

He leaned back on the bench, crossed his legs, and brushed a smudge of dirt off the sleeve of his shirt. His mother used to bring him to play in this park. She'd play games with him among the squirrels and birds, as if they all were family. Those were his earliest memories of the Park.

He shut his eyes, hoping to clear away further thoughts of her. He did not like thinking of her. It depressed him.

He was still a child when his father died in war. He was with his mother when she learned of her husband's death and every bit of expression drained from her face. From that moment on, she lived a life of unvarying routine. Every day she went to work at the business she'd created with her husband, and every afternoon she'd walk to the Park. She no longer laughed. No matter how hard he'd tried, he could not make his mother laugh.

Finally, he stopped trying, and soon after she ended her life. He'd never know whether his efforts had given her the modicum of joy she needed to keep on living, but he never forgave himself for giving up.

Unmarried and without children, he lived his life in testament to his mother, working at her business each day, and visiting the Park each afternoon, all in penance for having failed her.

He shook his head and opened his eyes. It was time to get back to work. He popped up off the bench and headed for the gate. The mid-afternoon crowd would soon be descending on his diner.

Mid-afternoon was a busy time for the diner. Shoppers taking a break from the rigors of running up credit-card debt, cops ending their shift and looking for a place to unwind away from alcohol, workers on their coffee break in search of a better brew than offered in their office—*and* at a lower price than the slick coffee chains—all made it to Gabriel's diner at roughly the same time.

The dinner crowd would come later, a quieter group made up largely of singles tired of cooking for one and looking for an inexpensive meal and the unobtrusive camaraderie of others seeking the same.

Mornings were his busiest time. He'd arrive well before dawn, readying the place for departing night-shift workers hungry for their dinnertime meal, early birds readying themselves for a hard day's work, and all-night partiers trying to regain a semblance of sobriety before heading wherever their mornings would take them.

The diner had its regulars. Gabriel knew what they wanted before they placed their orders. His grill man did too. The moment they walked through the door, he'd see them from his perch behind the counter and start cooking their meals on the grill. Rarely did either man disappoint a customer.

This morning, though, Gabriel thought they had.

The young girl in the gray coat had showed up a bit later than usual, but she'd still hung her coat and taken her seat at the counter, the same way she had for weeks. He assumed she worked nearby but did not speak the language, because each morning when he opened the diner he'd find an envelope containing cash and a breakfast order for "the girl in the gray coat" slid under the front door.

It was a strange way to do business, but none of his concern.

The grill man had fit her routine into his own. The moment she walked in, he'd start the order set out in the morning's note and personally serve it to her, along with a quiet smile. But today there was no envelope, so he had no order to prepare. By the time Gabriel thought to ask what she might want to eat, she'd left.

He'd wondered why she'd bolted so quickly . . . why there'd been no breakfast order for her.

He sternly reminded himself that it was none of his concern.

THREE

Michael found couples who sat on the benches most interesting of all. At least one half of every couple had a motive for drawing the other away from the clatter of the city to sit amid the relative tranquility of the Park. It might be to confide, explain, apologize, beseech, promise or betray, but it was on those benches that they found their courage. From his windowed perch, he joined the birds and squirrels as unseen witnesses to seductions practiced, proposals made, breakups announced, illnesses revealed, and deaths mourned.

Sometimes magic happened on those benches. Though he often watched smiles turn to frowns, laughter to tears, and cuddles to crossed arms, he also saw sadness transform into joy, anger to hugs, anxiety to calm.

Today, a well-dressed couple in their mid-to-late thirties he'd not seen before sat sharply angled toward one another, the man's forearm rested comfortably across a leather briefcase on his lap. He showed no expression, only sat with his eyes on the woman as she gesticulated wildly, pausing only long enough to lean in and jab in his direction with the forefinger of her right hand.

Was she angry or excited? Sometimes it was hard to tell the difference. Especially when you could not hear what's being said.

You have no idea how I feel. ABSOLUTELY NONE. Worse still, you DON'T CARE. You just sit in silence, offering nothing in response, like I'm some madwoman whose rants you can barely tolerate. Don't you have anything to say for yourself? Not even a word of understanding or compassion? Nothing I say matters to you. Your only passion is your work. I almost wish it were *another woman. It would at least be a sign that you still feel some desire. But you're empty of emotions, if not a soul. Life is too short. I will not go on like this.*

That's what Michael imagined she said, and his deduction seemed confirmed when she jumped up from the bench and stomped toward the exit, a traditional ending for such one-sided encounters. The man did not budge. As the woman neared the gate, she stopped, turned, and strode back to the man. She leaned down, kissed him on the cheek, and whispered in his ear. He nodded, and she hurried off.

Michael wondered what she'd whispered. He clearly did not imagine their exchange correctly.

So many troubled souls came here searching for transformation, as if the Park were home to some mysterious, redeeming alchemy. Could it have worked its magic once again on that couple? Michael certainly hoped so, for that was why he rarely strayed from his window. He dared not miss those moments of miraculous salvation.

There were far too few of them.

The well-dressed woman flailed her arms at the sky above the Park while staring at the man next to her on the bench. "I can't believe you don't see the huge mistake you're making."

She pointed at the briefcase on the man's lap. "What's in there is earth-shattering." She jabbed her finger into the leather. "We'll never get an opportunity to do good works like this again."

The man gave no response.

"How could you possibly consider selling it?"

Still no response.

"*How?*"

The woman drew in and let out a deep breath, struggling to contain her temper. "Taking into account all that we share in common, I simply cannot bring myself to believe that you fail to appreciate the magnitude of the decision you're about to make." She leaned in toward him. "I *beg* you to rethink this. You owe it to history to be certain before you act. Surely it can wait another day."

She shut her eyes. "OK, I'm leaving now. Please, at least think about waiting."

She opened her eyes, stood, and walked toward the Park gates. Halfway there she stopped, turned and walked back to the man. She leaned down and kissed him on the cheek. "Whatever you decide, I'll be waiting for you at the diner."

The man nodded.

* * *

Near the end of the mid-afternoon rush, a well-dressed woman entered the diner and sat in a rear booth, facing the door. She fixed her eyes on the entrance, glancing every minute or so at a diamond encrusted, rose-gold Rolex on her left wrist. Gabriel stood next to her, waiting to take her order. Without taking her eyes off the door she simply said, "Coffee," and did not acknowledge him when he served her.

Fifteen minutes passed and she'd not yet taken a sip of the coffee.

Gabriel stood from his chair behind the counter, next to the cash register, and walked over. "May I freshen your coffee?"

She looked at her watch, then fixed her eyes back on the front door. "No."

He turned and walked away.

"I'm sorry. No, thank you," she said to his back.

He nodded and kept walking to his chair.

Ten more minutes passed, and the woman now was the only customer in the diner. Gabriel and the grill man stood behind the counter, speaking quietly to one another.

The woman looked at her watch, then rested her elbows on the Formica tabletop, gripped her forehead with the fingers of both hands, shut her eyes, and drew deep breaths in and out.

"Are you all right, Miss?" said Gabriel, not moving from behind the counter.

Without releasing her hands or opening her eyes, she said, "Yes. I'm sorry for taking up your booth. My company is obviously delayed."

"Don't worry about it. Take all the time you like."

She nodded and sighed. "Thank you."

Five minutes later, a well-dressed man entered the diner and walked directly to the woman's booth. He sat down across from her, placing a leather briefcase on the seat between him and a mirrored wall running the length of the booths.

"What would you like, sir?" said Gabriel from behind the counter.

The man smiled at him. "Coffee and a bran muffin. Toasted, please."

"And you, Miss?"

"Nothing, thank you." Her eyes remained fixed on the man's face.

"Where have you been?"

"Sitting on the same park bench as I was when you left me."

"That's all?"

He nodded.

"Then it's still with you?"

He patted the briefcase and nodded again.

She scowled. "You really enjoy tormenting me. Are you trying to drive me insane?"

He said nothing.

She leaned in. "You've brought me to the verge of a full-scale panic attack. I've been sitting in this booth for more than a half-hour, wondering what sort of cataclysmic decision you might be making, only to have you waltz in here without a care in the world, order a bran muffin—*toasted*—and not say a single word to me."

"Chill."

"*Chill*?" She screamed the word, catching the attention of the men behind the counter.

She clenched her fists. "That's the worst possible word you could say to me." She blew out a deep breath. "As a psychiatrist, you know that, so I'll just add this to the long list of twisted efforts on your part to manipulate me."

"Now, now, you're a psychologist, so let's not get carried away. I said there was no reason for you to come with me today, but you insisted. And there's no need to work yourself up over something that didn't happen." He lowered his voice as he placed his hand on the briefcase. "As I've told you before, we need to explore alternatives, and no matter what we ultimately decide, disposing of this without a proper safeguard is not an option."

"What sort of safeguard?"

"A method that maintains our anonymity. No telling who's out there waiting for us to make a mistake with this." He patted the briefcase. "It's pure, blind luck that you and I are the only people on earth who know we have it." He patted the briefcase again. "As long as we keep it that way, we're safe. Unlike the many others who've had this."

"You're not a criminal. You're a doctor. How are you going to find a *safeguard*?"

He smiled, reached across the table, and patted her hand. "That's why I was in the Park today. I told you I was going there to meet a courier. One who'd allow me to make anonymous contact with the perfect person to dispose of it for us. His name is—"

Gabriel appeared with a toasted muffin, packets of butter and jam, and two cups of coffee. He set them on the table. "I took the liberty of bringing you a fresh cup of coffee, Miss."

She forced a smile. "Thank you."

He left.

"We really have to be careful where we talk about this," said the man.

"I doubt a guy working in a diner in this godforsaken part of the city would have any idea what we're talking about, even if we showed him what's in the briefcase."

The man leaned across the table and locked eyes with her. "Is your life worth the risk?"

She looked away.

"No."

"Good, then keep in mind that the sort of person with the kind of knowledge or savvy that could bring us down won't necessarily be wearing Gucci, Hermes, or Rolex."

She gritted her teeth. "OK, I get it."

He picked up the muffin and took a big bite. "Like I said, *chill*."

FOUR

The tremors enveloping the girl were not of the sort her cloth coat could overcome. She stood quietly in front of a six-story, rust-stained tenement building. A windblown array of uncollected trash swept about her feet.

She'd spent the day riding the subway from borough to borough, wondering whether she should risk returning to the top-floor walkup she shared with two other girls.

They were the type that any day could up and leave and never return, offering no goodbyes or explanations. She was used to that. In her world, people disappeared off the streets all the time and no one seemed to notice, much less care. There was always someone new to replace the departed.

She wondered whether she'd be the next to disappear.

She sighed as she pulled her keys out of the pocket of her jeans.

At least the apartment had locks to protect her from random predators looking to prey on those with no choice but to live on the streets. She was no Pollyanna and knew that real dangers lurked within the building, but they were the predictable sort that she'd long ago learned to avoid, or at least survive. What gave her pause now was none of that, but rather what might await her *in* the apartment. She'd still not heard from her boss; by now he'd be fuming at her. It was after five, and she was supposed to spend her afternoons waiting for him to stop by the apartment to verify how many pickups she'd made that day in the Park.

She climbed up five crumbling concrete steps to an equally shoddy landing and a badly weathered front door. As she reached with her building key for the lock, the door swung out and a huge black hound lunged toward her, driving her stumbling back down the steps.

"Sorry about that, angel," said the young man, pulling the dog back hard on its leash. "She's just anxious to get out." With his free hand he held the door open, and she hurried inside, not saying a word.

Angel. No one had called her that before. Not since her father died. She liked that name, though it wasn't hers.

She thought of her father as she climbed the flights of stairs, stepping over a junkie asleep in his own urine on the second-floor landing, ignoring the false moans of hookers turning tricks in their third-floor brothel, paying no mind to the stares of gang-bangers running the fourth floor as part of their drug-dealing operation, passing through the ceaseless hum of sewing machines of the fifth-floor sweatshop, and stopping at the far end of the sixth floor in front of a dented and scratched, battleship-gray metal door.

She put her father out of her mind and listened for sounds from within. She heard nothing. Still, her hand shook as she reached for the lock. She turned the apartment key, held her breath, and pressed against the door.

It swung inward but came to an abrupt halt after opening slightly. She pressed harder but the door wouldn't budge, so she wedged herself inside with her back to the door, then turned to see what was blocking the door.

Seconds later, she gathered together her few possessions and fled the apartment.

If her boss was angry over her unsuccessful morning pickup, his anger had died in that doorway with a single bullet in his forehead. She wanted no part of whatever had gotten him killed and could only hope that no one wanted any part of her.

Each evening, Gabriel locked the front door to his diner promptly at nine, a not-so-subtle prod to lingering customers to finish up and be on their way. After, he'd retreat to his apartment above the diner and reflect on his day before preparing for bed.

He'd once hired a couple to keep the place open 24/7, but that was a short-lived experiment. Almost immediately, he'd found that the boisterous, all-night partiers who took advantage of those hours served mostly to keep him awake.

Long days were nothing new to him. He'd learned that life from his mother. She'd even bought the building from their landlord to ensure they could always live above the business.

A locked door at the rear of the diner opened on to a dimly lit stairway leading to a second door at the entrance to the apartment. Its rooms reflected his mother's taste, and he kept them that way, not as a monument to her, but out of an utter lack of interest in such things. A table was a table, a chair a chair, and a bed a bed. Everything else was decoration, about which he cared not a bit.

He poured himself a glass of wine from a gallon jug set on a doily at the edge of an oak sideboard and settled into an overstuffed Chesterfield chair still covered in throws collected by his mother. He didn't feel like reading tonight, so he didn't bother turning on a light. He took a sip of wine and stared into the light seeping in from the street.

He liked sitting in the dark, reflecting on his day.

Today's business had covered his expenses. That made it a good day. Plus, most of his customers had paid in cash, making it an even better take. These days, paying his employees in cash was the only way he could afford to keep them. Cash simplified things for everyone, except of course, the government.

He took another sip of wine. The well-dressed couple from the afternoon intrigued him. Initially, he'd pegged her as revved up to play a 'hell hath no fury like a woman scorned' scenario with her tardy partner, but once the man showed up, their interaction didn't strike him as a lovers' spat. Perhaps it had something to do with the man's briefcase. Both of them seemed to relax whenever he patted it.

Strange.

Strange, too, how he paid.

He'd paid in cash, leaving a fifty for a meal costing five. Paying in cash can keep you anonymous but tipping as the man had guarantees you'll be remembered.

Oh well, just another thrilling day in a lifetime of waiting on the public.

He finished off his wine and headed to his bedroom.

And tomorrow I get to do it all over again.

Who in their right mind would risk spending the night sleeping on a park bench? thought Michael looking down from his window perch. The dim light from the lampposts wasn't enough to make out a face. There was barely enough light to see that the faceless shape still breathed . . . beneath a gray cloth coat.

Could it be the young woman? he wondered. The coat is hers. She must understand the danger. Something terrible must have happened for her to dare spending the night alone in the Park.

He thought to call the police. But that might make things worse for her. He shouldn't intervene without knowing her reason for being there. Not that he'd ever know . . . for he'll never meet her. He can only watch. Which is precisely what he'll do. All night, if necessary.

His body trembled as his mind flashed through images of colleagues and friends who'd suffered horrors and death at the hands of the ruthless, while he survived. He would not now risk adding to those nightmarish memories by involving himself in the actual lives of his anonymous imagined souls.

But he would make a phone call. To someone he'd not spoken to in decades.

After fleeing her apartment she'd wandered the streets until well past midnight. Her roommates must have found the body by now. She wondered how they'd reacted. Maybe they'd noticed that she'd taken her things and decided to leave as well.

Or maybe they'd called the police. She should have done that. But experience had taught her that nothing good ever came of interactions with the police. Her roommates felt the same way.

Then again, maybe they had called the police—and blamed her for the dead body. After all, the fact that they'd stayed after she'd fled would seem to be proof of their innocence.

Maybe everyone's gone and the body's still on the floor and will be until someone notices the smell and calls the police.

But maybe no one will ever call the police. No one in that building wants the police there. The gangbangers would know how to get rid of a body. Maybe they'll take care of it.

Her mind kept looping through the possibilities until one seemed as likely as all the others. She needed time to think, and a place to do it clearly. She paused by a familiar locale, perhaps the only place in the city where she'd ever felt comfortable.

She knew the dangers of hanging out in a park at night, especially for a girl alone. But on her bench beneath the lampposts she'd always felt safer than anywhere else, as if guarded by the ever-vigilant iron griffins above.

She sat, waiting for answers to come. But none did. God, she was tired. She decided to lie down, only for a moment. She closed her eyes and, while her mind drifted to thoughts of her father, her body drifted off to sleep.

She awoke at first light, her face tucked up against the rear of the bench, her side aching from a night spent upon its hard, wooden slats. It was nothing compared to the pain she'd endured on other nights alone on the streets. She listened for sounds but heard only birds. It was a chilly, damp morning, yet she felt warm and secure beneath the heavy blanket.

Blanket.

She bolted upright, staring down at the white wool blanket trimmed in broad green, red, yellow, and indigo stripes.

"It's called a Hudson's Bay blanket. That one's something of a collector's item."

She stared at a man sitting on the bench across from hers. "Who are you?"

"The person who gave you his mother's blanket to keep you warm and stayed with you all night."

"I didn't need your protection."

"I didn't do it for you. I did it to protect my blanket."

She almost smiled. "I think I know you."

"We've had breakfast together many times."

"You're the man from the diner."

He nodded.

"How did you know I was here? Why are you helping me? What do you want from me? Who—"

He held up his hand. "I'll answer all your questions, but later. Now that you're awake, I've got to get back to the diner. Come along and I'll buy you breakfast."

"I can't go there."

"Suit yourself, but from the way you left my place yesterday morning, I'm willing to bet you haven't had anything to eat in quite a while."

He stood up, walked over to her, and held out his hand. "I'll need my blanket back."

She bit her lip.

He smiled. "Come. It's only for breakfast. What else do you

have to do this morning? Besides, it's the only way you'll get answers to your questions."

She didn't respond.

He shrugged, took the blanket, and left the Park without looking back at the girl.

She followed a few paces behind.

Back at the diner, he pointed for her to sit in a booth near the back. "I think you'll be more comfortable there than sitting at the counter. No need for you to order, we know what you like." He nodded to the grill man, who smiled and waved to the girl.

She nodded at him but didn't smile.

"Things will be pretty busy in here for a while, but don't worry, just sit in the booth, have as much breakfast as you'd like, and we'll talk once the rush is over. OK?"

She hesitated. "OK."

"Good." He walked behind the counter and, with a wink to the grill man, said loud enough for her to hear, "Let's give her the most memorable breakfast ever."

Over the next hour and a half, the place was packed with customers eating in and taking out. The grill man looked to have five sets of hands, while the waiter bounced from customer to customer, taking orders and delivering food. The middle-aged man kept an eye on it all, pitching in where necessary, filling half-empty coffee cups, helping the busboy clear away dirty plates, and manning the cash register.

In the midst of all this madness, food kept coming to the girl's table. After rounds of orange juice, milk, eggs, bacon, hash browns, pancakes, fresh fruit, and yogurt, the girl told the waiter, "Please, no more."

That's when a hot-fudge sundae arrived. She'd worked her way through most of it by the time Gabriel dropped on to the booth seat across from her.

"How was breakfast?"

She nodded. "Really good."

"Best ever?"

She nodded, and he yelled to the grill man, "Bravo, Gee, you did it again. She loved it."

Gee smiled and gave a thumbs-up.

Gabriel looked back at the girl. “Would you like something else?”

She waved her hands in front of her. “No, no, please. I’ll be sick.” She dropped her hands to her lap and stared at him for a moment. “Why are you being so nice to me?”

“It’s not me. I’m not nice. I’m doing it because someone asked me to help you. And he’s paying for your breakfast.”

Her eyes darted around the room, panic seemingly blooming in her chest.

“Whoa, don’t worry. It’s no one in here, or for that matter anyone you know or even knows you.”

“What are you saying?”

“An old friend of my mother lives across from the Park. He saw you sleeping on the bench and was worried something bad might happen to you, so he called me and asked if I’d check on you.”

“How did you know it was me?”

“I didn’t, but like I said, he’s an old friend of my mother, and also a very good customer. I had no choice but to go.”

“But you brought me a blanket.”

“That wasn’t for you, it was for me. But when I got to the Park, I saw your gray coat and knew it was you.”

“And rather than using it to keep you warm, you gave it to me. See, you were being nice to me.”

He blushed. “No, it was just good business. I knew my customer could see us from his window, and if I’d kept the blanket for myself, it would have angered him.”

“So, I’m wrong. You’re a selfish bastard,” she said with a slight twinkle in her eye.

He leaned in across the table. “Now that we’ve settled that point, do you care to tell me why you were sleeping in the Park?”

Her face blanched. “I lost my apartment. I had no other place to sleep.”

“Where do you plan on sleeping tonight? Please don’t tell me in the Park.”

She picked at her sundae with a spoon. “I don’t know. I’ll find some place.”

“Look at me.”

She raised her head.

"What can I do to help you?"

"I could use a job."

"How old are you?"

"Twenty-two."

"Don't lie to me. How old are you?"

Her eyes welled up with tears. "Sixteen."

"Any family?"

"They're all dead."

He paused. "What's your name?"

She chewed at her lip. "Angel."

"Mine's Gabriel. Stay here. I'll be right back."

Her voice cracked. "Where are you going?"

"Don't worry, it's for something good. Just stay here."

He left, and she shut her eyes.

Go or stay ran through her mind. She had no idea what to do. Both frightened her.

A clatter of plates in front of her startled her. Gee pointed to a plate of croissants and a cup of coffee he'd placed on the tabletop.

He smiled. "Stay is better."

"Hello?"

"Mr. Michael, it's Gabriel from the diner."

"Yes, I wondered when I'd hear from you. I saw you leave with the girl at dawn. I commend you for spending the night as her protector. Thank you for responding to my request for assistance."

"That's why I'm calling you."

"If it's about the costs, just add them to my bill. They'll be paid by my bank in the normal course."

"No, that's not what I meant. The girl's sixteen, an orphan, and has no place to stay. She needs help."

"What can I do? I don't know her."

"Nor do I," said Gabriel. "But since you're the one who had me spend my night in the Park watching out for her, that makes you, not me, her Good Samaritan."

"I don't get involved in other people's lives," Michael said sternly.

"Great. I don't either, but now you've involved us both."

Michael cleared his throat. "As far as I know, neither of us has ever been a parent, and speaking for myself, I can't remember the last time I spoke to a sixteen-year-old, nor can I imagine what either of us could possibly do to help this child bring order to her life."

"My guess is, helping is like riding a bicycle," said Gabriel. "And today's as good a day as any for you to start up again."

"I never liked bicycles. Besides, I'm much older than you are."

"Not to mention far more dramatic."

"You're as difficult as your mother."

"Ah, we finally agree on something. Let's build on it."

Michael paused. "What do you have in mind?"

"Talk to her," said Gabriel. "She's willing to work, and with your connections and experience, you might come up with a way to help her."

"If she's willing to work, why don't you hire her at your diner?"

"I can't even afford to offer her a job as a dishwasher."

Gabriel heard a deep sigh on the other end of the phone.

"This is all highly unusual . . . bring her here in one hour."

"Thank you, Mr. Michael. We'll see you then."

Gabriel put down the phone, leaned back into the well-worn Chesterfield, and stared at a simply framed photo of his mother on the sideboard. "I haven't seen your friend Michael since your funeral. Some say his old war wounds finally caught up with him, mentally and physically. Others say he's just a crazy old eccentric. I guess I'm about to learn the truth."

He stood and headed toward the stairs leading down to the diner. In an hour, he'd be rid of the girl and back to his normal routine.

Gabriel's voice reminded Michael of Gabriel's father, and his quick and convincing repartee brought back memories of Gabriel's mother . . . before her husband died. None of them was the same after his death. Including Michael. He'd lost his best friend and begrudgingly resigned himself to the wishes of a perpetually grieving widow who wanted nothing to do with anyone who reminded her, or her son, of her husband. When she passed away, her son showed no interest in resurrecting a relationship with Michael, and to be honest with himself, nor had Michael tried.

He wondered what led him to reach out to Gabriel last night for help. And wondered even more why he agreed to meet with Gabriel over the fate of a girl barely known to either of them.

He sighed. Perhaps his age had played a subtle role in softening his attitude. After all, with neither man having family of his own to survive them, this could be a heaven-sent opportunity for reconnecting with his best friend's son.

Michael turned to look at a photograph in a silver frame. *We shall see.*

FIVE

Gabriel chatted with Gee for a moment before joining Angel at the booth. He sat across from her while she looked anywhere but at him.

"The man who asked me to keep an eye on you at the Park last night. He wants to meet you."

She began shaking like a puppy, still not daring to look him in the eye.

"There's no reason to be afraid."

She said nothing, still trembling.

"As I told you before, the man's an old friend of my mother's. He served with my father in the war." He paused. "He came back . . . my father didn't."

She looked at him at last. "How old were you when your father died?"

"A few years younger than you."

Angel looked away again. "So, you were about my age when my father died."

"Yes, that's how I know how you felt."

"How could you?" She didn't lift her eyes. "Your father died a brave soldier, mine a brutalized refugee. I never got to bury him. Or my mother. She died with him."

Gabriel patted the tabletop lightly. "You're right. Two very different experiences, *except* in one respect." He waited until she looked up. "Your father and mine left us to find our way without them. I chose to honor his memory by watching out for my mother. Whether or not I made the right choice is a fair question, but I made a conscious decision to do what I thought honored his memory. I think it's time you did the same."

"You sound like one of those social workers who work with runaways."

He laughed. "Trust me, I'm not." He leaned in across the table. "Michael—the man who wants to meet you—has led a very different life from mine and yours. He's in a much better position to help you than I am. And I promise there's no danger in meeting him. Certainly nothing of the order of whatever has you so spooked."

Angel clenched her teeth. "I'm not spooked."

He nodded toward Gee. "I don't know if you've ever been formally introduced to Gee, but he told me that while I was upstairs, every time the door opened, you practically jumped out of your skin." Gabriel stood. "Come, let's go. You can't sit here forever. Nor, I suspect, do you want to."

Angel slowly rose from the booth.

He offered her what he hoped was an encouraging smile. "I'm sure we're both in for a fascinating experience."

The nearer they came to the Park, the closer Angel stayed to Gabriel, her eyes darting from doorway to doorway and fixing on every passing face.

"Are you looking for any one in particular?" he asked.

She didn't answer, and he didn't ask again.

"Here we are."

They stood in front of a Gilded Age four-story townhouse, its rusticated brownstone facade rendered even more austere by ornate wrought-iron bars fitted snugly over its arching parlor-floor windows.

They made their way up a ten-step stone stoop to a massive, ebony-stained door surrounded by elaborate, foliated molding. Gabriel pressed a lone button beneath the house number: 221.

He turned and looked across the street toward the Park. "He must have a clear view of your bench from the upper floors."

Angel stood silently focused on the door. The moment it opened, she stepped inside, not waiting to be invited by the gray-haired fireplug of a woman who'd opened it.

Gabriel exchanged smiles with the woman. "We're here to see Mr. Michael. He's expecting us."

The woman opened the door wider. "Please," and gestured for him to enter. "He's one floor up, in his study at the front of the house. Do you want to take the stairs or the elevator?"

"We'll take the stairs," said Gabriel, taking Angel by the arm and leading her across an intricately patterned, polished marble and parquet-wood foyer toward a broad staircase. They passed between emerald-flocked, wainscoted walls lined with paintings of classic scenes, crystal sconces, and a clutter of antiques of varied styles and descriptions.

Angel's eyes took everything in, but she said nothing.

"Impressive, huh? I haven't been here since I was a child. But it all looks about the same as I remember it."

Gabriel gently held Angel's arm as they climbed the stairs. He dropped his hand when they reached the next floor.

"As I recall, Mr. Michael's study is down there." He pointed down a mahogany wainscoted hallway to a matching, floor-to-ceiling, six-panel cross-and-bible door.

She didn't move.

"Go ahead, he's expecting you." Gabriel waved his hand in the direction of the door.

She shuddered. "I don't want to do this."

"There is no *this*. He just wants to meet you. *If* he offers to help you, it's up to you to decide whether or not to accept it. It's a simple choice, Angel. Talk with him or walk out of here right now and back to your life on the streets. I know what I'd do but, as I said, it's up to you."

Tears began welling up in her eyes.

He put his hand on her shoulder. "There you go again, acting like a scared puppy. Some folks must have treated you really badly." He patted her shoulder. "I think it's time for you to take a leap of faith and trust someone." He lifted his hand from her shoulder. "If it makes you more comfortable, I won't leave. I'll wait out here while you're inside." He paused. "OK?"

Angel bit at her lip, nodded, and stepped slowly down the hall toward the door.

Gabriel whispered after her, "Don't forget to knock. And this time, don't step in until you're invited."

She stopped at the door, drew in and let out a breath, and knocked lightly once.

A deep voice on the other side of the door bellowed, "That sounds like the knock of an angel. Come on in, dear, there's nothing to be afraid of."

She hoped he was telling the truth.

* * *

"Welcome, Angel. That is your name, yes?"

She hesitated, then nodded at the silver-haired elderly man dressed in a jacket and tie seated behind the desk.

"No matter if it is or isn't, it's a lovely name that suits you." He gestured toward a pair of ornately carved, highly polished wooden chairs sitting in front of the similarly carved desk.

She stood at the edge of a deep rose and blue silk Persian carpet, her gaze drifting around the study.

In a softer voice, he said, "Please, child, come sit."

She hesitated before tentatively stepping on to the carpet and slowly walking toward the chairs.

"I expect you can see that I'm into old things. The place is pretty much the same as when I moved in. The woodwork is original. I added the rugs. All the dusting, polishing, and vacuuming they require drives my housekeeper crazy. But she's been here almost as long as I, so I guess some might say we've grown crazy together."

Angel fixed her eyes on a photograph sitting in a silver frame atop the credenza behind him.

"I see you have a sharp eye for detail." He spun in his desk chair, picked up the photo, spun back, and as Angel sat, handed her the frame.

"Do you know who they are?"

She stared at the image of two strapping men in military uniform, a woman and a boy. She shook her head and, at barely a whisper, said, "No." She handed it back to him.

"How would you? None of us is as we were then." He stared at the photograph. "I'm the young handsome chap on the right, next to the boy. The couple on the other side of him are the boy's parents." He sighed. "They're both dead."

"Is that Gabriel and his family?" she asked, reaching out for the photograph.

He nodded and handed it back to her.

"They look like nice people."

"Gabriel's father was my best friend." He hesitated. "I'm Gabriel's godfather."

She put the photo down on the desk. "In my culture, that's an important obligation."

"Mine too. Especially once his mother passed away, leaving him with no family."

"We both are without family."

"Do you mind if I ask how you lost yours?"

She looked down at her hands. "I was born in a rural village. My first memories were happy ones. My mother and father paid for me to be schooled. It's how I first learned to speak your language. Then came the violence, and everything changed."

She talked of her family, their efforts to survive in their village, the random violent deaths, the violations of family members and friends, the decision by her father that the family flee, the months spent trekking in search of a place of refuge, and the more than a year they'd spent in filthy, violent, overcrowded camps. She recounted the death in a camp of her baby brother, her father's desperate gamble to trust their lives to human smugglers, and the fatal journey in which all her family but she perished.

"I was twelve then. Now, I'm sixteen. Do you want to hear what I've been through in those four years, sir?"

All expression had faded from his face. He shook his head. "No, I've heard enough."

"Would you like me to leave now that you've heard my story?" Her voice held the tiniest hint of a challenge.

He leaned across his desk. "I did not ask Gabriel to bring you here to amuse me. I have watched you sit in the Park each morning at dawn for weeks and imagined what your life must be like. I was wrong about the details, but not about the spirit I saw in you. You've suffered greatly, and I suspect, still are."

"I find ways to get by."

"I'd say your life depends a lot on fate."

She shrugged. "I've been lucky."

He nodded. "That's good. But sleeping on park benches at night seems an unnecessary test of your relationship with luck."

"I do what I have to do."

He pushed himself to his feet from behind his desk and took up a blackthorn cane from beside the credenza. "I returned from war without a left foot. Like you, I was lucky. Many didn't return at all. But unlike you, I decided to test my luck by taking risks with greater financial rewards than that which comes from sleeping on park benches."

He limped around the desk, his trim athletic frame aged but

still there. "Now I get to do whatever I want, including sharing my luck anonymously with strangers who I believe could use some. In your case, you may not need any of mine, because you appear to have your own supply."

He sat in the chair next to her. "But I think you need to learn how to wisely spend your luck. Because once it's gone . . ." He shook his head and let the thought hang out there.

"What do you mean?"

"I think you need to find a place where you feel safe and can focus less on 'getting by' and more on creating a better life for yourself."

She smirked. "You and Gabriel both talk like social workers."

"I'll take that as a compliment, because they tend to know what they're talking about."

"But their talk never works."

"That's generally because of two things: an unwillingness on the part of their clients to be helped, and insufficient funding to implement the advice. I'm prepared to offer you the latter, if you're prepared to commit to the former."

She pointed at her chest. "You're going to pay me?"

He nodded.

"For doing what?"

"Hard work. Not so hard as to prevent you from going to school, but hopefully hard and worthwhile enough to keep you from being caught up in whatever it was that had you sleeping on that bench."

She did not respond.

"My proposal is this. My housekeeper needs help. You'll move into an apartment on the garden level and do whatever she asks you to do. She has Sundays off, so you'll get Saturdays. Beyond that, you'll work out your schedule with her. Your meals will be included, and I'll pay you the going rate for the type of work you'll be doing. Of course, we'll supply you with new clothes suitable for one working in this household."

Angel stared, her mouth wide open. "Why are you doing this for me?"

"I honestly don't know. I spend so much time over at that window, staring at lives foreign to me," he gestured toward binoculars mounted on a tripod, "that I've lost all context for how life is actually lived these days." He scratched his cheek. "Perhaps I see this as my chance to go back into the real world."

"But you have Gabriel."

"I haven't spent time with him in years. Other than watching him from my window."

"But he's your godson."

"After his father died, I tried to treat him as such, but his mother was so tortured by her husband's death that she couldn't accept me playing anything close to a paternal role. By the time she passed away, he'd grown up knowing me as only a neighborhood friend of the family." He jiggled his cane. "But in my own way, I've taken care of him, though he doesn't know it. All the orders I put into the restaurant are my way of helping, because I know he's too proud to accept money from me." He grinned. "It makes my housekeeper angry. She says I order too much food and never eat it, leaving it instead for her, which is why she's gained so much weight. If you come on board, you'll not only share her workload, but also the food. That should make her doubly happy."

Angel bit at her lip. "I don't have any references."

"That's honest of you to say, but I didn't expect you to. Just tell me this, are you wanted by the police?"

She blinked. "Not that I know of."

He studied her face.

She did not look away this time.

"So, when can you start?"

"As soon as you want me to."

"I assume you'd prefer sleeping in a room here tonight rather than on a park bench?"

"Yes, sir."

"Fine, then let me speak to my housekeeper so we can organize things for you to move in today."

"Thank you, sir." And for the first time in a long time, Angel smiled.

Angel found Gabriel sitting on a plush upholstered bench at the end of the hallway closest to the stairs.

"So, how did your meeting go?"

She smiled openly. "He offered me a job and said I could live *here*."

Gabriel grinned back at her. "You must have really impressed him. When do you start?"

"He's talking about that now with his housekeeper but said I could sleep here tonight."

"Ah, Mrs. Baker. She's a good customer of mine. Picks up food from the diner almost every day. I guess that'll be your job now."

Angel's smile vanished. "I can't do that."

Gabriel patted the seat next to him on the bench. "Come, sit here."

She shuffled over and sat.

"What has you so frightened? Is it the man who's been paying for your meals all these weeks?"

She shuddered. "No, it's not him."

"Then why are you afraid to come to the diner?"

"I'm worried about the other people who expect me to be there every morning."

"What people?"

She shook her head. "I don't know."

"And what would happen if they found you there?"

She shut her eyes and bowed her head. "I don't know. I can't risk it."

"What sort of risk are we talking about?"

"I don't know."

"If I understand you correctly, you can't accept this life-changing opportunity because of some unknown risk, from unknown people who may or may not be looking for you between here and my diner."

"You make it sound silly, but it isn't."

"I'm sure it isn't." Gabriel looked up at the ceiling, shook his head, and exhaled. "I'm going to hate myself for saying this, but here goes." He looked straight at her. "If you take the job, when Mrs. Baker places an order for you to pick up, I'll arrange to have it delivered to the house. OK?"

She leaned over and kissed him on the forehead. "No matter how you think about yourself, you really are a nice man. Thank you."

"You're welcome," he whispered back.

The door at the end of the hall opened, and Mrs. Baker stepped out. "Young lady, please come in here. You too, Gabriel."

"Me?"

"Yes, Mr. Michael wants to see you."

She led them to the two chairs in front of the desk, then stood next to Michael, facing Angel and Gabriel.

"It's been a long time since we've been together, Gabriel."

"Yes, sir, a very long time."

"The fault's all mine. I see you every day in the Park, sitting on the same bench where your mother always sat, and somehow that makes me feel we're still in touch."

Gabriel offered a sad smile. "I know what you mean, I sometimes notice you at your window."

"How are you doing?"

"About the same as always."

"I hope that's a good thing."

"It's a living."

Michael smiled. "You and your protégé seem to have a similar attitude toward life." He nodded at Angel.

"She's not my protégé. And I don't sleep in the Park."

Michael raised his hand. "I meant no offense."

"None taken." Gabriel shifted in his chair. "But I should say that you likely know more about her than I do. So, please don't consider me as vouching for her. This act of kindness you've offered her is one hundred percent your doing."

Michael nodded. "If that's how you wish me to look upon this, that's fine with me." He turned to Mrs. Baker. "So, Mrs. B, now that Gabriel has clarified that the decision whether to help Angel is strictly up to us, what's your opinion?"

Angel's eyes fixed nervously on Mrs. Baker.

She raised her hands from her sides, patted the tight bun of her hair, and crossed her arms over her broad bosom. "From the way she barged into the house, I'd say she needs to work on her manners. And from what she's been through, I doubt she's trustworthy."

Michael nodded, and Mrs. Baker continued. "She's led a dog-eat-dog life on the streets that's likely turned her into a thief who'll bite the hand that feeds her the first chance she gets."

When Mrs. Baker was finished, Angel appeared on the verge of tears, but said not a word as every eye in the room fixed on her face.

Gabriel broke the silence. "But what do you *really* think, Mrs. B?"

She didn't smile at the joke, keeping her eyes on Angel. "I'm a sucker for unwanted puppies, but if they're not trainable and can't break bad habits, I've no use for them."

"So, what is it, Angel?" asked Michael. "Are you trainable? Are you trustworthy?"

Angel's jaw tightened. "Do you expect the untrustworthy to say 'No'?"

"Watch your tongue, young lady," warned Mrs. Baker.

"She does have a point," Gabriel said with a smile.

Michael raised his hands. "Enough of this *My Fair Lady* routine." He turned his chair in the direction of Mrs. Baker. "Since she'll have to work with you, Mrs. B, I think it's only fair that I leave the decision on whether to hire her in your capable hands."

Mrs. Baker and Angel locked stares, neither breaking away.

"I'll tell you this, Mr. Michael," said Mrs. Baker, breaking off eye contact. "This pup has spunk. I think she's trainable."

Angel's taut expression dissolved into tears. "Thank you. Thank you. I—I promise you won't regret it."

"Let's hope not," said Mrs. Baker.

"Godspeed to you both," said Michael.

SIX

Dr. Brackett Fielding III spent much of his late morning sitting on the same park bench as he had the day before. The tooled leather briefcase clutched snugly to his side bore the same BF III monogram as the pale-blue shirt cuff protruding from the sleeve of his camel-hair topcoat. Today, though, he sat alone. Marilena's anxiety was simply too contagious. Not to him, for he'd trained himself to be immune to such weakness, but he could not risk her interfering with his plans again.

He'd told Marilena of his intention to connect with a courier here yesterday, and the importance of appearing calm. He'd patiently explained how couriers are a breed that existed to be sacrificed should something go wrong, their survival depended upon caution. Still, she'd insisted on coming, and she couldn't help bringing her anxieties along with her. A skittish deer among hunters is how he envisioned the courier. He would not risk Marilena spooking the courier a second time.

His gaze wandered down the path to the gate leading out of the Park, and across the road to fix upon a row of classic townhouses reminiscent of the neighborhood's long ago fashionable past. Some were shabby, some were not. They might be good real-estate investments, what with once iffy city neighborhoods drawing pioneering artists and avant-garde style-setters, followed by developers sensing vastly profitable opportunities.

He looked down at his briefcase, patted it, and smiled. *Why ponder speculative investments when what's in here's a sure thing?*

His mobile rang.

"Hello."

"Where are you?" barked an agitated Marilena. "Your patients are wondering why you canceled their appointments."

He crossed his right leg over his left and picked at a bit of lint on his charcoal-gray wool trousers. "What is the point of your call?"

"Do you think I'm a fool?"

He sighed. "Please, let's try to avoid getting into your insecurities."

"It's not about me. It's about you."

He shook his head and looked at his watch. "OK, talk to me."

"You are such a condescending prick."

"Tsk, tsk on the name-calling."

"You want a name? Well, here's one for you. *Dante Carlucci.*"

Brackett bolted upright on the bench. "Where are you?"

"Oh, so now you want to know where *I* am. My, how quickly the roles reverse."

"*Stop it.* This is serious."

"More so than you can imagine."

"Where are you?"

"In that diner from yesterday, the one close to where I'm guessing you are."

Brackett ended the call, jumped up and stormed for the gate. Five minutes later, he raged into the diner and headed straight for Marilena.

"Coffee and a toasted bran muffin?" asked Gabriel from behind the cash register.

Brackett ignored him as he dropped on to the seat across from Marilena. "Are you insane, saying that name over a mobile phone?"

"You're the psychiatrist. Why don't you tell me?"

"How did you know that name?"

"You mean . . ." She mouthed but did not say, *Dante Carlucci.*

Brackett's lip twitched. "Stop playing games."

She rolled her eyes. "We share an office, and through an extraordinary bit of unexpected good fortune, we also share something of priceless value—"

He crossed his arms in front of his chest. "Is this where you tell me you don't trust me?"

"No. My work has me continually dealing with the untrustworthy, and I don't consider you among them."

"Then what *are* you trying to say?"

She shook her head and leaned across the table. "You were absolutely right yesterday when you said we're caught up in something that could get us both killed. But what you don't get is that you're into something way beyond your skillset, and it's your arrogance that's going to do us both in."

He clenched a fist. "Are you done?"

"Almost. When you unilaterally announced yesterday that you'd taken it upon yourself to find us a 'safeguard,'" she used finger quotes for emphasis, "but never got around to telling me who you had in mind, I worried you might do something that would get us killed."

Brackett pounded his fist on the tabletop. "I *know* what I'm doing."

The man behind the cash register jerked his head toward their booth.

"Everything's OK, sir. My friend's just a bit dramatic about ordering. He'd like that coffee and muffin." She smiled at Brackett and whispered, "Stop being such an asshole."

"Just tell me how you got the name."

"It wasn't that hard. Yesterday, you went to the Park to launch your grand plan to protect us. But it didn't happen. You didn't make contact. So, this morning when you didn't show up at the office, I assumed you'd gone back to the Park to try again, no doubt blaming me for your unsuccessful first effort. I took that opportunity to see what I might find in your office, and lo and behold, sitting right out there on your calendar was the name Dante Carlucci."

"You had no right to go through my calendar."

"It's your anal-retentive notetaking that left his name out there for anyone to find. I don't consider that being careful."

He fumed silently.

"So, who's Dante Carlucci?"

"One of my patients mentioned him a few months ago in a session. He operates an auction business for disposing of valuable items that preserves the anonymity of the buyer and the seller. The only way to reach him is through a courier."

"Hasn't this auctioneer heard of telephones or the Internet?"

He shook his head. "He discourages electronic communications. He believes they're too easy to intercept."

"Why the Park?"

Brackett shrugged. "No idea, but my patient told me a female courier in a gray cloth coat circulated through there every day. The coat was a sort of uniform. It's how Carlucci's clients could identify his courier. I figured if I sat there long enough, I'd see her and pass along a letter asking Carlucci to take it to the next step."

"And you expected to make all these arrangements without describing what we have, or exposing our identities?"

"There's no need to worry. It'll all be done anonymously."

Marilena sighed. "Thank God you *figured* wrong."

He narrowed his eyes. "What does that mean?"

She reached into her bag and pulled out a newspaper. "Truth is, the name Dante Carlucci didn't mean anything to me when I first saw it on your calendar. But it all fell into place after I read the paper, something I assume you haven't done."

She spread the newspaper out between them on the table and turned to a story in the metro section. The headline read, *Gang Violence Claims Another Victim*.

"Dante Carlucci was murdered yesterday in a tenement not far from here."

The color drained from Brackett's face.

"Here you are, sir," said Gabriel, putting a toasted bran muffin and coffee down next to the newspaper.

Brackett said nothing, his eyes fixed on the article.

"Would you like anything else?" asked Gabriel.

"No thank you," said Marilena. "I think he has more than enough on his plate to digest for now."

So far, Gabriel's most interesting customers of the day were the same customers from yesterday. This time, though, the man appeared nervous and angry, the woman calm and in charge, and neither left a big tip. If Gabriel had to bet on a reason for the dramatic role reversal, he'd put his money on something in the newspaper the woman had pulled out of her purse.

Curiosity always got the better of Gabriel, and he wished they'd not taken the paper with them. But they had, and so he put it out of his mind.

On his afternoon stroll to the Park, Gabriel passed a trash can with a copy of that same newspaper edition plopped down on top. He wasn't a dumpster diver, but his curiosity wouldn't let him pass it up. Without breaking stride, he deftly lifted the newspaper and tucked it under his arm. He held off looking at it until comfortably seated on his favorite bench.

He found the page he'd seen the man reading and saw the gang-violence story. It said a man had been found dead in a nearby tenement notorious for all sorts of criminal activity.

No surprise, he thought. *Better there than out on the street.*

He didn't recognize the name of the victim, and there was no photograph. What gnawed at Gabriel was the couple from his diner did not seem part of the victim's world, yet by the man's reaction to the article, he had to have known the victim. Perhaps an estranged relative? Drugs dragged people down without regard to their social or economic rank.

He read the article's final line: "Police are looking for any information on a young woman believed to have lived in the apartment and observed leaving the scene on the night of the murder wearing a gray coat."

His eyes instinctively jumped from the page to Michael's window. Seconds later he was on his feet racing out of the Park, crossing the street, and pressing hard on the brownstone's buzzer.

Mrs. Baker opened the door, and Gabriel stormed inside. "I need to see Mr. Michael immediately."

Mrs. Baker raised her nose and looked down at him through her glasses. "Barging in like this makes me wonder if Angel didn't pick up her bad habits from you."

"I'm sorry, Mrs. B., but this is urgent. I need to talk to him immediately."

She waved him in the direction of the stairs. "He's up in his study."

"Where's Angel?"

"In her room."

"Fine, keep her there." He hurried up the steps, and five seconds later knocked on the study door.

"Come in."

Gabriel opened the door, stepped inside, and closed the door.

"Well, this is a surprise. I don't see you in my house for decades and now you visit me twice in one day." Michael gestured toward the chairs in front of his desk. "To what do I owe this second visit?"

Gabriel strode to the edge of the desk and handed Michael the newspaper, pointing at the story. "Read this. I just saw it a couple of minutes ago." He dropped into one of the chairs, his eyes focused on Michael's face as he read the article.

Michael read the article without expression. "This is troubling. I think we need to speak to Angel."

"I think we need to call the police."

"We may, but I think we owe it to Angel to hear her side of the story first. Bringing in the police could destroy her even if she had nothing to do with the victim's death."

"But she was living in that building."

Michael nodded. "Yes, which got her off the streets. As I said, I think we need to hear her side."

Gabriel raised his hands in a sign of surrender. "She's living in your house. I leave that call to you."

Michael picked up the phone on his desk and buzzed Mrs. Baker on the intercom. "Mrs. B., would you please have Angel come up to my study. Thank you." He put down the phone and looked at Gabriel. "Any other interesting news?"

"Not of this magnitude."

"How did you find the article?"

"A couple in my diner yesterday came back today, and when the woman showed the newspaper to the man, he fell apart. I couldn't resist getting a look at what she'd given him to read."

"What did the man and woman look like?"

Gabriel described them.

"They sound like the couple I saw in the Park yesterday. Today, I saw only the man."

A knock came at the door to the study.

"Come in."

Angel peeked through the doorway. "Mrs. B. said you wanted to see me, sir."

"Yes. Please come sit next to Gabriel."

Angel smiled at Gabriel as she sat down, but when he didn't return her smile, alarm spread across her face. "Is something wrong?" she asked Michael.

Michael leaned across his desk and handed her the newspaper. "Please, read this story."

She took it, and the moment she read the first line, she shut her eyes and dropped the paper into her lap. "I should have told you."

"Told us what?" said Gabriel.

"About where I was living, about what I had to do to stay there, and about finding the body when I went back to the apartment. That's why I was sleeping in the Park. I was afraid that I might be killed too."

"Please finish reading the story," said Michael.

Her hands shook as she read it to herself. "Oh, no, the police are looking for me. I'll be killed for sure."

"Why would you be a target?" asked Gabriel.

"Because whoever killed my boss for what he did might want me dead for the same reason."

"That man was your boss?" asked Michael.

"Yes."

"What precisely did you do for him?"

Angel described every detail of her daily routine, starting at dawn each morning on the bench in the Park and ending with breakfast in the diner, followed by her waiting in the apartment for her boss.

"I'd say you're one very lucky young lady, Angel. If you'd received a message on your morning route, and your boss hadn't neglected to give Gabriel your regular breakfast order, you'd likely have gone back to the apartment to wait for him. I hate to think what might have happened to you had you been there when the murder took place."

"Are you telling me that my diner was part of whatever got Carlucci killed?" Gabriel asked.

Angel shook her head. "I don't know. All I know is that every morning after I left the Park with whatever strangers put in the pocket of my coat, I'd hang my coat up in the back of your diner, have breakfast, and when I got my coat, the pocket would be empty."

Michael looked at Gabriel. "Sounds to me that if she goes to the police and tells her story, she's not the only one who'll be in trouble."

Gabriel bristled, but Michael held up his hands before Gabriel could speak. "I'm not saying that you did anything wrong, but the circumstances are going to require you to get a lawyer, and once the story gets out, your diner will get a lot of press. Whether that'll be good or bad for business I leave for you to decide. But one thing's for certain: if Angel's right about her life being at risk for what others think she might know, I assume you're at risk for the same reason."

Gabriel drew in and let out a deep breath, then looked up at the chubby cherubs merrily prancing about the pale blue trompe-l'oeil ceiling. "Ah, Angel . . . I wish I could blame this all on you. But I'm afraid we're both caught up in a mess not of our making." He dropped his eyes back to Michael. "So, what do we do about it? Just ignore it and pray it fades away?"

"That would be nice, but I'm afraid there are too many moving parts to safely leave your futures to fate."

"What moving parts?" asked Angel.

"Let's begin with the obvious. Your coat and hair. I've no doubt that your description is known to everyone who used Carlucci's services. You've got to change it all and give up your habit of sitting in the Park at dawn."

"Well, that's easy to do," said Gabriel. "What other moving parts are we talking about?"

Michael leaned back in his chair. "Those are far more complex, and I'm not nearly as sure about how to address them as I am with changing Angel's appearance. But what bothers me most is that couple from your diner."

"How so?" said Gabriel.

"For two days in a row, at least one of them was in the Park; both times the man clutched a briefcase and struck me as looking for someone. But I had the impression it wasn't for someone he knew. He focused too long on faces. And from what we now know of Angel's pickup schedule, he could have been looking for her but at the wrong time."

"Or maybe he was in the Park at the wrong time because he wasn't looking for her."

"I'd agree with you except for one thing." Michael paused. "The couple's reaction to the murder of Carlucci. Do you have any idea who they are?" he asked Angel.

"No," she said.

"I might," said Gabriel. "The initials on the guy's briefcase were BF III, and he called the woman Marilena. Come to think of it, she paid me by credit card, so her name should be on the receipt."

"Not very careful of her." Michael drummed the fingers of his right hand on the desktop. "If you can get me her full name, perhaps I can make some gentle inquiries into whether coincidence or something else is responsible for their crossing paths with Carlucci."

Angel looked at Gabriel. "I'm sorry I got you involved in this."

"You didn't get me involved in anything. Carlucci put the bullseyes on our backs. And if it weren't for you, I wouldn't even know."

"That's right," said Michael. "Get me that woman's name," he told Gabriel, then turned to Angel. "And you, young lady, go tell Mrs. B. to cut your hair. You can decide what color you want to dye it, but don't make it unusual. After all, you're trying to hide, not attract attention."

Angel stood and hurried out the door, pausing only to say a tearful, "Thank you."

After she'd left, Gabriel fixed his eyes on Michael's. "I have only one question."

"Which is?"

"Why?"

"Why am I doing this?" asked the older man.

"Exactly. All you need do to put this mess behind you is call the police, or if not that, tell the girl to leave your house immediately. You do realize you're making yourself a target by getting involved."

Michael nodded. "I do, and your concern is much appreciated." He paused. "I've done a lot in my life, though not much in recent decades beyond donating to causes I think worthy, and giving anonymously to souls I see in need of a helping hand." He hesitated, then sighed, "And yet, throughout those years I could not bring myself to undertake any effort that might require me to personally intervene in another's life."

Michael gazed off in the direction of the photograph of Gabriel's father. "If I am honest with myself, I'm an old man without family, who carries far more serious wounds in my mind than my body. They are the wounds that haunt my thoughts and hold me a recluse."

He turned his head toward the window. "For weeks I watched Angel spend each dawn sitting on the same park bench. I imagined who she might be, what she was doing there. Though I was wrong about what she was up to, I felt as if I'd come to understand her and, when we met, she was exactly as I'd envisioned." He shrugged. “I took that as a sign for me to trust my instincts, take a risk on her, and get back in the real game.”

“It could be dangerous.”

Michael smiled. “That’s why it’s called real.”

SEVEN

Angel sat barefoot on a straight-back chair, staring into a full-length mirror at her reflection and that of Mrs. Baker standing behind her.

Angel pressed her toes against the tiny white bathroom floor tiles and suppressed an urge to leap to her feet.

"Are you OK?" asked Mrs. Baker.

Angel bit at her lip. "My mother used to cut my hair. I haven't cut it since she died. It's . . . it's how I honor her memory."

Mrs. Baker patted Angel on her shoulders. "I'm sure your mother would far prefer that you honor her by not risking death over a haircut. After all, isn't that why your parents fled their home, to give you a better chance at life?"

Angel focused on the marble hexagons beneath her feet. "I know. You're right."

"Good, now take off your top, so we can get started."

Angel hesitated.

"Dearie, please don't tell me you're modest. I don't want to get hair all over that nice new blouse Mr. Michael had me buy for you."

"It's not modesty."

"Then what is it?"

Angel didn't answer, only pulled the blouse off over her head.

"Oh, my Lord," said Mrs. Baker, staring at rows of crisscrossing scars running down Angel's back. "Are they painful?"

Angel drew in and let out a deep breath. "No, not those." She paused to swallow. "I was eleven when my father paid traffickers to get us across the border to safety. The night we met them to make the crossing they demanded more money from my father. He refused, so they beat him. He still refused, so they whipped me until he paid. And even after he did, they beat me more."

"You poor child."

"They did worse things to my mother. In front of us all."

Mrs. Baker shut her eyes for a moment, then reached for a pair of scissors on a towel next to the sink. "Mr. Michael also has scars."

"He said he lost a foot in war."

"He has other scars, and like yours they're the kind you can't see, but still pain." She began clipping away at Angel's hair. "He, too, was tortured, but for information, not money. He lost his foot, one toenail and one toe at a time. Had he not been locked in a basement cage when an aerial bombing raid destroyed his captors and their building, they'd have killed him for sure. As it was, the air raid left his body riddled with shrapnel, and by the time friendly troops found him, infection had taken hold in his foot. He spent over a year in hospitals and rehabilitation." She kept cutting. "But even with his injuries, he remained on active duty in the intelligence services."

"You mean he was a spy?"

"He prefers the term patriot."

"Where did you meet him?"

"I was his nurse during his recovery. When he was released, he offered me this position."

"As his housekeeper?"

She smiled. "He likes to call me that, but we're more like confidantes. Two misfit loners united by a common attitude toward life."

"What does that mean?"

"I lost my little girl and husband in a road accident to a drunken driver. The driver got away with a fine and three months of community service." She snipped particularly hard at a long lock of hair. "But back to Mr. Michael . . . For years he drove himself close to madness trying to determine how his captors knew when and where to kidnap him. Finally, he found his answer, and it turned out to be the worst discovery of his life. He'd been betrayed by a member of his own team. If that weren't bad enough, his commanding officer had learned the identity of the traitor almost immediately but covered up the episode afterward to protect himself."

Mrs. Baker tousled Angel's hair with her free hand and snipped away with the scissors in her other. "That's when Mr. Michael decided to withdraw from the world. It didn't deserve him."

"Is that how you feel, too?"

"Life sure keeps trying its best to convince me that's the way to go." She gently ran the fingers of one hand along the scars on Angel's back. "Especially when I see things like these scars." She smiled. "But every once in a while, I run into someone who makes me think there's still hope for us." She put down the scissors. "So, how do you like your new look? I haven't given a haircut in years, but from what I see on the streets, I think it's in style."

Hair that once ran three-quarters of the way down Angel's back, now stopped in tapered ends at the level of her chin.

"It's not me."

"I'll take that as a compliment on a job well done. Now, on to picking a color."

"What's available?"

Mrs. Baker held up a bottle. "Dark brown or dark brown. Though we could call it chestnut, if you prefer."

Angel shut her eyes and shook her head. "Just do it."

Gabriel and a long-time customer sat at the counter drinking coffee while Gee, the waiter, and the busboy did the dinnertime prep work. Preparing ingredients in advance was key to the elaborate menus and fast service diners were famous for. Mountains of seasoned onions and potatoes sat steaming on the grill, soon to evolve into the ubiquitous hash browns found on practically every plate coming from the kitchen.

"That smell's making me hungry," said the customer.

Gabriel smiled. "It's supposed to. Old restaurateur's trick. The scent of simmering garlic stimulates the appetite, generating bigger orders."

The man laughed. "I wonder if I could arrest you for that hustle?"

"It's small-time compared to what bars and clubs do to keep customers drinking more."

"You mean the heavily salted free nuts and chips?"

"No, everyone knows that routine. I'm talking about gradually pumping up the sound level over the course of an evening; as the music volume goes up, so do booze sales. It's been scientifically proven."

"How do you know this stuff, Gabe?"

He didn't like being called Gabe, but a lot of his customers, especially cops, gave nicknames to their friends, and so he let it slide. "A life spent in the business," he answered with a shrug.

"I'll bet." The customer tapped his forefinger on the countertop. "You know what, you might be able to help me out with something."

"Sure, if I can."

"Have you heard about that murder a couple blocks over?"

"Which one?" Gabriel hoped he'd kept a straight face.

"Good point. A guy named Carlucci got whacked."

"Was that the one in the paper?"

"Yeah, this guy." He pulled a photo out of his jacket pocket, showed it to Gabriel, and put it back in his pocket. "Two women who lived in the apartment where the body was found phoned it in while I was the detective on duty, so the case landed on my desk."

"Lucky you."

He shrugged. "We had no trouble identifying the victim. He was well-known to us, but that's about all we know. The women said they found the body when they returned home. A third woman who lived with them in the apartment was seen leaving the building in a rush and hasn't returned."

"Sounds like you know a lot."

"Less than I'd like. We do know that Carlucci started out as a small-time drug dealer and pimp but moved on to other things."

Gabriel wanted to ask what he meant by *other things* but didn't dare risk sounding overly interested. "Sounds like a bad guy."

"He was, and I'm not surprised someone whacked him." He took a sip of coffee. "What surprised me was that it seemed a professional hit. This kind of guy usually gets taken out in a hail of bullets by some drugged-out cowboy gangbanger. But this was a single bullet to precisely the right spot in his skull."

Gabriel couldn't resist asking, "You think the woman who ran away did it?"

"Not likely. But who knows? We're just looking for leads."

"So, how can I help you?"

"You've got the best diner in the area."

Gabriel smiled. "Since we both know it's the *only* diner, I assume you're blowing smoke up my ass for a reason."

The detective smiled back. "People come in here from all walks of life. You might hear things, and if you do, I'd appreciate your letting me know."

"What sorts of things?"

"Like if anyone meeting the description of that third woman comes in here."

"Sure thing. What does she look like?"

He reached into another pocket and pulled out a piece of paper. "It's a composite sketch pieced together from descriptions given by her roommates."

The girl in the sketch had long, light brown hair and wore a gray coat. The image could fit many young women, but if you knew Angel, it was spot-on.

Gabriel stared at the sketch. "May I keep this?"

"Yep."

"Thanks." Gabriel paused. "I've got something to ask you."

"What is it?"

"We've known each other for a long time, and this is the first time you've ever asked me to do anything like this. What's really going on?"

The detective leaned in close to Gabriel. "Keep this to yourself, but Carlucci was a snitch."

"Snitch? Like an informer?"

"Yeah, one of our best. We got a lot of busts, thanks to him."

"What, like drug dealers and prostitutes?"

"Yeah, he gave us some of those, but that's not what made him so valuable to us." He looked around to make sure no one was listening. "Like I said, Carlucci had moved on to other things. He ran a specialized sort of fencing operation. Sellers used him to dispose of what they wanted to get rid of. Carlucci had a network of buyers for virtually anything they might want to unload. What made his operation unique was the auction process he set up. It allowed buyers to bid anonymously against one another, resulting in top prices for often extremely hot merchandise. Transactions were cash-only, and Carlucci personally handled the exchange, attended by third-party representatives of both sides."

"Wow. The ingenuity of bad guys never ceases to amaze me."

The detective shook his head. "Me neither."

"But how did he stay in business if he turned in his customers to you guys?"

"We let him run his business as he chose and never asked him to turn in one of his customers, buyer or seller. We didn't want to wreck his reputation as the go-to fence. His side of the deal was that when he had something significant come his way, he'd pass on handling it and let us know what he could about who was involved."

"So, he gave you some real leads?"

"Enough to justify our not dropping the hammer on him. We made a few big busts and got some great press coverage out of the arrangement. Meanwhile, Carlucci gained a rock-solid reputation for keeping his customers' identities hidden, allowing him to make a hell of a lot of money from commissions on the transactions he didn't have to pass up."

"How did sellers find him?"

"Word of mouth. He had a revolving door of street people he used to collect messages from potential sellers. He was a nut about security and always worried about saboteurs trying to ruin his business."

"I guess you could say a bullet to the head qualifies as ruining his business."

The detective grinned. "That's why we want to find the girl. Word on the street has it that she was his number one courier. She might be able to give us a lead on what got him killed."

"Is she in danger too?"

"Depends on what she knows." He raised a finger. "Let me amend that. It depends on what whoever killed Carlucci *thinks* she knows."

Gabriel shook his head and looked down at the sketch. "What a scary world we live in."

"Getting more so, and less comprehensible by the moment."

Gabriel tucked the sketch away in his shirt pocket and patted the detective on his back. "Coffee's on me."

"Why?"

"For bringing much-needed purpose to my life."

The detective laughed. "In that case, throw in a donut."

"Mr. Michael, it's Gabriel. I need to see you right away."

Michael sat with the phone next to his ear, staring through a lace curtain out into the Park.

"Three times in one day? There's no need for you to go to all that bother. Just tell me the woman's information." Michael heard what sounded like a hand slapping a forehead.

"Ah, I'm sorry. The diner was a total madhouse when I got back, and I forgot to look at her credit-card receipt. But that's not why I'm calling. It's about something else, something that I should only tell you in person."

Michael leaned back. "It's all sounding quite cloak-and-daggerish."

"More than you can imagine. I'll be there in ten minutes and will bring along the woman's information."

"Fine. See you then." Michael hung up the phone and paused for a moment before leaning forward and looking at the Park through the binoculars.

All this reality was beginning to impinge on his imaginary life. He'd been fixed on a matronly woman feeding pigeons, trying to guess what she might be thinking. But now his mind could only wonder what had Gabriel so wound up. Michael had never considered him to be an alarmist.

When he heard the doorbell ring, Michael pushed himself up from his window seat, buttoned his well-worn tweed sports jacket, and with the aid of his blackthorn cane, made it across to his desk before he heard the knock on his study door.

"Come in."

Gabriel opened the door and headed straight for Michael, a piece of paper in hand.

"This is her full name. She used a company credit card, so that's on it too."

"It amazes me how much personal information people willingly give away for simply the price of a coffee and muffin."

"These days, customers pay for a glass of water with a credit card."

"Psychological Perspectives," read Michael aloud. "An impressive name for a company." He put the paper down on his desk and fidgeted with his computer. "So, what has you so concerned?"

Gabriel recounted his conversation with the detective and concluded by pulling the sketch of Angel out of his shirt pocket and handing it to Michael. "We're just lucky the detective's routine didn't bring him into the diner when Angel was having her breakfasts there."

Michael nodded. "It's a good likeness. He'd have recognized her for sure. In my experience, eyewitness descriptions yield far less helpful sketches. We were right to change her appearance."

"Not sure that's gonna be enough to keep her safe. She's the only lead the cops have, and they're pressing hard to find her. Bad guys worried about what she might know are probably looking even harder."

"I agree." Michael looked at the sketch again. "They didn't get her nose or eyes quite right, and the chin's weaker than hers. We should change her eye color with contacts."

"You sound like you plan on letting her out of the house."

"At some point we'll have to. For now, though, I'm more concerned about someone who happens to see her in the house—a delivery person, worker, or casual passer-by. We don't want anyone thinking she might look like this sketch." He put the picture back down on the desk. "In time the police will lose interest. They'll get another snitch and forget all about Dante Carlucci."

"Yeah, but what about whoever killed Carlucci?"

"That's the troublesome part. If bad guys killed him because they figured out he was a police snitch, killing Carlucci accomplished their purpose. They have no reason to go after Angel." He leaned forward. "But if what got Carlucci killed was tied into something else, something the police think Angel might be able to help them with, whoever killed him might want to make sure she doesn't have that opportunity."

"Making Angel a prime target."

"Yes." Michael lowered his hand. "But you're also at risk if they learn Carlucci used your diner as his drop."

Gabriel rubbed his forehead with the fingers of his left hand. "How could they not? It's where she went every morning after making her pickups in the Park. Everyone Carlucci used to empty her coat pocket would know about the diner. There could be dozens, any one of whom could finger my place." He sighed.

"Carlucci didn't come to the diner himself?"

"Nope. Not if he was the guy in the photo my cop friend showed me. I'd seen him in the diner a few times, but never spoke with him or remember seeing him with anyone. And I never saw who left the envelopes inside my front door covering her breakfasts."

"Then who was emptying Angel's pocket?"

Gabriel shook his head. "No idea. He could have paid anyone to do it. Maybe a different person every day. People around here are desperate for money."

"I doubt he'd trust *anyone* to pick up sensitive messages. As you point out, people are desperate for money; they might betray him for a better price."

"Isn't that precisely what happened?"

"We don't know." Michael paused. "Put yourself in Carlucci's shoes and imagine who you'd pick as the most inconspicuous person to trust with your daily pickups."

"I've no idea."

"Well, think about it." Michael tinkered some more with his computer. "While you're doing that, I'll see if I can figure out how our Psychological Perspectives duo ties into all of this."

"Duo?"

Michael spun his computer around so Gabriel could see the screen. "Here's that company's website. It's a clinical practice in the toniest part of Manhattan, prominently featuring a photograph of one Dr. Brackett Fielding III—your *BF III*—and a much smaller photo of his colleague and diner companion, Dr. Marilena F. Sinclair."

Gabriel nodded. "I wonder what that pair would possibly want to sell or buy through Carlucci . . ."

"One of the primary teachings of my former life was trust your instincts, distrust coincidences."

"And what are your instincts telling you?"

Michael closed his computer. "That it's time I took a road trip."

Michael gave Mrs. Baker precise directions to pass along to the limousine rental company. At exactly nine a.m., the driver was to pick him up at home, drive him to a designated address, wait for him until his business was finished, and return him home. At no time was the driver to speak to him unless Michael spoke first.

Scheduling the 9:30 appointment for the next morning proved more difficult, because getting a psychiatrist to see a new patient on a rush basis was only slightly less daunting a task than Moses' parting of the Red Sea. Luckily both had help in high places. Michael's came in the form of the city's major patron of the arts making a personal request that the "distinguished doctor" please see one of her "dearest friends" soonest. She'd also confirmed Michael's suspicion that Brackett and Marilena were not husband and wife, but brother and sister.

Michael sat in the back of the limo, staring out the side window as they passed through neighborhoods he'd not seen in years. Some looked better, some worse, but all showed far more homeless on their streets than he remembered. A few held up placards expressing reasons for their plight, but most simply offered an outstretched hand and a doleful look.

He'd hoped things would be different, closer to the optimism he felt when looking at his people in the Park, not the dark vision portrayed by the media.

What he saw made him sad.

And the closer he came to the fashionable part of town, where the appearance of wealth, success, and power mattered above all else, the sadder he became.

The limo stopped outside a steel and glass office building emblazoned THE TOWER in shiny brass letters atop a rose and gold-speckled marble entrance. The driver hurried around to open Michael's door. He slowly swung himself out and up on to his feet, before moving off toward the entrance in as brisk a fashion as his prosthetic foot and cane would allow. A man dressed more like a grenadier than a doorman stood by the entrance, holding the door open for him.

Once inside, a concierge in a dark suit and regimental striped tie asked him who he was there to see, then directed him to an elevator that would take him to the twenty-fourth floor.

The location and glitz of the place confirmed Michael's instincts that the couple behind Psychological Perspectives held appearances in high esteem. That's why he chose to wear a dark blue pinstripe Brioni suit, crisp white Etro shirt, red Hermes tie, and custom-made John Lobb Oxfords. If that weren't enough to impress them, the white gold Patek-Philippe on his left wrist should do the trick.

He pressed a button beside a door bearing the names of the company and its two principals. At the sound of a buzzer, he pushed open the door and stepped into a small reception area, rendered decidedly tinier by a tall workspace counter running parallel to the far wall and cutting the room nearly in half.

"May I help you, sir?" said the woman sitting behind the counter.

"I have a nine thirty appointment with Dr. Brackett Fielding." Michael gave his name.

She handed him a clipboard, a set of forms, and a pen. "Since you're a new patient, sir, please fill these out."

A half-dozen matching straight-back chairs sat pressed up against every available bit of wall space. Michael chose the chair closest to the door; as the receptionist and he waited alone in the room. He wondered if that meant business was bad.

The door to the right of the counter opened and Marilena stuck out her head. "My eight thirty just left. I assume my nine thirty hasn't canceled."

"Not that I know of. She has five minutes left to get here."

Marilena noticed Michael and offered him a perfunctory professional smile, then ducked back into her office before he had a chance to speak.

"I didn't see her eight thirty come through here," Michael told the receptionist. "Is there another way out?"

She nodded. "We pride ourselves on preserving client confidentiality. Each doctor's office has another means of access."

"Is that why there's no one in here but us?"

"Usually there are patients waiting, sometimes they even chat with each other, but Dr. Fielding said to make sure you would not be disturbed."

"That's very kind of him. But what about her nine thirty?" gesturing with his hand toward Marilena's office.

"Don't worry. If you're still here when she arrives, I'll show her in through the doctor's other door." She looked down at her desk. "Oh, Dr. Fielding just sent me a message asking that I show you into his office." She pointed at the door by the end of the counter to Michael's left.

He stood, his right hand clutching the cane, his left cradling the clipboard, forms, and pen.

The receptionist hurried out from behind the counter to open the door for him and reached for the items in his left hand. As she took them, she glanced down at the forms. "But, sir, you haven't filled these out."

They stood in front of the open door. He raised his hand to the side of his mouth and whispered, "Don't worry. I'm sure the doctor will understand once he realizes that none of the questions on the form is relevant. And I'm paying cash."

Her face grew stern. "But we have procedures."

"Sir, welcome," bellowed a voice through the open doorway.

Michael smiled sweetly at the receptionist, turned, and made his way into the doctor's office.

EIGHT

The plush gray carpeting in Brackett's office stood so thickly piled that Michael nearly stumbled on his way across the room to where Brackett sat browsing through a file. He stopped and waited for the doctor to put down the file. The instant Brackett finished reading, he jumped to his feet and extended his hand.

"Brackett Fielding, sir. It is an honor to meet you."

Michael shook his hand. "I appreciate your seeing me on such short notice."

"Any friend of our city's most celebrated patron of the arts is a friend of mine."

"That's very gracious of you." Michael made a point of taking the time to stare at the paintings, sculptures, and objets d'art occupying virtually every available bit of wall and bookshelf space in a room twice the size of the reception area. "I see you share our mutual friend's taste in fine art."

"I try to learn from the best." Brackett pointed to the matching chair across from his. "Please." He glanced at Michael's cane. "Unless you'd be more comfortable on the sofa."

"No, this is fine." Michael carefully lowered himself into the chair. "If I may say, your entire office is quite comfortable. It's a brilliant idea not to have a desk or table between us." He waved his right hand at the paintings on the wall to his right. "From the quality of what you have here, you must serve a sophisticated clientele."

Brackett simply nodded, but Michael could tell he enjoyed the flattery.

"So, how can I help you Mr. Ark—" He stumbled on the name.

"Don't even bother to try. It happens to everyone. Just call me Mister Michael, or Michael, if you prefer."

"I apologize, Michael. I should know how to pronounce it. It sounds foreign."

"So does Fielding, depending on where you are when you say it."

"Touché," smiled Brackett. "So, how can I help you?"

"What do you know about me?"

Brackett blinked. "I'm generally the one who asks the questions."

"I'm just trying to see where I should start. I have a long story to tell, and since you could only spare me forty-five minutes today, I don't want to waste time going over things you already know about me." He pointed at the folder in Brackett's lap. "Things in that file, for example."

Brackett gaped at him, "How did you know this file was about you?"

Michael shrugged. "You're far too gracious a host not to have put down what you were reading and risen to greet me when I walked into the room. The only logical explanation was that you were reading something about me."

Brackett smiled. "I guess what I read about you is true." He opened the file. "You were born overseas, emigrated here with your parents when you were a child, and have lived in the same neighborhood all your life. You excelled in athletics and graduated with highest honors from college."

"That's all publicly known information," said Michael.

"What isn't in the public record is what you did after university. I think it's fair to characterize your reputation as one built on gossip, surmise, and legend." Fielding paused and fixed his eyes on Michael's. "You're said to have served our government in highly sensitive military intelligence operations and rumored to have used your access to secret information to build a vast private fortune for yourself."

Michael smiled. "So, when do we get to the legend part?"

"That ties into your military service. How you resisted torture," his eyes darted for an instant to Michael's foot, "and in so doing saved the lives of many of your comrades."

"Not enough of the right lives, sadly."

"Your injuries were severe but did not stop you from persevering in government and business, in a manner your fans call brilliant and your detractors ruthless."

Michael tapped his cane on the carpet between them. "So, based upon what you know of me, why do you think I'm here to see you today?"

"I understand you've become somewhat reclusive."

"I believe the clinical term for what you have in mind is agoraphobic."

"Are you?"

"No, I just gave up on interacting with the human race and decided to observe its members from a distance instead."

"I think you've given us a good place to start, Michael."

Michael nodded. "I agree. So, what do you want me to talk about first?"

"Why don't we start with how much of what's been said about you is true?"

"If you're talking about what you just told me, all of it."

Brackett showed a slight tinge of surprise.

"And more," added Michael.

"What sort of more?"

"I get to play the Wizard of Oz, but my character has balls."

Brackett stared at him. "How's that . . .?"

Michael kept an even tone. "I'm the invisible man behind the curtain. People come to me when there are nasty things to be arranged that they won't dare trust to anyone else." He stretched out his left hand and waved it around as if he were holding a wand, then dropped it on to the arm of his chair, his watch protruding out of his sleeve.

Brackett glanced at the watch, looked away for a second, then looked at it again. He blinked but kept his eyes fixed on the watch.

"Is everything OK, doctor?"

"Uh, yes, I was just admiring your watch."

"Thank you." Michael looked at his wrist. "Yes, this one's a beauty, but owning watches is like having children. You have to spread the affection around. Today was this one's turn to spend time with me."

Brackett bit at his lip. "What sort of nasty things are you talking about?"

"Don't worry, I haven't killed anyone in years."

Brackett tensed.

"That was meant as a joke."

Brackett forced a grin.

"Though it's also true." Michael leaned forward to stretch out his back. "When people are in need of contacts outside their normal channels of communication, they come to me to make the necessary introductions to do their business."

"Does that mean you're a fence?"

Michael laughed. "I think you watch too many crime shows. I'm more like an investment banker who brings people together but plays no part in the subject of whatever business they choose to do with one another."

Brackett leaned forward. "So, if a seller has something valuable but doesn't know who to trust to market it, you put the seller in touch with the right people?"

"That pretty well sums it up."

"How do you keep the two sides honest?"

Michael rested his hands on the crown of his cane. "Not sure I follow you."

"You said you deal with nasty things. I take that to mean nasty people are involved. So how do you keep them from being nasty to each other?"

"As I said, you've been watching too much television."

Brackett leaned in closer to Michael. "I meant it as a serious question. How do you protect normal people trying to do business with nasty people?"

"Doctor, are you still asking me professional questions, or is this something personal?"

Brackett slouched in his chair. "I'm just curious. I've never had a patient like you."

"I think I'm flattered. But to answer your question: people who use my services know that to betray the other side in a deal sanctioned by me could lead to irreversible consequences."

Brackett sat dumbfounded, then looked at the door. "Would you excuse me for a moment please? I just remembered I have to speak to my colleague about something urgent. I'll be right back."

"Take your time," said Michael, looking at his watch as Brackett hurried out.

Good job, Philippe.

Brackett marched straight for Marilena's office and barely knocked before barging in. A young woman sat sobbing at one end of a muted floral-pattern couch, Marilena at the other end.

"*Brackett* . . . what are you doing? Can't you see I'm in the middle of a session with a patient?"

"I'm sorry." He faced the young woman. "I apologize for the interruption, Miss, but there's an emergency that requires your doctor's immediate attention."

Perplexed, the woman looked at Marilena. "What should I do?"

"Just give me a minute and—"

Brackett interrupted, "If you could just wait in reception for a minute. Please."

Marilena silently fumed while the woman gathered up her things, grabbed the box of tissues next to her, and shuffled off to the reception area.

The moment the door shut behind the young woman, Marilena erupted. "How dare you storm into my office and order one of my patients to leave?"

"Keep your voice down. The soundproofing doesn't work at those decibel levels."

"Stop patronizing me."

He offered a calming gesture with his hands. "I think I have the answer to our problem."

"*What* problem?"

"Finding someone we can trust to help us market what we have."

Marilena shut her eyes and paused as if counting to ten. "*That's* your emergency? You couldn't wait twenty minutes?"

"No, I couldn't. There's a new patient sitting in my office, but he's a bit of a recluse and might not show up again. We can't afford to miss this opportunity to talk with him together, because if I'm right about him, he could be our savior."

Marilena stared at him without saying a word.

"What's wrong?"

"Do you have any idea what you sound like? You're talking about a patient—and one you just met, no less—as our *savior*. Are you out of your mind?"

Brackett clenched his teeth. "No, I'm certainly not. And the guy's for real."

"How can you possibly say that?"

"He was recommended by an impeccable source, and I checked him out."

"And he just happens to show up in our office when you're on the verge of driving us both to a nervous breakdown over the precise situation he can help us with?" She shook her head. "Sounds like a set-up to me."

"But who would know to set me up? Did you talk to anyone about what we have?"

"Of course not. But something about it doesn't feel right."

"That's why I want you to meet him."

She shook her head. "Give me one reason why I should think he's legitimate."

"His watch."

Marilena shut her eyes. "Tell me, Brackett. What in the world could his watch have to do with whether he's for real?"

"It's a Patek Grand Complication Tourbillon."

"I rest my case. He's likely as phony as his watch."

"It's not a phony."

"It must be. That watch is worth close to a million."

"Check it out for yourself."

"Are you seriously prepared to make a decision on whether or not to trust our lives to someone you've just met based upon his watch?"

"Stop with the drama. Will you meet him or not?"

"What about my patient?"

Brackett shrugged. "Have her wait or send her home. Just tell her you won't charge her for the session and she'll be happy. You have to apply tact and charm in these situations. Otherwise, your patients will control your life."

Marilena drew in and let out a deep breath. "I really shouldn't worry about your state of mind. Nothing's changed. You're still the same self-absorbed asshole you've always been."

"Coming from my little sister, I'll take it as a compliment." Brackett turned and headed toward the door. "Come, let's go meet him."

Marilena rose from the sofa, mumbling, "Asshole, asshole, asshole," all the way out the door.

Michael wondered what Fielding's patients thought of his insights. Perhaps they were distracted by all the glitz he tossed at them. It never failed to amaze Michael how willing people were to place their faith in shiny objects as a measure of their possessor's competence. How ironic that Fielding's reaction to him and his watch served as yet another example of the same.

From what Michael observed of their interaction in the Park, the brother viewed himself as the big dog, the one in charge. His was an arrogant breed, prone to resisting any idea that didn't originate with them. Yet, he wouldn't discuss what's plainly troubling him until first checking with his sister. Was that a sign of insecurity, a politic effort to involve her so she couldn't complain later, or true confidence in her judgment?

Or perhaps Michael's performance wasn't as impressive as he thought.

Whatever his reason, Michael was glad he'd decided to make his appointment with Brackett. A woman forced to endure his alpha-male condescension on a daily basis would be far warier and tougher to manipulate than he.

The door opened behind him.

"I apologize for having left you as I did, but I wanted you to meet my partner, Marilena."

Michael pushed himself up from his chair and turned to face the pair.

"No, need to get up, sir," said Marilena, stepping forward with her hand extended.

"Of course, there is. When I'm introduced to a distinguished doctor, I must show respect." He reached out and shook her hand.

Marilena's eyes lit up, but she quickly shot a nervous glance in Brackett's direction. "I think you're talking about my colleague, Dr. Fielding."

"No, I'm talking about you. Dr. Fielding came recommended to me coupled with the highest praise for you." He looked at Brackett, "Is there a chair for your partner, or should I give her mine?"

Brackett blinked. "Uh, yes, of course, there's one for her." He pulled a straight-back chair away from a small table by a window and hastily dragged it across the carpet to a place between his and Michael's chairs.

"Thank you," said Marilena to both men as she sat.

"I'm pleased we have this chance to meet," said Michael, sitting. "It makes my decision to pick today to venture out into the world feel all the wiser."

Marilena smiled. "I'm happy to hear that. I understand from Dr. Fielding that you feel more comfortable staying at home in familiar surroundings."

Michael smiled. "I see you're as reluctant as Dr. Fielding to mention agoraphobia around me. But, as I told him, I'm not that way. I just lost patience with the world and decided I could pursue my interests far more effectively without unnecessary human interaction."

"I see," said Marilena. "And what would those interests be?"

"Eclectic," said Michael. "And profitable."

"Michael brings parties together who otherwise don't circulate in the same spheres of influence," said Brackett.

"I like the way you put that," said Michael. "My business is based upon reading people and understanding what makes them tick. Their needs, their wants, their fears, their limits. Sort of like what you do. But different."

"Do you have references?" Marilena asked.

Michael offered a startled look. "Do I need references to be your patient?"

She blushed. "No, of course not. You, uh, had me so enthralled with that description of your business model that I got carried away at wondering who would use your services. Sorry about that."

Michael chuckled. "I can see why you're partners. You each reacted the same way when I described what I do."

"Perhaps that's because we're brother and sister," smiled Brackett.

Michael feigned surprise. "Now, *that's* what I call an interesting business model. Siblings sharing a psychiatric practice. But why the different names on the front door?"

"My friends all know me as Marilena Fielding, but I use my ex-husband's name professionally. It's less confusing that way to patients, and—"

Brackett interrupted. "It's my belief that if we had the same last name on the door, prospective patients might think we're husband and wife. With so much of our practice involved in counseling spouses working their way through troubled marriages and divorce, it makes no sense for us to risk losing patients who might be uncomfortable at the thought of discussing their marital problems with a husband-and-wife unit."

"That makes sense," said Michael.

"If only they knew the truth," joked Marilena.

Michael laughed. "Since you're being open with me, allow me to be the same with you." He looked directly at Marilena. "We all know you're not here to have social chit-chat with me. Especially since your nine thirty is probably out there wondering what's happened to her doctor. Whatever's troubling the two of you, you somehow think I might be able to help. So, I'd suggest that we stop beating around the bush."

Brackett and Marilena stared at each other, but neither spoke.

"If you're not interested in giving me at least an idea of what you think it is that I can do for you, that's fine with me. After all, I didn't come here looking for business, and I'm not in the mood to put on a show of my mind-reading skills. But if you want my help or even just my opinion, I'll need some overview of what's concerning you."

Marilena cleared her throat, "We have a very valuable item we want to dispose of, but we need help in deciding how best to arrange that."

"I assume it's not an item of the sort you'd want to put up for public auction."

"There's nothing illegal about this," Brackett protested.

"I wasn't suggesting there was, just confirming that you've rejected the conventional ways of disposing of something of great value."

Brackett hesitated. "It's the sort of item over which passions run high, and we're worried about what might happen if the wrong people learn we have it."

"Sounds like you're not just looking for the right buyer, but for protection from being ripped off."

"Or worse," admitted Marilena.

"Worse?"

"Just being identified with the item is fraught with peril."

Michael leaned back in his chair. "That's an intriguing description, but I think I get the picture." He paused. "Have you reached out to anyone for help with your predicament?"

Brackett answered quickly. "No."

"Not even tried?"

He shook his head.

"I assume that whatever this item is, it only recently came into your possession. I say that because if you'd had it for any meaningful period of time, from the level of anxiety you're broadcasting as we sit here in the confines of your comfortable office, by now you'd likely have made a horrible blunder if you'd tried to shop it around."

"What kind of horrible blunder?" asked the visibly nervous Marilena.

"A recent event strikes me as perhaps the most appropriate example for your likely situation, and it comes with an object lesson." Michael paused until he had Brackett's attention. "It's been common knowledge among the criminal element of our city that if you're looking for help in disposing of an item of the sort you're alluding to, you'd leave a message for a certain person in one of our city parks."

Brackett nodded for him to go on. Marilena was blinking rapidly.

"According to the fairy-tale version of this operation, you'd go to the Park and deliver your message to a courier to carry back to the person who'll then miraculously achieve what you want, allowing everyone to live happily ever after."

Marilena glanced anxiously at her brother, his poker face on the wane.

"But guess what? It was a scheme, not a fairy tale, and it had no fairy-tale ending. The mysterious miracle worker was a police snitch named Dante Carlucci who was murdered the other night for reasons unknown. His life had him into a lot of bad things, any one of which could explain his murder, but, then again, he'd been doing nasty things for years without a problem." Michael paused to allow his words to percolate. "Hopefully, the killer achieved what he wanted." He smiled at Marilena. "Or *she* achieved what she wanted. These days, who knows?"

"And what if the killer didn't achieve what he wanted?" asked Brackett.

Michael's expression turned grim. "He might just start working his way back down Carlucci's courier chain until he does."

Brackett strained to keep his voice from cracking. "What's the object lesson?"

"A simple one. Make sure you know who you're dealing with." Michael stood. "Now, if you'll excuse me, I really should be going."

Marilena jumped to her feet, followed by Brackett.

"How can we reach you?" Brackett asked.

"Your receptionist should have my contact details from when my colleague made my appointment."

Marilena grabbed and held Michael's left hand, eyeing his watch as she did. "Thank you. It was nice meeting you."

"You're welcome, doctor." He extended his right hand to Brackett. "I don't know precisely what you two have gotten yourselves into, but tread carefully. People die every day for reasons far less dramatic than what you've described to me. One wrong move and . . ." Michael shook his head. "Well, I don't have to add to the drama."

Marilena glared at her brother. "No, you don't."

That was an interesting exchange, thought Michael, sitting in the back of the limo. All was not well in the Fielding practice. Sister was more worried than Brother, but he was still extremely anxious. Michael wondered if they had engaged with each other this way all their lives. He guessed it worked for them. After all, they were still together.

The real question, though, was what they were trying to sell. It must be something with a life-changing payoff. They're so far out of their element that it's hard to imagine them taking such a huge risk for anything less. Yet, they're not the sort he saw as capable of handling the stresses attendant to participating in overtly illegal activity, like drugs or human trafficking, no matter the payoff. Whatever this priceless likely-pilfered property might be, in resorting to convoluted unlawful schemes to dispose of it, they were coming to fear it.

Which made him wonder: What sort of *item* generates sufficiently *high passions* that mere association with it is *fraught with peril*.

Hmm, perhaps he was going at this the wrong way. He might need to adopt a different way of looking at the state of affairs.

"Let me off at the edge of the Park," he told the driver. "I'll walk home from there."

If he was looking for a new perspective, the Park struck him as a good place to start.

NINE

"Mr. Michael, what are you doing here?"

He sat on the bench next to Gabriel. "Strolling through the Park, my friend. It's something I haven't done in a very long time. I thought today was a good day to start."

"Nothing wrong with some fresh air," Gabriel agreed. "So, how did your meeting go with the Fielding family?"

"I'm certain they have something valuable they wanted to market through Carlucci and were in the Park looking to hook up with him, but never connected."

"Do they know about Angel?"

"My guess is they didn't know of Angel specifically."

Two squirrels chased about the feet of the bench across from them.

"I wonder if what they wanted to get to Carlucci had anything to do with his murder?"

Michael nodded. "So do I. Which leads me to wonder how they came to possess it. I doubt it's an old family heirloom."

"What do you think they're trying to sell?"

"It could be a thing, an idea, something huge, something tiny . . ." Michael shrugged. "In other words, I don't have a clue."

Gabriel pointed to a passing businessman. "Do you see the briefcase that man's carrying?"

"Yes."

"Brackett Fielding never let his out of his sight when he was in my diner."

"Nor did he let go of it in the Park."

Gabriel shook his head. "I can't believe he'd be so dumb as to carry something that valuable around with him."

"I'd say anxiety-ridden rather than dumb," said Michael. "They're way out of their depth on this."

"So, what happens next?"

"It's their move, but my guess is they'll be getting in touch with me ASAP. With Carlucci dead, they're desperate."

"Do they know about my diner?"

"I don't know. It didn't come up."

"I can't help but look at every new customer and wonder if he's the one who came to pop me."

Michael pursed his lips and rested his hands atop his cane. "I'm not suggesting you not remain vigilant, but if I were you, I'd focus more energy on figuring out who did the pickups for Carlucci in your diner. Was it one person or many? One we can handle. More could prove difficult."

"What do you mean by *handle*?"

"We sit down with whoever it is and ask he or she to explain the arrangement with Carlucci, and whether anyone else knew of that arrangement. With any luck, the pickup person is the only one still alive, aside from Angel, who knows your diner was the drop."

"I don't like the sound of where this is headed."

Michael sat up straight. "How's that?"

"Getting rid of the pickup person."

Michael laughed. "You're starting to sound like Brackett Fielding. All I'm suggesting is that once we know who's involved, we tell them that if Carlucci and they are the only ones who knew of the diner's involvement, it's in everyone's interest to keep it that way."

Gabriel fixed his eyes on Michael's face. "So, you want me to locate the pickup person in order to help him?"

"Yes, help *him*, as you put it. And in the process help yourself."

Gabriel stared up at the bare trees. "I wish spring would come already."

"It's on its way. What's wrong, Gabriel?"

"I'm thinking if the pickup person's on my staff, then he's worked for me for years. Hard to imagine he turned on me."

"Whoever *he* is, I doubt he'd think of what he did as betraying you. After all, Carlucci was paying him simply to pickup and deliver packages to him. He wasn't stealing from you."

Gabriel sighed. "I guess that's one way to look at it. Besides, he needed the money."

"So, which of your employees was it?"

"By process of elimination it can only be one. No way my grill man, Gee, had the opportunity to get to Angel's coat during our morning rush and empty her pocket. Same thing holds true for my waiter and dishwasher. They were crazy-busy whenever Angel was there."

"Who's that leave?"

"The busboy. He's always running around between the front and the back, and up and down the stairs to my apartment. He also made deliveries when we weren't busy. Retrieving items from Angel's coat would have been a no-brainer. Deliveries were the perfect means for doing Carlucci's work on the side." Gabriel looked down at the ground. "I guess I better fire him."

Michael raised a hand. "I voice a very strong *objection* to that idea. We should stick to the approach we discussed. Point out to him that the best way to avoid anyone getting harmed is to make sure no one else ever learns of his involvement with Carlucci. Kicking him out of the tent strikes me as a bad idea. Let's not forget he also knows about Angel. Just convince him to keep his mouth shut and stay out of the courier business."

"What if he won't agree?"

Michael offered a mischievous grin. "I thought you didn't want to talk about that alternative." He patted Gabriel's knee. "Don't worry, most people faced with these sorts of circumstances act rationally. I'm sure he will too."

Gabriel stood up. "I've got to get back to work." He shook his head. "Just when you think you've seen everything in this business, the wildest off-the-wall thing drops in your lap. And now I've got to figure out how to handle it. Well, so long."

Michael nodded to Gabriel but said not a word as he watched him walk away.

Drops in your lap.

Michael burst into a smile and called out in Gabriel's direction. "That's it! You gave me the perspective I needed!"

But Gabriel had left the Park and didn't hear him.

Michael hurried home as fast as he could. He didn't want to miss the Fieldings' call.

Angel had spent her morning working through the daily schedule of chores that Mrs. Baker had listed for her to do.

"They're to be done every day, divided into morning, afternoon, and evening responsibilities, all organized around Mr. Michael's daily routine. Before his breakfast, prepare his study, making certain all supplies are in place, each pencil is sharp, and every surface free of dust. Under no circumstances do you vacuum until Mr. Michael is at breakfast, and once he's moved on to his study, you service his bedroom and bath."

Angel's daily schedule slated every room for at least some attention, on top of which were the special schedules: laundry days, window-washing days, pantry-stocking days, backyard-tidying days, and shopping days, though for the time being, her involvement in shopping was confined to making lists of needed items.

Mrs. Baker did the cooking and dealt with anyone having anything to do with the outside world. That, she said, would leave Angel free to concentrate on her tasks.

Angel faced a daunting amount of work, but once into it, felt strangely liberated. She sensed something she'd not felt in a very long time: control over her day-to-day existence.

At least as long as she pleased Mrs. Baker.

Michael returned home a little before noon and told Mrs. Baker he'd take his lunch in his study. Mrs. Baker instructed Angel to deliver it.

Angel knocked on the study door.

"Come in."

She opened the door and wheeled in a white linen-covered serving cart, bearing bone chinaware, crystal glassware, silver cutlery, and a single red rose in a Baccarat bud vase.

Michael said, "My God, girl, there was no reason to go to all that trouble just for my lunch."

"Mrs. B. said I should learn from the start how to do things the right way, so that I don't pick up bad habits."

Michael grinned. "That sounds like Mrs. B." He pointed from behind his desk to a leather-covered gaming table on the far side of the room. "Please, set it up on that table, but make sure you cover the leather with a tablecloth."

"Yes, sir." She wheeled the cart over to the table, covered the tabletop, and transferred everything on the cart to corresponding positions on the table.

"Very nicely done. My compliments to you and your teacher."

"Thank you, sir."

He pointed to a chair in front of his desk. "I know you're busy, Angel, but I'd appreciate if you'd come sit for a moment, please."

He waited for her to sit. "You might be able to help me clear up this mess surrounding your ex-boss Carlucci."

Angel bit at her lip.

"I know you'd prefer not to talk about him, but I have only a few questions, and you're the only person I know who could possibly answer them. So, what do you say?"

Angel kept biting at her lip. "OK."

"Thank you." He held up a photograph of the Fieldings. "Have you ever seen these people?"

She leaned in, staring. "No, I don't think so."

"They were trying to get in touch with Carlucci the day he was murdered. They'd been in the Park around lunchtime looking for his courier."

"But I was only there in the early mornings."

"I know. And that's what's bothering me. If they knew Carlucci ran a courier service in the Park, why wouldn't they also know you'd only be there early in the morning?"

"I don't know."

"Did he have other couriers working in the Park at other hours?"

"I don't think so, but I wouldn't know for sure."

"Did he ever make pickups on his own?"

"I don't think he'd take the risk. That's what he used me for. He didn't want to be tied to whatever people stuck in my coat pocket. Too easy to be set up that way."

Michael nodded. "I can't figure out why this pair knew everything about Carlucci's courier arrangement *except* for the right time to make contact. It makes no sense."

"When he offered me the job, he gave me the choice of working early mornings and joining the diner's breakfast rush, or early afternoons and getting there for the lunchtime crowd."

"Giving whoever emptied your pocket the cover of a crowded place in which to do it."

Angel nodded. "That's what I thought, too."

"But how does that explain why they didn't know you worked in the early mornings?"

"Possibly because the girl he used as his courier before me ran her route during lunchtime."

Michael's face lit up, and he slapped the desktop lightly with his hand. "That's it, Angel. Brilliant thinking. This couple was working off old information. Either whoever gave it to them wasn't well-informed, *or*," he tapped his forefinger on the photograph, "they got their information *before* you were the courier and never were updated on how to make contact with Carlucci."

Angel leaned forward. "How is that helpful?"

"This couple's been relying on outdated information or unreliable third parties, most likely both. They're desperate, and beginning to appreciate that if they continue down the path they're on, their journey will most certainly end in tears. They need to turn to someone else for help with whatever they have in mind."

"You?"

Michael smiled. "Possibly. But if they do, I trust I can call upon you for more of your insights. Just consider it something else to add to Mrs. B's lists."

"You know about the lists?"

"Of course, and I think structure is good for you."

"I just want to make sure I do everything right."

He smiled. "Don't worry about that. If you don't, I'm certain Mrs. B. will tell you."

"Oh, I'd better get back to work." She jumped up from her chair. "May I leave, sir?"

"Of course, but just one more thing. Do you happen to know the name of the woman who preceded you as Carlucci's courier?"

"I think it was Maria, but I'm not sure, and I never knew her last name."

"Too bad. I'd like to talk with her."

Angel blinked twice. "That's not possible, sir."

"Why not?"

"She's dead."

According to Angel, Maria was a runaway fourteen-year-old addict Carlucci had used for a month or so as his courier in the Park. When Maria died from an overdose, Carlucci decided not to trust his courier business to junkies and recruited Angel, a non-user, as his next courier. He moved her into Maria's apartment the day after she passed away, gave her a gray cloth coat, and through his breakfast arrangements with Gabriel, kept tighter reins on Angel's courier activities than he had with Maria.

Angel learned all of that a week or so after living in the apartment. One of the girls she shared it with began rambling on in her own druggy state about the girl who used to have Angel's job, talking about how Maria died on the very bed where Angel now slept, and two guys showed up out of nowhere to dump her body. According to Angel's roommate, "That's how all of Carlucci's girls end up."

From that moment on Angel lived in mortal fear of Carlucci.

Michael waited until Angel had finished explaining. "All that's behind you now. You have the chance for a different life. As for Carlucci," he smiled, "from the way he ended up, I think it's fair to say, karma's a bitch."

It was close to dinner time when Michael's intercom buzzed with a message from Mrs. Baker. He had a phone call from a man who "would not give his name."

He took the call in his study. "Hello, this is Michael."

"It's me."

"Me? Oh yes Dr. . . ."

"Please, don't say my name."

Michael paused. "I know that my phones aren't bugged, and if you believe yours are, I'd say it's a bit late to be worrying about an eavesdropper knowing your name or who you might be talking to."

"I just want to be careful."

Michael smiled to himself. "OK, what can I do for you?"

"We'd like to meet with you."

"I thought we just did. Whoops, am I allowed to say that?"

Brackett's voice bristled. "This is serious."

Michael's smile broadened. "I know, that's why I asked. So, when and where do you want to meet?"

"I know a place on your side of town. It's inconspicuous."

Michael sensed what was coming. "And when?"

"In an hour?"

"But it's dinner time."

"We can eat there. It's a diner with serviceable food."

As much as Michael didn't like changing his mealtime routine, in Brackett's highly anxious state of mind, this could be an opportunity to learn more from him than ordinary prudence would otherwise dictate.

"OK, I'll see you there in an hour."

"Don't you want the address?"

"I think I know it. There's only one diner in the neighborhood."

Brackett gave him the address anyway and hung up.

Michael stared at the phone in his hand, wondering: *If Fielding believes his phones are bugged, why did he just guarantee us an audience for dinner?*

Michael decided to walk to the diner. He hadn't done anything like that in years, instead getting in his daily exercise on a treadmill in the basement, but today seemed a good day for "busting routines," he told Mrs. Baker.

She offered to walk with him to the diner, but he refused. "I'm not crippled. All I need for company is my cane."

"Suit yourself, but at least tell Gabriel you're coming. You could give the poor man a heart attack walking into his place unannounced after all these years."

"I already called him. I wanted him to know who I'll be meeting there, otherwise he might have that heart attack. I also wanted to make sure we get a booth where we won't be overheard."

"Good luck with that. Sticking one's nose in other people's business is a national pastime around here."

Michael feigned a scowl. "Is that meant as a dig at me?"

She scowled back. "No, just saying."

As Angel watched, Mrs. Baker helped him slip a charcoal-gray raincoat over a double-breasted navy wool blazer and smoke-gray gabardine trousers. After he'd carefully tied a classic silk Hermes scarf around his neck, he took the gray fedora Angel handed him.

"Wow, aren't you a sight," said Mrs. Baker.

"It always pays to dress for the part."

"Mr. Gabriel might raise his prices if people dressed like you start eating there," said Angel with a smile.

Michael smiled back. "I'm happy to see you're up to making jokes . . . even if they're at my expense."

"We've got a ton of that kind. Been rehearsing them all afternoon," joked Mrs. Baker.

"My happiness does not extend to the *quality* of your humor, Mrs. B."

She wagged a finger at him. "Be sure to call me when you're leaving the diner, and if for any reason you'd prefer a ride home, or don't want to walk back alone, just tell Gabriel and he'll get you here."

Michael stared at her. "After all these years, I'd think you'd have learned that the surest way to get me doing something you think I shouldn't be doing is to make it seem as if you believe I can't do it."

"You sound like a child."

"That's it," said Michael, heading for the front door, cane in hand. "I just might stay out all night."

"Good," said Mrs. Baker, opening the door. "Angel and I will take turns watching you sleep on a park bench." She patted him on the back as he passed by. "Talk about a routine-busting day."

TEN

Michael slowly set out on the walk from his home to the diner, keeping an eye on groups of young men and boys milling around apartment doorways. This was his neighborhood, but he hadn't been out and about in years, making him a likely stranger to everyone who saw him, even if he recognized faces from his vigil above the Park. He wasn't worried about being attacked, certainly not at this hour with so many walking the streets, but remaining alert to his environment was an old habit he'd never abandoned.

As he walked, he thought of the phone conversation he'd just had with Gabriel. He hadn't told Mrs. Baker everything about the call, because Angel was with her, and he didn't want to risk upsetting her by mentioning Maria.

He'd asked Gabriel whether he'd had any young female customers other than Angel who might have been tied into Carlucci. Gabriel said it was the middle of the dinner rush, and he was crazy busy, so what the hell was Michael driving at? Michael said he wondered whether any young girls who'd been regulars at the diner stopped showing up once Angel began eating there.

Gabriel barked that he had no idea, then paused. "For about a month before Angel showed up, a young girl ate lunch at the diner most days, but I haven't seen her since, and unlike Angel's arrangement she'd ordered and paid for her own meals. I'd pegged her for a junkie with enough sense not to spend her lunch money on drugs, but I wasn't surprised when she just disappeared. If she worked for Carlucci, his experience with her must have led him to change the rules for Angel, because he obviously didn't trust Angel to pay for her own breakfast."

Michael told him the girl's name was Maria, she was fourteen years-old and died of an overdose.

The only words Gabriel said after that, before hanging up were, "This world sucks."

* * *

Michael paused outside the diner to look up at the second floor. He'd once lived in a third-floor tenement apartment not far from here. He thought back to when Gabriel's father and he had hung out together on these same streets, looking for ways to beat the boredom of growing up. Many of those people he'd passed this evening were searching for the same thing, except these days they had electronic gizmos to replace conversation and sophisticated drugs to fry their brains.

So much for modern times.

Michael pulled open the front door and headed straight for the booth farthest from the door, passing Gabriel on the way without either man acknowledging the other. The Fieldings sat perched side-by-side, facing the front door, eyes on Michael. He stopped at the booth next to theirs. A sign on that adjacent tabletop read RESERVED. Michael took off his hat and coat, carefully placed them next to the sign, and joined the Fieldings.

"You're late," said a visibly anxious Brackett from across the table.

"I know."

"That booth is reserved," said Marilena.

"I know that too. If and when someone shows up to claim it, I'll remove my things. Until then, consider that my humble effort at discouraging a potential interloper from robbing us of our privacy. Considering your brother's concern about being bugged, I suggest you keep your eyes out for potential eavesdroppers, and *your voices down.*"

He turned and waved for Gabriel. "Might I suggest we take advantage of our current relative solitude by you telling me what has you so worked up?"

"Sir, may I help you?" asked Gabriel, arriving at the table.

"Yes, thank you. I'd like black coffee and a toasted cheese sandwich. With tomato, please."

Gabriel looked at Brackett. "Toasted bran muffin and coffee?"

Brackett nodded brusquely. "Yes, and please don't disturb us after we're served."

"And you, Miss?"

"Just water."

"Thank you," said Gabriel, turning and walking away.

"So, which of you would like to begin?"

Brackett crossed his arms, sat back in the booth, and stared at Michael.

Michael leaned in toward him. "If you have no interest in conversation, I think I'll just excuse myself so that I can return home to a proper dinner."

Brackett scowled but said nothing.

Michael looked at Marilena. "Is this how it's going to be?"

She gestured no. "He just can't bring himself to admit how badly we're fucked."

"Ah, so we're into technical terms."

"I don't agree," said Brackett. "It's just a temporary setback."

"Really?" said Marilena. "How do you figure that?"

Brackett rolled his eyes. "We're in no hurry. No one knows what we have nor has any way of finding out that we have it—unless we're dumb enough to tell someone. All we have to do is wait until the right opportunity comes along. And it will, trust me. Time is on our side."

Michael coughed. "As the presumed *someone* in your hypothetical, permit me to say that I feel safer not knowing, so please don't tell me what *it* is. But your problem isn't with me, or whoever you choose to work with. It's with the hunters out there looking for your *it*. Contrary to your rosy outlook, time is *not* on your side . . . sooner or later, they'll find you."

"How can they possibly find us?" said Marilena.

"It's simple—"

"Here you are folks, a toasted cheese with tomato, two coffees, a bran muffin, and one water. Will there be anything else?" asked Gabriel.

"No, thank you. Not at the moment," said Michael, taking a bite of the sandwich. "This is very good."

"Thank you," said Gabriel, nodding and walking away.

"Get on with what you were saying," pressed Brackett.

Michael took another bite and sipped his coffee. "Your Achilles heel is how you came to possess the item. Once the hunters figure that out," he pointed to the sandwich, "you're toast."

"They'll never figure that out," said Brackett.

"I don't know how you can say that, because if it's obvious to me how you came to possess it, what makes you think they can't figure it out?"

"You couldn't possibly know," snapped Brackett.

"How do you think we got it?" asked Marilena.

"With the right perspective, it's obvious." Michael picked up his coffee and took another sip. "From one of your patients."

Marilena's mouth dropped and Brackett's face blanched.

"How did you know that?" she asked.

"I'll accept that as a compliment to my reasoning, and press my luck by venturing to say that, from the fact your brother included you in this operation, the patient was yours, not his."

"*Jesus,*" said Brackett loudly.

"I suggest you keep your voice down." Michael picked up the sandwich. "I'll get to all of that, but there's another, more troubling factor I'm also certain of." He took a bite.

"Please, enough with the sandwich," said Brackett, visibly struggling to contain his impatience.

Michael dabbed at his chin with a napkin. "Whoever entrusted you with the item is no longer around."

"Who could have told you that?" said Marilena, clutching her hands on the tabletop.

"No one had to tell me anything. It's obvious. How else could an unworldly, straitlaced pair of innocents such as yourselves possibly come to possess such an inherently dangerous item? You had to get it from someone involved with the seamier side of life, someone who trusted you implicitly. Voila, a patient." He took a sip of coffee. "As for the current status of your patient, it's hard to imagine you blindly flailing out to the criminal underworld for help in finding someone to dispose of what you have if the original owner was still around." He put down the cup. "My guess is your patient is now dead. As to how the patient died, I'd prefer not to guess."

"We had nothing to do with her death," said Brackett.

Marilena dropped her chin to her chest. "She was my patient. She was going through a vicious divorce."

"You don't have to tell him details," said Brackett.

Marilena glared. "We're way beyond that point."

Brackett shut his eyes and leaned back in the booth, gripping his arms tightly across his chest.

"At our last session, she said she'd discovered something of great value to her husband, something giving her all the leverage she needed to get what she wanted in her divorce. Her husband didn't know she had it, and she needed a place to hide it. I suggested she take it to her lawyer. She said that would be the first place her husband would look. That's when she asked if I would keep it for her until she found a better hiding place. I said yes, and she took a package the size of a large hardcover book out of her bag and handed it to me." Marilena paused to take a long sip of water. "I put it in our office safe. The next day, I read in the newspaper that she'd been killed by a hit-and-run driver. It happened after leaving our office on her way to a nearby parking garage."

"Do you think it was an accident or something else?"

Marilena sighed. "I've no idea."

"Of course, you do," said Brackett. "She said she was in mortal fear of her husband arranging to have her killed, but you convinced her that her fears were unrealistic."

"Are you suggesting I'm somehow to blame for what happened to my patient? God, why did I ever tell you about the package?"

"Uh, yes, the package. Let's get back to that," said Michael. "Why didn't you turn it over to the authorities?"

"Because my brilliant brother wanted to see what was in it."

"Yes, and after we opened it, *you* pointed out how valuable it was," Brackett said. "It would set us up for life and beyond, I believe were your exact words."

Michael spoke up. "And because your patient was dead, and she'd said her husband didn't know she'd taken whatever she'd given to you, you assumed no one could ever trace it back to you."

"Yes," said Marilena. "And a patient of my brother's had once mentioned Carlucci as someone who disposed of valuable things of questionable provenance anonymously."

"Who's the patient?"

Brackett pounced. "Sorry, that's a matter of doctor–patient confidentiality."

Michael exhaled deeply and looked at Marilena. "Did her husband know she was seeing you?"

"I doubt it. She had no reason to tell him."

"What about her lawyer? Did he know?"

"I don't know."

"Did she ever talk to a friend or family member about seeing you?"

"I don't know."

"How did she find you?"

"I treated a close friend of hers. But the friend died long before the wife started seeing me as a patient."

"How did she get to her appointments?"

"She drove herself."

"Did she pay for her sessions by check or credit card?"

"Cash."

"I thought about all that," smirked Brackett. "There's no payment record for her husband to trace back to us." He looked at his sister. "Like I keep saying, there's nothing to worry about."

Michael folded his paper napkin. "Sorry to rain on your parade, but I think you're overlooking the most likely consequences of your being tied to a murder victim."

"Carlucci?" said Brackett.

"No. Your patient."

Brackett shook his head. "How can a hit-and-run possibly tie back to us."

"If you want to bet your life trusting coincidences, go for it." Michael leaned back. "But if your patient's fears were well-founded, the driver was more likely an assassin who'd been looking for the right opportunity to strike."

Brackett fidgeted in his seat.

"If he hasn't already, at some point her husband will discover he's missing his treasure and start tearing the world apart looking for it. Sooner or later he'll realize his wife's the likely culprit and retrace her steps . . . including her coming out of your building before she died. How long do you think it will take him to learn she'd been to your office?" Michael leaned back. "I doubt your subsequent interactions with her husband and his colleagues will be pleasant ones."

"Stop trying to frighten my sister!"

"Frankly, I'm trying to frighten you."

Brackett bit at his lower lip.

Michael picked up his sandwich. "Isn't it interesting how a toasted cheese sandwich, even when cold, has a decidedly different taste than an untoasted one." He took a bite.

Brackett stared into his coffee cup. “What should we do?”

Michael finished chewing. “I presume you invited me here this evening hoping for an answer to that question.”

Brackett and Marilena nodded.

“Although I’d genuinely like to do business with you, for it sounds like an immensely profitable opportunity, in good conscience, the only course I see open to you that will protect you from what you fear is to turn the package over to the authorities.”

Brackett vigorously shook his head. “It’s not the sort of thing we can trust the authorities to deal with appropriately.”

“What’s that mean?”

“We’d have to do it anonymously. But word of its discovery will inevitably leak to the press, drawing widespread attention and a clamoring for the identity of whoever turned it over. Even if the authorities don’t give into pressures to investigate, the media won’t stop until they find us. Once that happens, we’ll be the husband’s number-one target for revenge.”

Michael stared at Brackett. “You’re really tempting me to ask what it is, but I won’t bite.”

“And I won’t say.”

“At least tell me the name of the husband?”

“Victor Persky.”

“Can’t say I’ve heard of him.”

Marilena leaned in and whispered, “His wife told me he’s very secretive. And rich enough to pay people to keep his name out of the news and social media. On top of that he kept her a virtual recluse from every aspect of his life.”

Michael looked back and forth between Marilena and Brackett. “And you actually believed that the two of you could pull off this hustle against someone with that sort of power? There’s no doubt in my mind he’ll find you once he starts looking.” He ran a hand through his hair. “You two are crazier than your patients.”

“Our patients aren’t crazy,” said a suddenly indignant Brackett.

“Modification accepted.” Michael drew in a breath, shut his eyes, exhaled, and opened them. “I’ll have to think about this and get back to you. It’s not going to be easy straightening this out if you’re insisting that turning it over to the authorities is off the table.”

Brackett fumed. "You mean you won't help us sell it?"

"I don't want to be responsible for your demise. I'll repeat what I said: Your safest bet is to turn it over to the authorities anonymously and be done with it."

Brackett waved to Gabriel for the check. "And I've already told *you*: I'm an adamant *no* on that point." He stood and gestured for his sister to do the same.

Marilena didn't move. "Couldn't we just give it back to my patient's husband?"

"That depends on whether or not he's willing to risk living out his days knowing that the two of you could at any time point to him as the possessor of what I assume is a priceless, purloined treasure. If he isn't comfortable with that . . ."

"It's as I've always said," muttered Brackett. "Our only option is to find a buyer who's as concerned about maintaining lifelong secrecy as are we. But as Michael's not interested in helping us find such a buyer, we no longer need bother him with any of this. Come, let's go."

Marilena slid out of the booth, as Brackett threw a fifty on the table and stormed toward the door without saying good-bye.

Marilena stood and reached out to shake Michael's hand. "Thank you. I apologize for my brother. He's generally not this rude. He's just anxious about our situation."

Michael shook her hand without standing. "He should be. To borrow from your lexicon of technical terms, I'd say the two of you should be *scared shitless*."

Michael remained in the booth, nibbling at his sandwich.

"You can stop eating that," said Gabriel, sitting down across from him. "They just drove away."

"I happen to like it. It's quite tasty. Mrs. Baker keeps me on a rather bland diet."

"If you think a toasted cheese sandwich is stimulating, wait until you try what Gee's cooked up. It's his country's national dish, a spicy lamb stew made with tomatoes, okra, onions, and spices I can't pronounce."

Michael feigned a smile. "Sounds charming. The perfect cap to an agita-inducing evening."

"Was it that bad?"

"Worse. He's arrogant and narcissistic; she's the rational one but she's intimidated by him, and both are overcome with anxiety."

"Sounds like they should be treating each other."

"Amazing, isn't it?" Michael pushed his plate away. "What really troubles me is this nagging feeling in the pit of my stomach that anyone who gets involved with them in their mess runs a bigger risk of getting killed than they do."

"Sounds like you're having second thoughts on your decision to re-enter the real world."

"From what I just said you might think so. But no, I'm not. At least I don't think so. It's just frustrating when people who come to you for help won't listen to reason." Michael drummed his fingertips on the tabletop. "At least two people tied into whatever the Fieldings are trying to unload have turned up dead."

"Two?"

Michael recounted his conversation with the Fieldings. "Carlucci's one, but their patient was the first, also likely murdered."

"Maybe that girl Maria was too?"

"Anything's possible."

Gabriel shut his eyes. "I'm upset about that poor girl. Perhaps I could have done something."

"I know how you feel, but don't beat yourself up over what happened to her. She was a junkie, and I seriously doubt anything you could have said to her would have mattered."

Gabriel opened his eyes. "I at least could have spoken to her friend."

"Carlucci? Not a chance."

"No, the young man who met her for lunch once a week."

Michael sat up. "You never told me about any young man."

"You never brought up the subject of female ex-customers of mine until our last conversation, which happened to take place in the middle of my dinner rush hour after you'd announced you were on the way over here."

Michael waved his hand. "Fine, get on with it."

"Every Sunday, he'd tie his dog up out front, come inside, and wait until a seat at the counter opened up next to her. I once offered them a booth, but she refused. I sensed she didn't want to make it obvious they knew each other."

"Was he her boyfriend?"

"Could be, but I don't think so. He looked to be in his mid-twenties, and spoke to her seriously, as if he were a parent. My guess was he worked the rest of the week and Sunday was his day off."

"If he were family, why didn't he take her home? Get her out of her hellhole life?"

"Maybe he'd tried and it didn't work. Runaways will run away again if what drove them away in the first place hasn't changed. He might have thought lunch once a week was the best way to keep a communication line open to her."

"Her death must have come as quite a shock, especially if he thought he was helping her. Has he been back since her death?"

"Only once. It was the first Sunday after what I now know was Angel taking over for Maria. He showed up at his normal Sunday lunchtime, but Maria never did. He was visibly upset and asked if she'd been there earlier. I told him I hadn't seen her in a few days. He left without eating, untied his dog, and took off. I've not seen him since."

"Any chance you caught a name or something that might help identify him?"

"Nope. They both always paid for their lunch in cash."

"Did he know Carlucci?"

"I never heard him mention his name."

Michael shook his head. "Anything else you haven't told me?"

Gabriel flashed a sarcastic smile. "Yes, I confronted my busboy."

"And?"

"He broke down and cried like a baby. Said he had no idea he was doing anything wrong, let alone something that might put me in danger or hurt the diner. He swore he'd never do anything like that again, or talk about what he'd done for Carlucci with anyone."

"Since I see he's still working here, I assume you believed him."

He shrugged. "What can I say, I'm a soft touch."

"I'm sure." Michael stretched out his arms and yawned. "Speaking of generosity, I'm happy the Fieldings paid for the glorious meal they treated me to." He started to slide across the booth.

"What are you doing?" said Gabriel.

"Heading home."

"Not unless you're prepared to offend a very emotional man's national pride in a dish I told you he made especially for you."

At that moment a large casserole arrived at the table, delivered by an even larger, smiling man.

Michael returned Gee's smile and abruptly turned to Gabriel. "That's very kind of each of you, but I'm afraid Mrs. Baker is expecting me home for dinner."

"No problem. I already called and told her you'd be dining here tonight. She thought it was a good idea. Said you could use a night out in the real world, away from your window seat."

"How very thoughtful of you both," said Michael through tightly compressed lips.

"Think nothing of it," grinned Gabriel. "Besides, it's just the first course. Bon appétit."

Michael had to admit he ate more than he usually did, and that the meal generated far more pizzazz than he was used to. Some of that he attributed to the wine Gabriel had surreptitiously supplied, camouflaged in water tumblers to keep any curious customers from wondering when the diner had obtained a liquor license.

It also had gone on far longer than Michael expected, in large measure because of his reminiscences of his exploits with Gabriel's father, including their time together in war. Gabriel asked whether Michael had been with his father when he died. At that, Michael gave an abrupt side-to-side shake of his head and moments later excused himself, saying he had to return home.

Gabriel offered to call a taxi or walk Michael home, but he declined both. "I need to walk off as much of this meal as possible, but don't worry about me, I'm like an old warhorse. I can find my way home from here with my eyes shut."

He thanked Gabriel for the company, praised Gee for the food, donned his coat and hat, picked up his cane, and made his way out the door.

The evening air struck him as crisp, and surprisingly fresh for the city. He drew in and let out a deep breath before starting out toward home. The street lay patched in random light seeping out through gated storefronts and snuggly curtained upper story windows. Every sound of life seemed to come from someplace far way. This was not how Michael remembered the street. These days, neighbors stayed inside past dark, leaving the street to care for itself.

Michael paused. *Perhaps company on the walk home wouldn't be such a bad idea, after all.* He felt silly at the thought of going back to ask Gabriel for an escort on a simple, few blocks walk through his own childhood neighborhood.

He kept walking.

He sensed the man pressed back in the doorway's shadows before he saw him. Michael scanned ahead and behind and out along the row of parked cars, searching for an accomplice. He saw none.

Nor was there anyone else on the street. Only the two of them.

Michael knew he was about to be attacked and had no way to outrun his assailant.

"Top of the evening, sir," said Michael stopping ten paces before the doorway, staring straight at the man.

The man paused for an instant, as if startled, but stepped far enough into the light to show the blade in his hand.

"Ah, so that's what this is," said Michael, raising his blackthorn cane in front of him as a conductor would his wand. "Well, let's get on with it."

With a flick of his wrist, the cane twirled in the air, in and out, then back and forth and side-to-side. As if this left any doubt in the stranger's mind as to whether Michael knew how to wield a club, he ended by spinning the cane over his head before bringing it abruptly to rest pinned beneath his armpit.

"Are you going to bring it on or not? I really would like to get home."

Michael wasn't sure, but thought he saw the man smile.

The man stepped out of the doorway. "I gotta lot easier ways to make a livin' than takin' a chance getting my head cracked open by a crazy old man with a shillelagh."

And with that, the man walked away.

ELEVEN

Michael stood at his front door jiggling his key as he aimed for the lock. He'd made it the rest of the way home without incident, but the adrenaline rush from his run-in had left him shaking. He'd not felt this way in a very long time. What he felt wasn't fear, but a renewed sense of being alive. He needed to digest the feeling and determine what it meant.

He wasn't a young man anymore and held no misconceptions about how his engagement with the stranger likely would have ended, had it gone to battle; nor did he feel helpless—as he had so long ago when his friends perished and he'd survived.

"A bit tipsy, are we?" bellowed Mrs. Baker, pulling open the front door.

"I'm just a bit out of practice with the key." Michael stepped inside, handing Mrs. Baker his hat and coat.

"How was your evening?"

"We had dinner, reminisced about old times, and I came home. What's to tell?" He'd decided that mentioning his episode with the mugger would inevitably lead to a pitched battle with Mrs. Baker when he next needed to go out alone.

"I meant with those Fielding people."

"Hello, Mr. Michael," said Angel, standing in the kitchen doorway.

"Good evening, Angel." He smiled at Mrs. Baker. "And what have you two been up to while I was out and about?"

"I'm teaching Angel how to mend clothing."

"And she lectures me on world events."

"Two important disciplines to master," nodded Michael. "Perhaps someday you'll be able the use the former to better the latter."

"Would you like tea?" asked Mrs. Baker.

"No, thank you." He paused. "But I could use a sherry."

"Haven't you had enough to drink?"

Michael cocked his head. "Sounds like you managed to squeeze some details out of Gabriel about our evening."

She grinned. "He tried being wily, but I got it out of him. Every glassful."

Michael nodded. "I bet you did."

"Would you like your sherry served in your study?"

"If it's OK with you, I'd prefer joining the two of you in the kitchen."

Mrs. Baker blinked twice and turned to Angel. "Dearie, please clean up that mess we made on the kitchen table." She looked at Michael. "After all, we wouldn't want our clutter distracting you from telling us *everything* that happened tonight."

"You seem suspicious."

"Me?" she said, pointing at her bosom in mock surprise. "For the first time in recent memory, you ventured out of the house on your own, not once, but twice in a single day. Now you return home only to announce that you suddenly prefer sitting with us around the kitchen table. How could I be anything but suspicious?"

Michael looked down at his cane. "You made me agree to move the kitchen up here from downstairs as a condition of your employment. So, I could say I'm just getting around to taking advantage of it." He headed toward the kitchen, passing Angel on her way out, and made his way to the far end of a long, oak-plank table, before dropping on to a cherry Windsor dining chair. Mrs. Baker followed, stopping by the chair next to his.

He looked up at her. "Actually, something about the people I met today made me want to be more involved in life than watching it from afar."

Mrs. Baker feigned a swoon into the chair. "I don't know what kind of wine you had at dinner, but whatever it is I'm going to get the name from Gabriel and make sure we always have plenty on hand."

Michael laughed. "It wasn't the wine."

Angel walked in carrying a sherry bottle and two glasses. "Is this what you wanted?" She put the bottle on the table between Michael and Mrs. Baker and set a sherry glass down in front of each of them.

"Yes, thank you," said Michael, opening the bottle. "I see you're teaching her well," he said, pouring Mrs. Baker a glass before pouring one for himself.

"Um . . . I didn't say I wanted a drink."

"Indulge me. It will make it easier for you to take what I'm about to tell you." He motioned for Angel to join them. She picked up a glass of apple juice from a countertop and sat across from them,

"OK, what happened?" said Mrs. Baker.

"When it comes to rating evenings, I'd say my toasted cheese sandwich was the highlight of tonight's get-together." He told them of his conversation with the Fieldings, but not of his subsequent conversation with Gabriel.

"With instincts like that, it's amazing those two have survived this long," said Mrs. Baker.

"Blind luck, I'd say."

"I know what you told them, but I also know how you think. So, my guess is you have something percolating in there," she pointed at Michael's head, "to get them out of the mess they're in."

He took a sip of sherry. "I'm tempted to let them figure their way out of this on their own. After all, it's a situation of their own creation, and I see no sign of any willingness on the brother's part to listen to anyone offering advice he doesn't want to hear."

"You have to help them, sir," said Angel.

Michael looked at her. "Why?"

"If only for the sister. He has her doing whatever he says. Without your help, it will only get worse for her."

"She's not exactly an innocent in this mess," said Mrs. Baker.

"Who among us is?" said Angel.

Michael smiled at Mrs. Baker. "She seems to know her Bible."

Angel sat up straight in her chair. "I think the sister's doing what she has to do to please her brother, even if she realizes it's wrong. They may be rich, but it's the same sort of twisted relationship I've seen over and over on the streets. Demean and dominate."

Michael stared at her.

"You don't have to say it. I know what you're thinking. And you're right. I know what I said is true because I've been a victim of that same sort of relationship."

He smiled. “Perhaps your insights can help me with something else. The young woman you replaced as Carlucci’s courier, Maria, was a regular at the diner for lunch, and every Sunday she had company.” Michael described Maria’s young man and what Gabriel had told him about their lunches together. “Do you have any idea who the young man might be?”

Angel shook her head. “I know nothing about her life.”

“What about your roommates who used to share the apartment with her. Did they ever talk about Maria or her family?”

“Not to me.” Angel shut her eyes, as if struggling to concentrate. “But I remember one girl saying, ‘Someone should let her brother know she’s dead.’” Angel paused, her eyes still shut. “The other girl said forget about it.” She opened her eyes. “I guess that could explain the man.”

“Where are those girls now?”

“I don’t know. I left as soon as I saw Carlucci’s body, but they might still be there. It’s not as if they had many choices if they wanted a roof over their heads.” Angel sighed. “Who knows, if you hadn’t taken me in, I might have gone back there.”

Michael patted her hand. “That’s all behind you now.” He leaned back. “According to the newspaper, they’ve spoken to the police. Do you think they’d be willing to talk about things they didn’t tell the police?”

“It depends on what they’re offered.”

Mrs. Baker perked up. “Don’t you dare tell me you’re thinking of bringing those girls here.”

He lifted the sherry to his lips. “Don’t worry Mrs. B., I’m not about to turn this into a home for lost souls. Three in one household are more than enough.”

“This new leaf of yours is going to drive me mad,” said Mrs. Baker, picking up her sherry and slugging it down.

Michael refilled her glass, and raised his own in a toast, “To life. And to madness. May one never outdistance the other.”

Angel raised her glass. “Amen.”

The screaming had begun the moment Brackett and Marilena got into their car outside the diner. He raged on about how she had seen to reveal so much to a stranger. She yelled back that he was the one who’d introduced her to Michael as their “savior.”

"I don't trust him," he shouted, pounding on the steering wheel. "There's no way he could have guessed how we got the package."

She stared at the side of her brother's head and calmly said, "I realize your fragile ego is terribly offended by how easily he figured out both the identity and fate of the package's source. But the bottom line is, *he did*. So get over it."

"He must be working for your dead patient's husband."

"I certainly hope you're wrong, because if he is, after what we told him tonight, we're both as good as dead. On the other hand, if he isn't, and we don't listen to him, we soon will be."

Brackett's voice took on a familiar, silky tone. "You need to have faith in me. I need your confidence and support to get us through this."

"Don't try pulling your condescending clinical-voice bullshit on me, Brackett. Either we do what Michael says or I'm out of this practice, this town, and your life."

He jerked his head around to face her. "You wouldn't dare. You can't survive without me."

She pointed straight ahead. "Keep your eyes on the road." She waited until he had. "Co-dependency works two ways. I don't know anyone who'd be willing to indulge your narcissistic insecurities by catering to your fantasy-world whims and schemes like I do. But even I have limits."

"What's that supposed to mean?"

"Either you and I work our way through this mess with Michael's help or you'll be dealing with this on your own."

"I don't believe you."

"I'm not surprised, because it's a rational decision, something you seem incapable of making."

He cursed under his breath.

"Let me put it this way: If I do what you're asking, there's a very high probability I'll end up murdered. On the other hand, if I leave you to pursue your craziness on your own, I'm far more likely to end up attending your funeral than being a participant in my own."

He pulled the car over to the curb and stared at her. "You're serious?"

"Of course, I'm serious. I'm not into suicide pacts."

Brackett chewed at his lip. "I have another plan."

She sighed. "What is it?"

"Just trust me."

She laughed. "You have got to be kidding. Read my lips: *not a chance.*"

"OK, OK. Here's what I have in mind: The patient who told me about Carlucci must have connections to others like him. I'll just ask my patient for another recommendation."

Marilena fixed her eyes on his. "In my professional opinion, you're in serious need of help."

"Stop with the—"

She stuck her finger in his face. "Listen to me. Your patient likely knows Carlucci was murdered, but he's also likely forgotten that he ever mentioned Carlucci's name to you, and even if he hasn't forgotten, it's hard to imagine him conceiving of any connection between you and Carlucci or Carlucci's death." She struggled to maintain her poise. "But all that changes the instant you ask him for a second recommendation. Criminals like your patient are suspicious by nature, always doubting coincidences and always looking for an underlying motive. It's how they profit, how they keep out of jail, how they survive. At the very least, you'll get him to wondering whether you knew Carlucci was dead. By raising the subject with him, you risk getting the wheels turning in his mind and triggering serious thinking on his part about why you need a replacement for Carlucci."

"But we had nothing to do with Carlucci or his death."

"Who knows why he was murdered? But assuming his death had nothing to do with us, or what we wanted him to do, once your criminally connected patient starts snooping around, there's no telling what he might turn up or who else might get interested." She shook her head. "We can't forget Michael's warning. The husband of my patient will soon be knocking on our door, looking for his package. We don't need any more bad guys suddenly taking up an interest in us."

Brackett's knuckles whitened as he grasped the gear shift. "I don't see things the same way you do."

"No kidding."

"But, since you feel so strongly, I'll go along with you on this."

Marilena studied her brother's face. "Are you serious?"

He smiled. "Absolutely. After all, you're not just my sister, but my only living relative. Even though I don't agree with you about this, I'll do what you say."

Marilena's eyes welled-up as she leaned across to kiss him on the cheek.

He smiled and turned back on to the road, muttering to himself. "For now."

After dropping his sister off at her apartment in Douglaston, Queens, Brackett instinctively headed for the highways that would take him west over the George Washington Bridge to the Palisades Parkway and his mini mansion in fashionable Alpine, New Jersey. But his confrontation with Marilena had left him far too wound up to head directly home. Rush hour had long passed, and a leisurely drive snuggled in his big BMW seemed the perfect way to calm down and organize his thoughts. He selected EASY LISTENING on the audio playlist, fixed cruise control at slightly above the speed limit, and headed north toward the Tappan Zee Bridge. He, like most long-time users of the bridge, still called it by its old name despite its recent rechristening to honor a former New York governor. There he'd cross the broad Hudson River and wind home south along Route 9W.

Marilena had surprised him with the ferocity of her reaction. It wasn't like her. She'd always done what he asked. She'd argue, sure, but in the end, she'd do what he said. He knew the gears and levers that made her work. He'd even convinced her to abandon her lifelong desire for a medical degree, something he'd obtained, arguing that if she chose to be a psychologist instead, they could team up together in a practice offering different psychological services to patients.

He wasn't sure what was driving her behavioral change, but one thing was clear: Michael had emerged as a direct threat to his authority. He had Marilena deferring to his opinions over her own brother's. He couldn't allow that erosion to continue. He had to nip it in the bud.

He pressed the phone icon on the steering wheel. "Dial Anthony Bodine."

"Dialing Anthony Bodine," came over the speaker, followed by three rings.

"Hello?"

"Mr. Bodine, hello, it's Dr. Fielding."

"Dr. Fielding? Oh, sorry, I wasn't expecting your call. Is everything all right?"

"Oh, yes, what I'm calling about has nothing to do with you. It concerns another patient."

"Another patient? I'm sorry. I don't follow."

"He came to me today with a problem that's outside my ability to help him with. But if my memory served me correctly, in the course of one of our sessions you described someone who might be just the person he needs."

"I'm drawing a blank. Could you give me a bit of a hint of what I said?"

"No problem. It was such an inconsequential conversation, I'm surprised I remembered it at all. He's looking for someone who could resolve what he called a 'delicate matter.'"

The line went quiet for a moment. "What sort of *delicate matter*?"

"He's trying to find a buyer for something valuable, but I've no idea what it is."

"Ah, now I remember . . ."

"Terrific."

"Sadly, the man I mentioned left the business."

Brackett hesitated at Bodine's cagey answer. He wondered whether he should risk raising the man's suspicion by pressing him for another name. He decided to try to get Bodine to suggest an alternate on his own.

"That's too, bad."

"Yeah, and he gave it up only a few days ago. A lousy coincidence, him dropping out of the business just as your patient needs his help."

"Such are the fates." Brackett paused. "But I do so hate disappointing patients."

"Sorry, I wish there were some way I could help you."

Brackett took that to be as good an opening as he was likely to get. "Perhaps there is . . . if there's someone else who might be able to help him . . .?"

A moment of silence, then: "How urgent is it?"

Brackett forced a laugh. "From my take on the level of my patient's anxiety, I'd say he considers it quite urgent."

"I'll get right on it for you. Can you give me your patient's name?"

"As I'm certain you can appreciate, my patient is anxious to keep his identity secret, which is why he asked that I call you rather than simply introduce you."

"I see. So, all contacts are to run through you?"

"Yes, but strictly as the conduit for my patient."

"Gotcha."

"Um . . . when do you think you might have something for me to pass along?"

"Soon."

"Thank you."

"Sure, no problem. Bye."

The line went dead, and the music resumed playing in the background.

Brackett smiled. *That went well.* Soon his sister would see that he was right, he'd regain her unquestioned trust in his judgment, and Michael would be out of the picture.

Anthony Bodine was getting ready for bed when Dr. Fielding called. Though he'd once been a serious hypochondriac, he wasn't used to receiving calls from his doctors at such late hours. For years, every little twitch, blemish, or pain sent him running to the hospital in a paranoid frenzy. That's what had initially driven him to see Dr. Fielding.

With the doctor's counseling and prescriptions for anti-anxiety medication, he'd been able to regain control of his life. He owed Dr. Fielding a lot. Which was why he decided to play along with the good doctor's obvious charade about a patient looking for a hook-up to replace the now-dead Carlucci.

Bodine wasn't about to judge why his doctor would be mixed up in something shady. After all, Bodine's business was all about helping otherwise upstanding members of society defraud their partners, shareholders, creditors, spouses, and governments.

He performed what he considered unofficial bank-clearinghouse operations out of nondescript second- and third-floor offices in an off-the-beaten-path South Bronx neighborhood filled with cheaply constructed early twentieth-century two- and three-story brick buildings. Clients seeking to siphon money undetected out of their businesses brought Bodine checks payable against phony invoices purportedly issued by major corporations. He cashed their checks, less his three to five percent fee, then submitted the checks to his bribed contacts at the appropriate banks for full payment to him, not the corporations named on the checks.

The beauty of his business lay in its simplicity. The checks were returned to his clients by their banks in the normal course of business, marked as canceled and paid to the issuers of the invoices, leaving no one to question the transactions. The clients who wrote the checks would not complain and, as the invoices were phony, they left no record at the corporations of any unpaid invoices. The only risk to the client was a tax audit, but rarely did the government ever seek to verify that a third-party invoice was legitimate. There was, however, an overriding additional risk for those foolish enough to give Bodine a check with not enough money in the account to cover it: his fee instantly quadrupled and less than immediate payment came with potentially fatal consequences.

He'd been providing his services for years and over that time had cultivated deep contacts within the legitimate and illegitimate business worlds. That was precisely the sort of help Dr. Fielding needed. But Bodine wasn't about to simply give him a name and turn him loose. The doctor was far too naive. If he had something valuable, he risked being ripped off in any number of ways, plus setting himself up for blackmail or worse, such as serving as a "bigger fish to fry" bargaining chip in some down-the-road plea deal with a prosecutor.

He would have had a much easier time finding the right person for Dr. Fielding if the doctor had simply told him what he wanted to unload. Obviously, that wasn't going to happen, which meant Bodine would have to do a bit of snooping on his own to see what it might be. He knew where to start looking and planned to turn to that first thing in the morning.

He sat on the edge of his bed and stared at the floor. Given all that Dr. Fielding had done to calm Bodine's anxieties, the least he could do was help to settle the good doctor's own bad case of nerves.

"Good morning, Rachel."

The woman behind the counter looked up at the stocky man carrying a shopping bag and headed straight for her. The puzzled look on her face morphed into a broad smile. "Mr. Bodine, we haven't seen you here in a long time."

He stopped at the counter, lifted a huge box of chocolates out of the bag, and placed it on the counter in front of her. "This is for you."

She almost blushed but pulled the chocolates down on to her desktop. "Oh, you're always so thoughtful."

"It's the least I can do for what you and Dr. Fielding did for me."

Her face took on a look of concern. "Is everything all right?"

"Absolutely. I was in the neighborhood and thought I'd stop by for quick hello."

"That's nice, but Dr. Fielding isn't in the office this morning. This is his day to see patients at a clinic across town."

Bodine snapped his fingers. "Darn, I should have remembered that, but when he called me last night, he never mentioned he wouldn't be in this morning. I guess he thought I already knew that."

Rachel leaned toward him. "Don't blame yourself. Between you and me, these days he's not been himself. Something's bothering him."

Bodine rested his forearms on the counter and leaned in toward Rachel. "I had precisely the same feeling after I hung up with him."

"Oh?"

"Yeah. And, frankly, he had me a bit concerned." He smiled. "And I thought *I* was the one with the anxiety disorder."

She shut her eyes and nodded. "He hasn't been the same since our patient died." She opened her eyes.

Bodine mirrored her nod. "That's probably it. The death of someone whose innermost thoughts you've shared must be horribly disturbing."

"But she wasn't his patient. She was his sister's patient."

He nodded. "I guess that's the curse of being such an empathetic man."

She shrugged. "I've never seen him react like that before. Or her. The woman's death rocked both of them to the core."

"Why do you think that is?"

She shrugged. "Perhaps because she was killed right after leaving our office."

Bodine jerked back. "What?"

"A hit-and-run driver killed her as she crossed the street on her way to where she'd parked her car."

"When did it happen?"

"About ten days ago. It was all over the news."

"What a tragedy." He patted the countertop. "Let's hope that Dr. Fielding and his sister work through this soon."

"Amen to that. Every day seems to present a new surprise. They've gone from missing appointments or canceling them at the last minute, to shouting at each other over whether or not a new patient is their savior. Can you believe it? Doctors arguing over whether a *patient* is *their* savior?"

"Hard to imagine. I could use a savior myself." Bodine smiled. "Is the new patient listed in the phonebook under 'savior'?"

She laughed. "If you ask me, he's just a curmudgeonly old man, but Dr. Fielding told me he's a very important man."

"Maybe I know him?"

"I wish I could tell you, but you know that I can't."

"Of course."

"Maybe Dr. Fielding will tell you."

"Yeah, I'll ask him if I still need a savior the next time we speak." He smiled. "Well, I guess I'll be going. No reason to take up any more of your valuable time."

"You're always welcome here, Mr. Bodine."

"I'll call ahead next time I'm in the neighborhood. I leave it to your judgment, but I see no reason to tell him I was here. He might blame himself for missing me, and he already has more than enough on his mind."

"You're a kind man."

"Thank you, my love." He blew her a kiss as he left the office.

While Bodine waited for the elevator, he opened his smart phone and searched for the name of a female victim of a hit-and-run driver, ten days before. He found what he was looking for, felt a chill on the back of his neck, and breathed aloud: "Oh my God."

TWELVE

Angel spent the hour before dawn finding chores for herself to do in the small garden behind the house. No one had asked her to do any of that, but the work reminded her of happier days watching her father work his fields, learning to do things she'd thought she'd never have the opportunity to practice again.

A door down the hall from her room opened out on to the garden, and she'd taken care not to make any noise that might disturb Mr. Michael or Mrs. Baker. She paused as dawn began to creep into the sky, and smiled to herself at how rapidly her life had changed from her days of sitting on a park bench, waiting for dawn to arrive. She shifted her gaze from the sky to the house and wondered how many other homeowners kept the back sides of their properties as pristinely as Mr. Michael did his. She guessed that most preened their public facades, but here, out of sight from the street, each window frame shone neatly painted, each stone fit firmly in place, and each gutter properly drained away from the foundation. Even the exterior rear stairs, running from the garden up to the kitchen, matched the stonework of the house.

As Angel's gaze drifted from one kitchen level window to the next, she caught sight of Mr. Michael standing by a parlor window. He waved, she waved back, and he gestured for her to come inside. She replaced the trowel in the basket where she'd found it and hurried up the stairs to the kitchen door.

Mr. Michael opened the door for her. "I see you're still an early riser."

"I hope I didn't disturb you," she said with a tinge of anxiety.

"No, not at all. I'm a rather early bird myself. I'm happy to see you like working in the garden. That shall be of great assistance to Mrs. B. She detests gardening, though our occasional gardeners may feel somewhat challenged by your obvious skills."

"Thank you."

"Come, please sit with me at the kitchen table."

"Would you like me to make your breakfast?"

He smiled. "*Those* skills might threaten Mrs. B. She considers cooking her domain."

"Oh."

"But a tea would be nice, if you don't mind."

"Certainly."

Michael read a newspaper as Angel prepared his tea, then served it to him on a silver tray with two biscuits.

"Hopefully Mrs. B won't consider me giving you biscuits 'cooking.'"

He put down the paper. "I think we're safe." He fiddled with his tea for a moment. "So, is everything to your liking?"

"Oh, yes, sir."

He gestured to a chair across from him. "Please fix something for yourself and sit down."

"I'm not hungry."

"Of course, you are. You've been working since well before sunup. At least have some of these biscuits."

She paused, then brought a bottle of milk, the tin of biscuits, a plate, and a glass to the table, and sat where he'd pointed.

"That's better." He poured his tea. "I want to talk to you about the girls who lived with you in your old apartment."

Angel nodded.

"Do you happen to still have your keys to that apartment?"

She shook her head. "I threw them away after I fled the apartment. I imagined that every police officer I saw was looking for me, and I feared the keys would tie me to the murder if they found them on me." She paused. "Why do you ask?"

"I've decided to pay them a visit today. When do you think I'll have the best chance of catching them at home?"

Her eyes widened. "Oh, you can't do *that*. The building's run by gangs. You won't be safe. They'll rob you for sure and might do worse."

"Oh, don't worry about that. I can handle them."

She started blinking wildly. "No, you can't. You don't understand. A lot of them are on drugs, they act crazy, and there's no telling what harm they might do to someone like you."

"I appreciate your concern, but I really do have to speak to those girls."

"Why?"

"I want to learn about Maria's brother. And your former roommates are the only links I see to him."

"I don't think you should be going there. It's too dangerous."

"Shouldn't be going where?" came echoing through the kitchen doorway, followed by Mrs. Baker.

Angel's eyes jumped between Mrs. Baker and Michael, her face looking lost at what to say.

"Angel doesn't think it's safe for me to pay a visit on the apartment where she lived before joining us."

Mrs. Baker walked over to the refrigerator, opened it, and began removing ingredients. "I told you she was a smart girl." She put everything down on a countertop next to the stove and reached for a frying pan. She held the pan in the air and wielded it in Michael's direction. "And if you won't listen to her advice, perhaps my banging you over the head with this will pound some sense into you."

"I appreciate your dramatic gesture, but there's really no stopping me."

"Let me go in your place," said Angel.

"That's very noble of you," said Michael, "but I've no doubt the police are waiting for you to return to the apartment, and even with your new appearance they'll likely recognize you if they see you anywhere near the building. The risk is greater for you than for me."

"You can't go alone. Period, end of story," said Mrs. Baker, stepping toward him, still gripping the frying pan.

"Maybe Gabriel could go with him," injected Angel.

"It's his busy time," said Michael.

"The girls probably won't be there anymore anyway," Angel pointed out. "But if they are, the best time to catch them would be between two and four in the afternoon, and the diner isn't busy then."

"I take back what I said about you being smart," said Mrs. Baker. "Now he'll be putting two old men at risk."

"Gabriel's much younger than I am."

Mrs. Baker glared at him. "The whole world is younger than you. That's why I'm saying *you can't go*."

Michael smiled. "I'll have my breakfast now, please. Preferably with that pan serving as the means to an omelet rather than the source of a concussion."

She turned, walked to the stove, and slammed the pan down onto a burner. "Fine, but on one condition."

"Which is?"

"Gabriel's grill man Gee goes with you two."

Michael winked at Angel. "Deal."

Michael called Gabriel to ask for his help. Gabriel said he'd be available at three but didn't understand why it was necessary for Gee to join them. When Michael told him where they were going and for what purpose, Gabriel sighed and wondered aloud if they should have Gee bring along a few comrades from his Balkan Special Forces days.

The chauffeured, black SUV with darkly tinted windows arrived at the diner precisely at three. Gabriel and Gee slid into the back seat.

"Thank you for coming," said Michael, as he turned to face them from his seat next to the driver.

"'Think nothing of it' does not strike me as an appropriate response, considering what you have in mind," said Gabriel.

Michael ignored Gabriel and looked directly at Gee. "Mrs. B thinks very highly of you. So much so that she said I shouldn't dare do this without you."

Gee nodded. "Very nice lady." He spread his catcher's-mitt-sized hands apart. "Big heart."

"I agree, but I'm curious how she knows so much about you."

"I can answer that," said Gabriel. "Whenever she stops by the diner, it's generally late in the afternoon, when we're not busy, and she likes chatting with my staff about their lives."

Michael looked surprised. "Why?"

"It's all part of how she looks out for you."

"I don't understand."

Gabriel leaned in toward Michael. "Considering your somewhat adventurous past, she's taken it upon herself to check out everyone with access to you or what you consume, just to make sure you're not at risk from someone who might be harboring a grudge."

"Really?"

"And then she verifies what they tell her. In our friend's case," Gabriel patted Gee on the knee, "she was profoundly impressed by what she learned. A true hero who did what was right, rather than what his superiors ordered him to do, for which he and his family had to flee their country with only their lives."

"I'm impressed as well," said Michael, nodding at Gee.

"So, what's the plan?" asked Gabriel.

"I thought we'd just stroll up to the apartment where Angel once lived, knock on the door, and ask to interview her former roommates."

Gabriel rolled his eyes. "And are you expecting Alice in Wonderland to be joining us on this fairy tale junket of yours? You do know the reputation of the building where we're headed?"

"How could I not? It's said to be a veritable haunted house of potential cut-throat surprises situated only a few blocks further away from my house than is your diner."

"And one of the most notorious gang hangouts in the neighborhood," added Gabriel as the big SUV pulled to a stop in front of the building.

"Nothing but top-shelf for us," said Michael. He waited until the driver came around to open his door before stepping out, dressed as elegantly as he had for his first meeting with the Fieldings, minus the watch.

Gabriel and Gee slid out and stood beside him.

"A bit overdressed for the neighborhood, wouldn't you say?" said Gabriel.

Michael twirled his cane. "I don't want to leave any doubt in anyone's mind who's coming to visit them. It's my best defense."

"Frankly, I've got my money on Gee."

Gee winked.

"OK, let's get this show on the road. Just follow my lead." Michael carefully worked his way up the crumbling concrete steps to the front door.

"I take that to mean you don't have a plan. Like for example, how we're going to get into the building without a key?"

"Oh, ye of little faith. The Lord will provide." At that moment the door burst open and a wild-eyed, preppy-dressed young man came rushing out. Michael caught the door with his cane and held it open. "After you," he told his companions with a smile.

Once inside, they started up the stairway in single file, Gabriel first, Michael second, and Gee bringing up the rear.

"How many flights?" asked Gabriel.

"All the way up to the sixth floor."

"Are you going to be able to make it?"

"I'm missing a foot, not the breath or heart for the climb."

As they reached the second-floor landing Gabriel said, "Just let us know if you want to stop to rest."

"Don't worry, I'll—"

They heard an enormous BOOM as the front door slammed open and ricocheted off a wall. Three young men dressed in gang colors raced up the stairs behind them, two steps at a time, pushing by Gee, bumping into Michael, and aiming to knock Gabriel over had he not jumped out of their way to let them pass to the next flight.

Gabriel started to say something to them but Michael stopped him. "Their mothers didn't hug them enough. Let's leave it at that and continue on our way."

The next flight involved a bit less adventure, though a man coming down from the third-floor bordello blushed crimson red when he realized he'd instinctively said hello to Gabriel.

"Just another of my upstanding customers," quipped Gabriel.

When they reached the fourth-floor landing, a half dozen young men, including the three who'd passed them on the stairs, stood blocking their way to the next flight.

"So, what do we have here?" said a bear-like, shirtless man in a black leather vest worn to accentuate his massive, tattooed biceps.

Michael stepped forward, relying heavily on his cane. "We're just on a social call."

Bear looked at his colleagues and laughed. "Dude, the whores are downstairs."

Michael shook his head. "Oh, I'm long past that stage in my life. It's nothing like that."

"Looks to me that you're pretty close to the end of your life."

Gee slipped in behind Michael.

"I certainly hope not. I wouldn't want to disappoint my granddaughter."

Bear looked puzzled. "Granddaughter?"

"Yes, she lives on the sixth floor, and we haven't heard from her in quite a while. I'm worried about her."

"What's her name?" said a lanky man in a black leather vest over a black shirt that covered his arms.

Michael turned to him. "Maria."

Bear shot a look at Lanky but said nothing.

"We don't know any Maria here," said Lanky.

Michael nodded. "She may have moved, but I know she lived with roommates. Perhaps one of them can tell me where she's gone."

"I think you should just leave." Lanky nodded to Bear.

"You heard the man," said Bear, taking a step toward Michael.

Michael shook his head and smiled as he turned sideways to Bear, looking directly at Lanky. "My, oh my, the errors of judgment made by youth." His smile turned into a hard glare. "You obviously have no idea who the fuck you're talking to. So, let me explain what your choices are, young men."

Bear took another step toward Michael, reaching for Michael's throat. Without turning away from Lanky, Michael jammed the steel tip of his cane hard into Bear's throat. As Bear gasped for breath, Michael used his cane's crook to catch Bear's ankle, then yanked hard enough to send him crashing head-first on to the concrete floor, unconscious.

For an instant, no one moved. Then hands everywhere pulled guns.

"Cool it!" screamed Lanky, staring down the barrel of a cocked .45 in Gee's hand.

"A wise decision," said Michael. "Now let's relax, everyone. Put your guns down, so we can carry on our conversation in a civilized manner."

Lanky's eyes darted from one solemn face to the next, "Put them away."

Gee was the last to lower his gun, and then only to his side.

"As I was saying, here are your choices. Either I get to speak to my granddaughter's roommates today, or tomorrow morning demolition begins on this building. And if for some reason my colleagues and I don't leave this building unharmed, I've left instructions for the building to be demolished, along with you and all of your colleagues still in it."

"You're fuckin' crazy," said Lanky.

Michael locked eyes with him. "Absolutely, ragingly so. It's how I got to where I am, and why you should take everything I just told you very seriously."

A man standing next to Lanky whispered something in his ear. Lanky looked at Gabriel. "Aren't you the guy with the diner over by the Park?"

Gabriel forced a smile as Gee tightened his grip on the .45. "At your service."

"What do you have to do with this?"

Michael hoped it did not show that he was holding his breath.

"My customer asked me to show him where the building was and to help him climb the stairs." Gabriel swallowed. "And he's not a man whose request you dare refuse."

Lanky studied Gabriel's face, then smiled. "I like your diner. If you introduced yourself in the first place, we could have avoided this misunderstanding."

He motioned for those blocking the stairs to move aside. "And move Bear on to a bed. When he wakes up, tell him he slipped and knocked himself out. We wouldn't want him to think he was knocked silly by an old man with a cane."

They all laughed.

Michael gave quick salute to Lanky before following a fast-moving Gabriel up the stairs. Gee trailed them, .45 in hand and eyes on the stairs behind as they climbed.

"That was the perfect answer," whispered Michael to Gabriel. "You gave him the out he needed to save face. Angel was right to have me bring you along."

"I was scared to death."

"Who wasn't?"

"I don't want to think what would have happened if Gee didn't have that gun and hadn't figured out which guy was their leader."

"Didn't you tell him to bring the gun?" said Michael.

"No."

Michael shook his head. "I have to give Mrs. B credit. Her instincts are impeccable." He smiled. "But don't tell her I said that."

"Think where you'd be right now if you hadn't listened to her and Angel."

"I'd hold off on the self-congratulations for now. We're not out of the woods yet."

Gabriel smiled. "But at least there's one less bear in the woods to worry about. That was some impressive cane work."

Michael waved him off. "I was aiming for his nose."

Gabriel sighed. "Enough jokes. Let's just get this done and out of here ASAP."

When they'd reached the top floor, Michael whispered to the others, "Angel said the apartment's the last one on the left. You two stay here, just in case any of the guys from the fourth floor change their minds. Also, an old man showing up unannounced at their door won't be as intimidating as a crew."

Without giving either man the chance to object, Michael turned and hurriedly hobbled down the hallway. He stopped at the apartment and listened. From the screaming he heard filtering through the door, either mass slaughter was in progress, or the current occupants had decidedly different musical tastes than he.

He glanced down the hall at Gabriel, offered a *cheerio* wave, and knocked on the door.

Here goes nothing.

No one asked who'd knocked before the door swung wide open. A girl slightly older than Angel with dirty blonde hair and puffy red eyes stood in her underwear, yelling back over her shoulder, "It's some old man."

"What's he want?" came from within the apartment, barely audible over the music.

"What do you want?" asked the blonde.

Michael spoke softly. "I'd like to talk with you."

"What? I can't hear you?"

Michael repeated, "I'd like to talk with you."

The blonde yelled back into the apartment, "Turn down the fucking music. I can't hear what the old man's saying."

"Fuck him, fuck you, fuck everybody! I'm not turning down my fucking music."

The blonde spun around and raced out of sight into the next room, exchanging loud, vile obscenities with another and leaving Michael standing at the open door.

He stepped inside and closed the door, but the shouting and

music continued, unabated. Michael reopened the door and slammed it shut hard enough to shake the floor.

Instantly, the shouting stopped, and seconds later, so did the music. Michael walked into the room. The blonde, and a gaunt brunette in a threadbare robe sat huddled together on a badly stained couch, staring fearfully up at him.

"We're not whores," said the brunette.

"Good, because I'm not looking for whores. I'm looking for young ladies who'd like to make some money by answering a few questions."

"What are you, some kind of weirdo?" asked the blonde.

"No, just a man looking for his granddaughter."

The brunette smirked. "You think one of us is your granddaughter?"

"No, but your roommate was."

"Which one?"

"Maria."

The girls exchanged a panicked look.

"We don't know any Maria," said the blonde.

"Of course, you do. She lived here with you until another young lady moved in." He paused. "Who's since moved out."

"I don't know what you're talking about."

Michael reached into his jacket pocket and pulled out a roll of bank notes. "I can either be the best thing that's ever happened to you, or the worst. It all depends on you." He riffled the bills in his hand. "For every answer you give that I believe is true, I'll give you one."

"And what if we don't play your game?" said the brunette.

Michael shrugged. "Take a look outside, down the hall. I have two men out there, one a very large man. I leave to your imagination what that means."

The blonde started to shake. "I told you we should have left after we found Carlucci. But you said no, we'd be safe here, no one had any reason to bother us here. Well, guess what?"

"Fuck you."

"Now, ladies, let's not digress. And, Miss, for that outburst of honesty, here's something for you." He handed the blonde a fifty.

The brunette's eyes widened. "What do you want to know?"

"Did you know Maria?"

"Yeah, she was our roommate."

He handed her a twenty.

"Why only a twenty? You gave her a fifty?"

"Because you told me something I already knew. Now tell me something I don't."

"She worked for someone who's dead, picking up things for him."

"Carlucci?"

"Yes."

He gave her another twenty. "Did either of you ever do that for him?"

"Yes," they said in unison.

"Well, sort of. Maria did pickups. We did deliveries," said the blonde.

He gave them each a twenty. "What sort of deliveries?"

"Envelopes to drop off all over town," said the blonde.

"They looked like invitations," added the brunette.

Michael gave them each another twenty.

"Did Maria ever deliver the invitations?"

"No, she only did pickups."

"We did all the deliveries, because people were used to seeing us around town."

"When did you last see Maria?"

The brunette bit at her lower lip. "About a month ago. Just before that other girl moved in."

He gave her a fifty.

"Now for the big money-round." Michael cleared his throat. "Tell me everyone Maria knew."

The girls looked at each other.

The blonde shook her head. "Well, she may have known some people in the building, and of course she knew Carlucci, but I don't know anybody else she knew."

"Did she ever talk about any friends or family?"

"She talked about her brother a couple of times," said the brunette.

"Did you ever meet him?"

She bit at her lip again. "No."

"Did she ever describe him by name?"

"Uh, we're talking about your grandson," said the blonde.

He shrugged and waved the wad of bills. "Think hard, and make sure you come up with the right name."

The two argued until finally looking at Michael. "We think it was David."

He waved a hundred in front of each girl. "And the last name would be?"

"I never knew it," said the blonde.

"Me either. Last names aren't used much around here. At least not real ones."

"Fair enough." Michael gave them each a hundred. "Anything else you can tell me about David? Where he works, an address, a phone number?"

"How come you don't already know this?" said the blonde.

"Shut the fuck up and just answer the man's questions," said the brunette. "He lives and works in the city. He also has a big dog."

"And neither the brother or Maria got along with their parents," said the blonde.

"I know," said Michael, handing each a fifty. "That's why I'm looking for her."

Blonde looked down at the floor. "I wish I had a grandfather who cared enough to look for me."

Michael turned to face her and waited until she looked up. "I'll tell you the same thing I want to tell my granddaughter. Think where each of you could be in ten years if you took back control of your life today. You'll have families of your own, raising children who'll make you proud, and someday, God willing, be a grandparent. And all of that depends on what you decide to do today."

The brunette shut her eyes. "I met the brother once."

"You never told *me* that," said the blonde.

"It was the Saturday after Maria . . ." her voice trailed off.

"After Maria what?" said Michael.

The brunette fixed her eyes on the floor. "Maria's dead. She OD'd in this apartment. We found her dead on the bed. Some guys showed up and took away her body. I have no idea what they did with it." She looked up. "I'm sorry."

Michael shut his eyes in a show of grief. "I feared as much. Thank you for being honest." He paused. "What did you tell her brother?"

"The same thing I just told you. We came home, found her

dead on the bed from an overdose, and some guys we didn't know took away her body."

"How did he react?"

"I was pretty high when he showed up, and I didn't let him in the apartment. I told him everything standing at the front door. He had dark hair and dark eyes, but what I remember most about him was his anger. When I told him his sister was dead, he kicked the front door harder than you slammed it."

"Did he happen to ask whether you called Carlucci to tell him Maria was dead?"

The brunette shook her head. "We told him we never called anybody, and Carlucci's name never came up."

"Not even in a curse when he kicked at the door?"

"No. Besides, like I said, we never called Carlucci." She looked at the blonde. "Did we?"

"No, the two guys just showed up and took her away."

"When's the last time you saw Carlucci alive?"

"The morning he was killed," said the blonde.

The brunette added, "He showed up at the apartment early in the morning to tell us he'd canceled everything for that day. There'd be no pickups or deliveries, and we had to stay away from the apartment between two and eight."

Michael cringed. Angel had not told him of that morning warning from Carlucci.

With tears in her eyes, the brunette held the bills out. "Here's your money back."

"Not necessary," said Michael.

"But we can't help you find your granddaughter. She's dead."

"That's not your fault." Michael hesitated, then held his breath as he asked, "Was your other roommate with you when Carlucci gave you those instructions?"

"No, she'd left to do her route before Carlucci showed up."

Michael exhaled and handed each of them five hundred more. "Use this to help get yourselves the hell out of here and into a rehab program. Do it before you end up like Maria."

He turned and hurried out before they saw the tear running down his cheek.

* * *

"What happened?" said Gabriel, walking toward Michael as he came down the hallway. "It sounded like a bomb went off in there. I wanted to see if you were OK, but Gee told me to stay back."

Michael spoke tight-lipped. "I got what I needed."

"Care to share?"

"I know how to find Maria's brother."

"Yeah?" said Gabriel. "Where?"

"The morgue."

THIRTEEN

Michael had his driver drop Gabriel and Gee off at the diner before taking him to the Chief Medical Examiner's office over by Bellevue Hospital and the East River. He arrived just before closing time, went straight to the Chief's office, and asked to see the Chief on an urgent matter. The secretary sitting outside the Chief's office said her boss was unavailable and suggested the next time Michael wanted to see her boss, he should call in advance to arrange for an appointment.

Michael politely asked if he might use her phone. She nodded. He pulled out a tiny leather address book, found a number, and dialed.

After introducing himself and asking to be put through to "the boss," ten seconds passed before he spoke. "Hello, old friend, how are you?"

A minute of personal chit-chat ran between the two, and the secretary began to look at her watch and scowl.

"Oh, sorry to interrupt you, but I'm using the phone of the secretary to our City's illustrious Chief Medical Examiner and I think she wants it back. So please permit me to explain why I'm bothering you."

Michael explained what he was looking for and that he would greatly appreciate any assistance his friend could lend to expediting the process.

Michael nodded, said, "Thank you," and handed the phone to the secretary. "My friend would like to speak with you."

"Sir, I have no time for your theatrics." She took back the phone and hung it up without bothering to put it to her ear. "Now, please leave. Our office is closed."

Michael chuckled. "I think I'll wait until you answer your next phone call."

"I'll call the police . . ."

The phone rang.

She paused but answered. “Who is this?” she said in what must have been her most officious tone.

Michael watched as all color faded from her face.

“Yes, sir. Absolutely sir. No problem at all, sir.” She handed the phone back to Michael. “He wants to speak to you.”

“Hello.”

Pause.

“Yes, I’m sure all will go smoothly from here on out. Thank you, Mr. Mayor.”

All my years of contributing generously to his campaigns just paid off. He handed the phone back to the secretary. “So, where were we?”

“Just tell me what you want and I’ll get it for you.”

“Thank you. I need any information you have on an approximately fourteen-to-sixteen-year-old girl who turned up dead in the last thirty days. Possibly as a Jane Doe, later identified by a family member.”

“Where was the body found?”

“I don’t know. I understand she died of a drug overdose in an apartment, but the body was moved and dumped somewhere else.”

“Any other details?”

“If her brother claimed the body, I believe his first name is David. He may have given her name as Maria.”

She reached for her keyboard and began typing. “Thankfully, we don’t have a lot of Jane Does. It’s nice of you to have taken such an interest in this one.”

Michael nodded, not interested in adding to the gossip she’d soon be spreading about the mysterious man who sicced the mayor on her. “Thank you.”

She continued her search.

Her face lit up. “I think this is it. Four weeks ago, kids playing at an inactive construction site found the body of a teenage girl in an abandoned dumpster. Originally recorded as a Jane Doe, a relative identified the body.”

“Was her name, Maria?”

“Yes. But her brother’s name isn’t David. It’s Daniel.”

“Close enough. Do you have a last name?”

"Rudolph."

"What about an address or telephone number for Daniel?"

She wrote them down on a Post-it and handed it to Michael. "I wouldn't put much faith in either of those."

"Why's that?"

"According to notes in the file, our office has never been able to contact him at either that phone number or address."

"Why are you trying to reach him?"

"To find out what to do with his sister's body. He said he'd claim it but never has. He signed for her personal effects and that's the last we've heard from him. We're about to dispose of her remains under public-health laws."

"Hart's Island?"

She nodded.

"Do me a favor, please, and hold off on doing any of that for another few days. If I'm not able to find her brother, I'll bear the cost of the funeral. Is that OK?"

"Sure, whatever you say."

He stood. "Thank you."

Leaving the office, Michael's thoughts drifted to the many others he'd known who died far too young, alone and, at best, in unmarked graves.

Anthony Bodine's career had progressed from street-corner loan-sharking to a more civilized style of usury, almost legitimate to his way of thinking. Most who used services such as his worried about their names wending back to authorities seeking to catch tax cheats and frauds, but Bodine had a golden reputation for protecting his customers' identities. So much so, that his customers paid him a premium. Never would Anthony Bodine betray a customer, even those who pushed him to violence for failing to keep up their end of the bargain.

But Dr. Brackett Fielding wasn't a customer.

The instant he recognized the name of Fielding's deceased hit-and-run patient, he saw trouble. Her husband was a long-time major customer of his, a secretive man with a finger in virtually every major construction project in the region. His name never appeared on a contract or invoice, but if you wanted your project to go forward, twice a month like clockwork, you delivered a check to Bodine payable to an above-reproach corporate vendor. Bodine then diverted the payment into whatever offshore account Victor Persky instructed him to use.

He'd heard gossip about the man's divorce, a messy one the wife kept making messier. He'd never met the wife, not even seen a photograph of her before reading of her death in the newspaper. But, considering how much her husband detested publicity, Bodine wasn't surprised to learn of her demise.

He wondered why the Fielding siblings were so upset over the death of the wife. It had to tie into something more than the sister serving as the woman's shrink. From his conversation with their receptionist, Bodine's instincts told him that Brackett Fielding's bizarre nighttime call about a replacement for Carlucci had to do with Persky's wife's death. If his instincts were correct, Fielding was trying to unload something of the wife's. And not likely for the benefit of her estate.

Bodine didn't care what Fielding was up to, as long as it didn't put him into conflict with the husband. If what Fielding was trying to sell was something of interest to Persky, Bodine had no doubt that sooner or later Fielding would do something to attract Persky's attention. And once that happened, the first words out of Fielding's mouth would likely be Bodine's name, followed by some story intended to save his skin at the cost of Bodine's own. At best, Bodine would have a lot of explaining to do to a very angry, very important customer. At worst . . . well, he didn't want to think about that.

On the other hand, if Fielding's gambit had nothing to do with Bodine's customer's wife, then casually mentioning the coincidence of his sharing the same doctor with Persky's wife would be taken by Persky as nothing more than idle small talk. But if there were a tie-in, then raising the subject ASAP would present him to Persky as an innocent in whatever Fielding had going on.

Bodine saw no choice. The only decision left for him to make was whether to immediately call Persky or wait until Persky called him. They spoke regularly, but considering Persky's naturally suspicious criminal mind, Bodine had to raise the subject in the most matter-of-fact way.

He shut his eyes, drew in and let out a very deep breath, and decided for now to wait until Persky called him.

Which could happen at any moment.

Or not.

Bodine opened his eyes and sighed. *God, I'm anxious. I wish I had a doctor to call.*

For so long I'd taken such great care to maintain a detached existence for myself, a life safely confined to conjecture, reflection, and surmise; far removed from taking part in those human dramas that inexorably draw so many to misfortune, pain, and loss. I'd found my Walden Pond in the Park. Or so I'd thought.

Michael leaned forward and told the driver to take him to the diner. He had too much on his mind to go directly home from the morgue and face one of Mrs. Baker's relentless cross-examinations.

He thought to send the driver home, but on reflection told him to wait. One cane battle per day was more than enough to risk at his age.

The diner was jumping, every booth filled and only two stools open at the counter.

Gabriel waved him over to the counter and asked a customer to slide over one stool so he could sit next to Michael. "I'm surprised to see you here. Isn't Mrs. B expecting you for dinner?"

"Probably, but I'm sure she'll find me if she wants to. After all, my partying days are behind me."

"Yes, but the myth lives on." He pointed to a booth toward the rear. "Recognize anyone?"

He turned to see a group of five young men waving at him.

"How you doing, cane man?" several yelled.

"Fine, thank you, and glad to see you're eating well."

Michael turned back to Gabriel as a few in the group laughed before going back to their food. "I hope this means our gangbanger friends from earlier this afternoon aren't holding a grudge."

"Far from it. No one but us knows what happened, and as long as we keep it that way, they're looking at us as comrades-in-arms who proved themselves in battle. When they came in here, Gee and I treated them like family, and they loved it. Everybody likes to be recognized in a restaurant."

"I didn't notice the big fellow."

"He's still resting."

"Lucky for me."

"You've got nothing to worry about. They checked you out, heard you're one of those secret-agent types from the golden old days, and now you're a legend to them."

"I wonder who sold them that story."

"Whatever . . . it worked. Just treat 'em with respect and it'll be fine."

"Considering what they do, that will be hard for me."

"Surely you can fake it while you're in here. If a war starts with them, I lose. It's too easy to firebomb this place." He jerked his head up toward the ceiling and his apartment above, "While I'm in it."

Michael exhaled. "Too many moral dilemmas. I never should have changed my routine. The worst thing I've done in a long time is call you about Angel sleeping in the Park. My life hasn't been the same since. Up until then, everything was going fine."

"Really?"

"Yes, and now I've got one problem after another to deal with. Angel, the Fieldings, that girl Maria, her brother." He took a breath. "I found out her brother's name. Daniel Rudolph. At least that's what he told the morgue. But the address and phone number he gave are bogus. He's also not claimed her body. If I don't find him, I'll be paying for her funeral."

"I'll split the cost with you."

"That's not why I said it. This is what's happened to my simple life."

"Another way to put that might be to say you've gone from waiting around to die, to living life with gusto."

Michael stared at him.

"Hey, you know I'm right. And to a lesser degree, it's been the same for me. Somewhere along the way, we lost the balance in our lives." Gabriel smiled. "It's that yin and yang thing."

Michael coughed. "I wouldn't exactly describe it like that, but I do get your point." He swallowed. "I'd like you to stop by the house tomorrow when you take your customary stroll to the Park. I think it's time we get together for a brainstorming session. There are too many intrigues, too many players, too many loose ends literally dying to be connected, and too many possibilities lurking about. We need to come up with a real-time take on what's happening and stop playing catch up watching re-runs."

"Works for me."

"Good, I'll see you tomorrow."

"Don't you want something to eat?"

"Despite my earlier bravado, I dare not miss Mrs. B's dinner without having given her appropriate advance notice."

Michael stood, waved goodbye to the guys in the booth, gave a smile and thumbs-up to Gee at the grill, and tipped his hat to Gabriel. "Thanks for your advice. Someday I just might take it."

Gabriel smiled. "Until tomorrow, *cane man.*"

Marilena lived at the Water View Apartments in a highly stylized two-bedroom penthouse overlooking Little Neck Bay. It was close enough to her office to be convenient, and far enough away from her brother's elaborate sprawling home to be restful.

If left to her brother, she knew she'd have no life of her own. He had undermined her marriage and every relationship that followed, finding a way to burrow deep into her feelings for a lover, hollow out all but the thinnest shell of a relationship, and then when an otherwise minor lover's tiff blew away what remained, he'd act blameless for the breakup.

After killing her last romance in the crib, he'd pressed for her to move into his home's tiny casita. When she refused, he spent weeks making guilt-invoking pleas for her not to forsake him. His campaign only ended when she told him she'd entered into a long-term apartment lease, and unless he was prepared to assume her rent obligations for the term of the lease, there was no way she could afford to move to his property.

She had long ago learned that the only way to convince her brother to drop one of his self-absorbed, master of the universe fantasies, was to point out a serious downside risk to his personal financial well-being. Appealing to emotion or good works? Useless. Brackett was driven by what he saw as enhancing his image, infected by the acquisitive bug for all manner of pretentious accoutrements. A curse he'd spread to his sister, though thankfully to a lesser degree.

She sat staring out the window at the moonlight reflecting silver off still water.

How could she not have realized that her brother's narcissistic failings would put them on this course to doom?

She had known what was in the package long before her patient had entrusted it to her. She'd talked to Marilena about it in their sessions, told her of its incalculable value to so many, and emphasized the need to keep its existence between only the two of them.

But when her patient died, Marilena panicked.

The only person she could think of to turn to for help was her brother. But she also knew he'd never appreciate the item's true value to the world but instead insist on adding it to his private collection for "safekeeping." It would become just another possession in testament to his ego.

That's why she'd told him from the outset that the item would "set us up for life and beyond." The lure of *real money*, as he called it, was too much for him to resist. She'd thought he'd go for the reward or some legitimate disposition, but he had a different idea: a black-market auction.

She told him he was crazy, but her brother was too far into his fantasy to listen. Even now, with everything having gone so wrong, he was still desperate to prove he was right.

Even if it gets us both killed.

Brackett put down his brandy and looked at his watch. Twenty-four hours had passed since he'd spoken to Bodine and he'd not yet heard back from him. Normally, Brackett would call his sister and push his anxieties off on to her, but he couldn't do that this time. He'd have to work through it on his own.

Damn her.

His eyes wandered over shelves of leather-bound volumes and fixed on a pair of French doors leading out to the garden. Once this troublesome distraction was resolved, he'd move to a grander residence, one in keeping with the elevated societal rank his new-found wealth would bring him. Perhaps he'd endow a hospital. The Fielding Clinic struck him as an appropriate name.

No.

The *Brackett* Fielding Clinic. Since his sister had no faith in his plan, why should she share in the glory?

Again he glanced at his watch, then picked up his brandy and took a sip.

No reason to worry, he thought, trying to reassure himself.

It's *only* been twenty-four hours and delicate arrangements like this must take time.

Unless he has something else in mind. He chewed at his lower lip. *Bodine's a criminal, and the criminal mind cannot resist temptation.*

But to Bodine, Brackett was more than just his doctor, he was his savior. No way Bodine would betray him. Besides, Bodine only knew what Brackett had told him—a nameless patient had something valuable to sell—and he had no idea what the item was, who possessed it, or how to find out.

He lifted his brandy toward a growing smile.

Unless he forces me to tell him.

With the smile now gone, blinking uncontrollably, he slugged down the balance of his drink, ran to the French doors to make certain they were securely locked, and hastily set the burglar alarm.

He took in and let out deep breaths, trying to slow his pulse. He wanted to feel safe. He wanted to call his sister.

But he couldn't.

Damn her. Damn her. Damn her.

FOURTEEN

It had been raining for hours when Angel awoke. She took that as a good sign, for planting time was near. When she'd told Mrs. Baker of her plans for a garden, her boss had told her to "have at it." She'd planned to work outside this morning, but the weather would be keeping her in. So, she spent the time plotting out the garden, trying to fit in what she wanted to grow in the available space. She liked the idea of sunflowers and corn; both reminded her of home, but they'd take up too much space.

Perhaps just a sunflower or two.

She finished her plans and made a list, which she'd have to run by Mrs. Baker. Angel knew that the cost of a garden was far less than the market prices they'd otherwise pay for what it yielded. So, she hoped that her plans were within budget, but she'd do whatever Mrs. Baker thought best.

Once Mr. Michael was up and about, she began her morning cleaning chores. She didn't mind them, because unlike so much of what she'd lived through, they came with a decided beginning and end. Be it cleaning a bathroom, changing a bed, doing laundry, all were finite tasks. So different from life on the streets, constantly wondering where she'd find her next meal, a safe place to sleep, or someone to trust.

Yes, she definitely preferred her chores.

Her favorite time, though, was the early afternoon, after the luncheon dishes were washed and put away. That's when Mrs. Baker sat her down in front of a computer screen as an enrolled member of an on-line school classroom. She'd almost forgotten how much she loved to learn new things. This afternoon, though, she'd have to cut those classes short. Mr. Michael had told them at breakfast that they'd be meeting in early afternoon with Gabriel in the parlor.

He didn't say what the meeting was about, but as long as it didn't put her back on the streets, she didn't care.

She'd do whatever was asked of her.

* * *

Michael had an uncommonly restless night's sleep. His mind wouldn't shut down long enough for him to catch more than an hour and a half of sleep at a time, separated by a nearly equal amount of wakeful tossing and turning.

He lay in his bed long past dawn, staring at the ceiling.

If only he could turn back the clock a few days, when he had no trouble sleeping. But if he had that power, he'd not waste it on a couple of days, but go back decades to the moment when he wished that he'd died with his mates.

He'd received a medal for not giving in to torture, while those who valiantly sought to protect him received nothing but death. They were innocents, attacked and slaughtered except Michael—because a traitor had told the enemy that Michael alone knew what they wanted to know. The traitor had long since died, not as painfully as Michael had prayed, but the guilt over his colleagues' deaths still plagued him.

Now other innocents faced mortal danger. Hopefully this time he would save them, not curse them.

Loose ends dangled everywhere he turned. Gabriel's diner as a drop, Angel in her coat as a courier, all made sense. But the murder of Carlucci, the killing of Marilena's patient, the mysterious package, and the potential murder of Maria made to look like an OD death, all cried out for a unifying answer other than coincidence. Too many possible explanations, too many dangerous players involved, and too little time before someone else might die.

He sat up and swung his legs out over the side of the bed.

Time to eliminate the impossible and focus on the improbable.

The rain had stopped by the time Gabriel arrived to join Michael, Mrs. Baker, and Angel in the Victorian-style parlor. They gathered around a highly polished walnut coffee table laden with tea, coffee, assorted pastries, and all the appropriate china and silver. Mrs. Baker had provided the beverages, Gabriel the pastries.

Michael waited until everyone had a drink in hand. "I think it's fair to say that four days ago, none of us thought we'd be where we are today." He smiled at Angel, "And in your instance, young lady, I mean that literally."

Angel tried to hide a blush.

"But here we are, squarely in the middle of a difficult situation in search of a solution." Michael took a sip of tea and put his cup and saucer down in front of him. "Based upon the years we've worked together," he nodded at Mrs. Baker, "how long I've known you and your family," a nod to Gabriel, "and my instincts," indicating Angel, "I have great faith in your demonstrated collective *good judgment*."

He leaned back in a well-worn leather wingback chair. "We all know the facts. I've talked to each of you about them in detail. So, unless one of you is holding something back from the rest of us—which I do not for a moment believe—the question left for us to address is a simple one: What do we do now?"

Michael looked at each face, waiting for someone to speak.

Gabriel broke the silence. "Why do we have to do anything?"

"That's a powerful question, especially coming as it does from the one who faces the greatest potential peril on every front. Carlucci used your diner as both the drop for his couriers and the place to feed them. He also recruited your busboy into his scheme. His former courier Maria ate there daily and met her brother there every Sunday until she turned up dead." Michael paused. "Even the Fieldings were drawn to your diner as their meeting place of choice." Michael looked straight at Gabriel. "I'd say the *last* person who'd want to do nothing is you. Your diner turns up in every scenario, inevitably leading anyone, good or bad, who puts faith in the adage, 'Where there's smoke there's fire,' to fix on the diner as a five-alarm blaze in the middle of this mess."

Gabriel shrugged. "I thought you said I had good judgment."

Michael smiled. "You do, except when it comes to protecting your own best interests. You say you don't get involved in other people's problems, but I don't see that. Your suggestion that we do nothing has everything to do with protecting the rest of us—and it's a strategy that just might work . . . for us. But it definitely won't work for you."

Gabriel wagged a finger at Michael. "Talk about the non-involved pot calling the kettle black."

Michael grinned. "That's old news, and I stand guilty as charged."

"How do you propose we get Gabriel out of the middle of this?" asked Mrs. Baker.

"That's the primary impediment to my coming up with a plan."

"Why don't you just tell the Fieldings to give the dead client's husband what he wants?" asked Angel.

"That should get the Fieldings out of the picture," said Gabriel.

"Possibly in more ways than one," said Michael. "I suggested that to them, along with the alternative of turning it over to the police. They refused both options, claiming the husband's not only vengeful but murderously paranoid over his possessions. They're frightened to death at what he might do to them should he learn they're involved, something I think he's going to figure out soon enough anyway. Frankly, when he does, I'm more concerned about how the Fieldings will try to implicate us in an effort to save themselves."

"Sounds like we better hurry up and find a way to separate the Fieldings from whatever the husband's after that doesn't link it back to them," said Mrs. Baker.

"Or us," added Gabriel.

"And there's still the Carlucci angle to worry about," said Michael. "Who killed him and why?"

"How about the husband?" said Mrs. Baker. "He might have learned Carlucci was arranging to sell the item and stopped him."

"I don't think so," said Michael. "Carlucci died before the Fieldings made contact with him. There's no way Carlucci knew what the Fieldings had, or for the husband to have known of Carlucci's potential involvement."

"Then who killed him?" asked Angel.

"The possible enemies of someone like Carlucci are endless," said Michael.

"But what about Maria?" asked Gabriel. "If she didn't overdose, someone must have had a reason to kill her. And if it happened to tie into her role as Carlucci's courier . . . " His voice trailed off.

"Am I at risk?" said Angel.

"I don't think so," said Michael in a calming voice. "But until we determine who killed Carlucci, and how and why Maria died, we have to be careful not to let our guard down."

"What about Maria's brother as Carlucci's possible killer?" asked Mrs. Baker.

"An obvious possibility," said Michael, "but what would lead him to blame Carlucci for her death? Was Carlucci responsible for his sister's drug habit? She was a junkie when Carlucci hired her, and her brother had to know that."

"But according to what Angel told us," said Gabriel, "Carlucci didn't want a drug user as a courier."

"Apparently that applied only to his couriers making pickups, because he continued using Angel's two addicted roommates to deliver what I assume were invitations to bid on what was coming up for auction. But even if he wanted to get rid of her because of her drug use, all he had to do was boot her out of the apartment and find someone else."

"Like me," said Angel.

"Well, she knew about Carlucci's business," said Mrs. Baker.

"So what? That still gave him no reason to kill her," said Michael. "Let's not forget what Gabriel's police friend told him: Carlucci was a protected snitch, meaning that even if Maria had gone to the police to inform on him, he knew nothing would likely happen to him. So why kill her?"

"But Maria's brother wouldn't know about Carlucci's deal with the police," said Mrs. Baker. "Maybe the brother acted out of emotion, assumed Carlucci had killed his sister, and took revenge."

Michael picked up his tea and took a sip. "The brother learned of Maria's death from her roommate weeks before Carlucci's murder, and when he did, he exploded in front of her without ever mentioning Carlucci in his outburst. If his temper was driving him to blame Carlucci, why would he wait even more weeks to kill him?"

"It could have taken him that long to identify Carlucci," Gabriel ventured.

Michael put down his tea and shook his head in disagreement. "My instincts tell me Carlucci would have needed a much stronger motive for killing her than terminating her services as his courier. Plus, her brother would have had to know about that motive in order to blame Carlucci."

"Perhaps it was passion, a romance?" said Mrs. Baker.

"Even though his sister was only fourteen, that's always a possibility with dirt bags like Carlucci," said Angel.

"Yes, but it strikes me as unlikely from the way Carlucci treated her. Look at how she lived, in a hellhole of an apartment building with two other junkies. Not exactly Camelot." Michael looked at Gabriel. "Another possibility is that the brother is a headstrong psychopath, not capable of reason. You're the only one who's ever met the brother. Did he seem like a madman to you?"

"Quite the contrary. From the bits and snatches of their conversations I can remember overhearing, he kept trying to convince her that she deserved a better life, and he wanted to help her, if she'd only let him."

"I don't know about any of that," said Angel. "But how could the brother have gotten into the apartment? Carlucci was manic about security in the building. He'd installed a steel front door with a non-pickable lock and even deadbolts that went into the floor, ceiling, and doorframe. No way you could force your way in, and Carlucci would never have let in a stranger."

"So much for the brother," said Gabriel.

"Where's that leave us?" said Mrs. Baker.

Angel nodded agreement, biting at her nails.

Mrs. Baker gently pulled Angel's hand away from her mouth. "Don't worry, dear, nothing's going to happen to you."

"I completely get the Fielding part of the puzzle," said Michael. "A husband who arranged for the murder of his wife is now hellbent on finding whoever has his treasure, and once he learns who they are, he might want to kill them. I don't like it, but I get it.

"Next, we have the Carlucci part of the puzzle. We're missing way too many pieces to picture what's happened there. We're missing motive in Maria's murder, and if Carlucci wasn't killed *because* of Maria's death, we're missing motive for that too. Plus, we're missing their killer, or killers. Until we gain some clarity on that, I'd hate to set a plan in action that might have us stumbling into an even bigger and more dangerous mess."

"Where do you suggest we start looking for your clarity?" said Gabriel.

"With the only member of the Carlucci cast I haven't spoken to yet. The brother."

"But you only have phony contact information for him."

"Which makes me want to find him even more. What could possibly have him so afraid of being found that he'd give false information to the morgue and abandon his sister's body unclaimed?"

"So, how do you find him?"

"For that, I think we'll have to involve your friend on the police force."

"What exactly do we tell him?"

Michael smiled. "Perhaps that you're trying to help an old friend locate his grandson."

"Homicide."

"Detective? It's Gabriel. From the diner."

"Oh, hi, Gabe. What's up? Did I walk out on a check or something?" He laughed.

"No, I'm used to that."

He laughed more.

"I need a favor. A little one I think."

"What is it?"

"It's for a long-time customer of mine. He hadn't heard from his granddaughter in over a month, and with her history of addiction he was worried. Yesterday he checked with the morgue, and that's when he learned she'd died of an overdose."

"Oh, wow, that's rough. How old was she?"

"Fourteen."

"Damn. I really feel for the guy."

"On top of all that, he can't find her older brother either."

"How old is he?"

"Mid-twenties."

"Is he a junkie, too?"

"Not that the grandfather knows. He's worried the boy might be having a nervous breakdown."

"Why's he think that?"

"The brother and sister were very close. They used to have breakfast together in my place on Sundays. But the boy never told anyone in the family about his sister's death, even though he identified her at the morgue."

"So, everyone missed her funeral?"

"There's been no funeral. The brother never claimed the body. Just left it there for the morgue to dispose of, along with a fake address and number."

"Jeez."

"Tell me about it . . . The grandfather's at his wit's end."

"What are the parents like?"

"My customer says he has no contact with them."

"Sounds like a pretty screwed-up family."

"The grandfather strikes me as a solid sort of guy, but who knows?"

"OK. What's the brother's name?"

"Daniel Rudolph." Gabriel paused. "Though sometimes he goes by David."

"Something doesn't smell right, Gabe."

"That's why I'm calling you."

"What's the girl's name?"

"Maria."

"You say the body's in the morgue?"

"Was yesterday."

"I'll ask a buddy in missing-persons to see what he can do for you on this. He'll likely want to speak to the grandfather."

"No problem. Just have him call me and I'll put them in touch."

"What's the grandfather's name?"

"Michael."

"Rudolph?"

"I guess. I don't know most of my customers last names. I have trouble enough trying to remember the kind of donuts they like."

The detective laughed. "That remark's going to cost you."

"I figured as much. I'll definitely be indebted to you. Thanks."

"You're welcome, and my sympathies to your customer. Losing a child is horrible. Losing one this way is . . . what can I say?"

"I know. Thanks again. Bye, my friend."

"Bye."

Gabriel shut off his mobile, drew in and let out a deep breath, and looked at the faces sitting around the coffee table. "So, how did I do?"

"Great," said Michael. "No hesitant pauses, no outright lies."

"Other than the fact you're not anyone's grandfather," said Gabriel.

"But that's my lie to you, not yours to your detective friend. You didn't even have to lie about my last name. Clever how you handled that."

"I guess I'm learning how to do that sort of thing from you."

"So, what do you think's going to happen?" asked Mrs. Baker.

Michael leaned back in his chair. "He's going to call the morgue to check out what Gabriel told him before he reaches out to his buddy. If everything seems on the up and up, he'll turn it over to his buddy and they'll do their thing."

"I assume that includes checking to see if the brother has a criminal record," said Gabriel.

Michael nodded.

"Then I think you'd best be prepared to be disappointed at how your grandson turned out."

"Who knows? He might be a lawyer," said Michael with a shrug.

"That's what I meant," Gabriel shot back.

Angel laughed.

"Don't encourage him," said Michael. "When missing-persons calls you looking for me, give them this number." He handed Gabriel a business card embossed with only a telephone number.

"What's this?"

"An answering service I use when I don't want callers to know my location or true identity. As of now, it will be answered as 'Michael Rudolph's line.'"

"You're one mysterious S.O.B.," said Gabriel.

Mrs. Baker sighed loudly. "Language."

"Hey, I only used initials."

"Are we done with your comedy routine?" Mrs. Baker asked, standing. "Angel and I have work to do."

Angel stood too.

"Sure, Gabriel and I can take it from here. Thank you both. You've been very helpful."

As the women left, Gabriel reached for a pastry. "How long do you think it will be before we hear back from the police?"

"Depending on your detective friend's relationship with his buddy, it could be quick. And if, as you suggest, the brother has a police record, or better yet is on parole, they may have a real address for him. On the other hand, if they can't come up with a quick answer, there probably won't be one in the offing."

Gabriel took a bite of the pastry. "One thing I don't get, is why you have me using my low-level contact to get information when you'd have a much better and faster chance of obtaining it through one of your higher-power connections."

"I thought about that. The problem is, asking questions inevitably makes people curious about the questioner's motives. Asking too many questions makes those same people *very* curious. I'm sure my single phone call to the mayor started tongues wagging in both his and the Medical Examiner's offices. If I ask another powerful person to intervene on that same matter, I have no doubt someone will think to take a closer look at why I'm so interested. With Angel living here, I don't want to take that risk. It's far less conspicuous, and therefore safer for her, if an unrelated party—that's you—comes in looking for a low-level favor from a cop friend."

Gabriel shrugged and nodded. "Who knows. Maybe we'll get lucky and some Sunday morning Maria's brother will stroll into my diner like he used to." He took another bite.

Michael frowned. "Whether or not I'd call that luck depends on what's on his mind when he walks through your front door."

Gabriel choked on his last bite.

FIFTEEN

"Hi, Sis."

Marilena struggled to keep her tone calm. "Where have you been? You never showed up at the office for your appointments. Rachel's spent her entire day placating very angry patients."

"That's what I pay her for. As for my clients, they need to learn to process their anger more efficiently when confronted with disappointment."

Marilena held her breath and began counting to ten.

"You still there?"

She finished counting. "It's a waste of time calling you self-absorbed and utterly narcissistic. You wear those labels proudly."

"Now, now, is that any way to talk about your only brother?"

"Yes, and that's something I'll forever hold against our parents."

A giggle came through the phone. "That's actually funny."

"So, what ruse are you about to pull on me?"

"No ruse. Last night, I wasn't feeling myself so I decided to take a few days off."

"And you couldn't be bothered to call Rachel or me to inform us of your decision, or answer your phone?"

His tone turned testy. "I did what I had to do to get better."

"Sounds like depression, or a full-blown anxiety attack."

"Whatever it was, I'm better now."

"And since you didn't call me about it, as you often do, I can only assume it bears directly on something you dared not raise with me."

"That's rubbish. There's no subject I dare not raise with you."

"Yeah, right. So why are you calling me now?"

"Just to check in."

"Good, you've checked in. Now I'm going to hang up. I'm busy doing double duty in the office, covering your patients as well as mine. Bye."

"*Wait*," yelled Brackett.

Marilena shook her head at the phone. "Yes?"

"I thought you should know that I've put our plan into action to resolve our problem."

"What do you mean *our* plan?" her voice cracking with anger as she spoke.

"The one about speaking to my patient regarding . . . an alternative recommendation."

"*You what*?" she screamed.

"No need to get hysterical. It all went precisely as I expected."

"But you promised you wouldn't do that. *You promised*."

"I know you better than you know yourself, Sis. You were just testing me to see if I knew what you really wanted."

Marilena said nothing.

"Oh, by the way, if you happen to receive a call from an Anthony Bodine, just forward it on to me. I'll take care of it. Love you. Bye."

Marilena sat holding the phone in a hand that would not stop shaking. She didn't know if it was vibrating out of fear or anger. Her delusional brother had gone off the deep end, taking her with him.

She dropped the phone on to her desk, followed by her head into her hands. She didn't move until the shaking stopped, then sat up straight, shook her head hard, and picked up the phone.

It was time to change the rules of engagement with her brother.

The call hadn't surprised Michael, but Marilena's frantic tone of voice added an unanticipated urgency to her plea to see him immediately. She offered to come to his home, but Michael said he preferred meeting at her office. Now he sat in the rear of a limousine, listening to the driver mumble to himself in a language Michael did not understand. He assumed it was a curse-laced soliloquy on rush-hour traffic. He'd not been out and about in such evening rush-hour traffic in years, and from how slowly they crept along, he almost questioned the wisdom of his decision to keep his residence off-limits to the Fieldings.

So many people herding in the same direction—to places they called home—away from where they spent the great majority of their waking adult lives laboring among souls they often know better than their own relatives.

He wondered how many realized how little time they actually spent with their families. Each new day launched practiced morning rituals, followed perhaps by a brief kiss and a scoot out the door on a routinized commute into eight or more solid hours of work. Then back home, perhaps interrupted by an errand or two, before catching up at dinner on each other's day, followed by a bit of TV or a book, and off to bed.

People speak of "family time" in reverential tones, yet for most of the working world, it's far more scarce than sacred.

Then you have families who work together, creating an entirely different dynamic. Like the Fieldings . . .

Michael looked at his watch, shook his head, and muttered to himself, "Happy families are all alike; every unhappy family is unhappy in its own way."

By the time Michael made it to THE TOWER building, normal business hours had passed. That required him to show identification to the concierge and wait for him to call Marilena's office for permission to send him up. When Michael stepped off the elevator, Marilena stood waiting in her doorway, her head looking up and down the hall, and her hand waving frantically for him to come inside. "Please, hurry."

The instant Michael stepped inside, Marilena shut the door and locked it.

"Are you expecting someone else?"

"I don't know *what* to expect anymore." She pressed the fingers of her right hand tightly up against her cheek, and, with her thumb anchored snugly under her chin, drew her fingertips up and down the side of her face.

"Are you all right?"

She shut her eyes and took in several deep breaths. "No, I'm definitely not all right."

"Let's sit down." He pointed toward her office.

She hesitated.

"Is there anyone else here?"

"No. I sent Rachel home."

"The receptionist?"

"Yes." Marilena moved slowly toward her office, still rubbing at her face.

Michael followed. He waited until she picked where to sit, and when she chose her couch, Michael sat beside her.

She shut her eyes again.

"So, where do you want to start?"

Marilena forced a smile. "You make it sound like I'm the patient."

Michael shrugged. "I think that's a fair way to look at where we are at the moment. The only way I'm possibly going to be able to help is if you tell me what has you so bothered."

She drew in another deep breath. "My bastard of a brother is going to get us both killed."

"Since I've already warned you of that possibility, I assume something's happened that has you thinking it's now more of a probability."

"He promised me he wouldn't do anything. *He promised*. But now he tells me he did it anyway. We're both going to die."

She pressed her fingernails into her cheek. Michael grabbed her hand and pulled it away from her face. "Stop. This is not a time for that."

Marilena glared at Michael and tried to wrench her hand away from his grip. But he didn't let go.

She stopped struggling, drooped her head, and began to sob.

Michael let go of her hand, handed her a box of tissues from a table beside the couch, and waited for the moment to pass.

After she regained her composure, Michael took back the box of tissues, hoping she'd take it as a signal to begin talking.

"Where do I start?"

"At the beginning would be good."

She slowly twisted her head from side to side, sat up straight, looked off into the middle distance, and in the most clinical of tones, recited everything that had happened, starting at the moment her patient confided in her about the great treasure she'd taken from her husband; continuing through her brother's plan to profit off the wife's death by using Carlucci—the middleman referred by her brother's patient, Anthony Bodine—to sell the treasure; to just having learned that her brother broke his promise not to go to Bodine in search of a replacement for Carlucci.

When she finished, she turned to look at Michael. "So, what do you think?"

Michael paused. "I think you're right to be alarmed. As I've said, your brother is in way over his head, and as you say, likely jeopardizing you both."

"Then what can I do to protect myself?"

Michael smiled. "I see we're making progress."

"I don't want anything to happen to him, but if he's going to keep putting our lives at risk, despite all my pleading with him not to, what alternative do I have?"

"Definite progress." He smiled, hoping to ease her tension another notch. "One question. What had you so worried when you met me at the door?"

"I don't know. The simplest things are setting me off now."

"What sort of simple things."

"Rachel and I spent the past few days placating angry patients my brother had ignored. Today I asked her to give me a list of every patient he'd stood up for an appointment or failed to call back." She paused. "After I asked you to meet me here, I looked at the list. On it was Anthony Bodine."

"The patient your brother reached out to for a new contact?"

"Yes. I asked Rachel if he had an appointment, and she said no. He'd just stopped by yesterday morning to say hello. But she wasn't sure my brother *didn't* have an appointment with him, because, as she said, 'Mr. Bodine is such a nice man he wouldn't have wanted to upset us if Brackett had stood him up.'"

"I take it your receptionist can be chatty."

"Sadly, yes. Especially with patients she likes."

"So, there's no telling what she might have told him."

"I'm afraid so."

Michael bit at his lower lip. "What might she have known about this mess you're in?"

"Nothing. I can't imagine Brackett would have told her anything about Bodine or Carlucci. He mostly wants to fire her."

"What about your now-deceased patient?"

"All Rachel would know about her is her name. But she'd never tell anyone a patient's name."

"Would she talk about a patient of yours being killed by a hit-and-run driver?"

"Well, yes, probably. Of course, it was all over the newspapers . . . But she still wouldn't say her name."

Michael sat quietly.

Marilena blinked twice. "Oh, my God. All he'd have to do is look up her name in the newspapers. And because of his line of work, he'd likely know her husband."

"Not likely, most certainly."

Marilena's breathing became labored again.

"Perhaps you should take a pill," Michael said.

"I'd prefer to work through this on my own, thank you."

"Whatever you say."

Ring-ring.

"What's that?" said Michael.

"The building's concierge is calling." She answered the phone. "Hello."

Her face lost color and her breathing quickened.

"I'm sorry, could you repeat that, please." She held up the phone so that Michael could overhear.

"There are three men here to see your brother. I told them he's not here, so they've asked to see you."

"Could you repeat their names again."

"Victor Persky, Anthony Bodine, and Matthew Shuey."

She pressed her hand over the mouthpiece. "Persky's my dead patient's husband. What do I do?"

Michael exhaled. "Tell him you're with a patient and he should send them up in ten minutes."

"Are you crazy?"

"Would you rather confront them alone in your home in the middle of the night? They've come to your office using their real names, looking for your brother, not you. This might be the best chance you'll ever have to work this out."

"Doctor, are you there?"

Marilena took her hand away from the mouthpiece.

"I'm with a patient at the moment. Send them up in ten minutes." She hung up the phone, her hand shaking. "What am I going to say? I can't possibly face them. I'm scared to death."

"Don't worry, I'll be with you the entire time."

"To do what?" Panic was rising in her voice.

"We'll improvise. Give me a minute to think, and I'll give you our storyline. Just follow my lead and use your common sense. Like you did with that box of tissues."

Marilena jumped up from the couch, ran to her desk, and rummaged through her middle drawer.

"What are you doing?"

"I'm looking for that pill you suggested. There's no way I'm going to get through this without one." She pulled a sample pack out of her desk, ripped it open, and two pills fell out. Ignoring the bottle of water on her desk, she swallowed one dry. She looked at Michael. "Make that two." She swallowed the second.

The sound of the buzzer signaled *showtime* to Michael, and he raised the curtain by swinging the office-suite door open with a flourish.

Three men stood in the hallway, two middle-aged men and one Middle-Earth giant. All wore dark suits and ties. As if dressed for a funeral.

"Who are *you*?" said the taller and stockier of the middle-aged men.

"I'm a patient. You interrupted my session." Michael leaned forward on his cane. "And you gentlemen are?"

"None of your business," said the shorter man, pushing his way past Michael into the waiting area. The others followed.

"I'd say that's a matter for the doctor to decide."

"Just go home, old man. It'll be better that way for everyone, especially you," snapped the shorter man.

"That's a pretty good movie line," said Michael, "but this is real life."

The short man jerked his head in the giant's direction. "You want real life, wise guy, meet Shuey."

Michael extended his hand toward the giant. "Pleased to meet you, Goliath."

Shuey looked at the shorter man.

"His name's Shuey."

"And yours is?"

"Persky."

Michael looked at the stockier man. "Making you?"

"Bodine. Anthony Bodine." He extended his hand and Michael shook it.

Michael smiled at the trio. "Now, that wasn't so difficult, was it?"

"What's *your* name?" snapped Persky.

"Michael," extending his hand.

Persky pointed to the open front door. "It's time, Michael."

Michael nodded, stepped up to the door, and firmly shut it. He paused, turned, and looked at Persky. "Now what?"

Persky turned to Shuey and jerked his head in Michael's direction. "OK, wiseass, have it your way."

"You're certainly one for drama, Mr. Persky. Too bad I'm an old man who's beyond caring about threats. Besides, unless you kill me—and of course dispose of the body in a way that no one ever discovers what happened to me—you're, as they say in French, *fucked*."

As Shuey moved toward him, Michael raised a warning finger in his direction. "I assume killing me also means you'll have to do the same to the good doctor, the concierge downstairs who copied your IDs, and the building's security folks, who've recorded your every move in the building." He shook his head. "A lot of bodies to get rid of."

"How about just some broken bones, then?" said Persky. "Like a broken hip?"

"That's an interesting suggestion, and a clever one for you to use at your criminal trial. I'm sure the two of you will claim that your colleague here acted solely on his own, and you were mortified by his conduct."

Michael locked gazes with Shuey. "But have they mentioned to you, young man, that intentionally inflicting such grievous bodily harm on a man of my age will undoubtedly land you a sentence of attempted murder?"

"What are you, a lawyer?" asked Bodine.

"No, but I know a lot of them. Some very good ones that I can assure you you'll soon be meeting in both civil and criminal proceedings, should any harm befall me."

Shuey stopped a step away from Michael and looked at Persky.

Persky glared. "What's your interest in this?"

"Merely the well-being of my doctor. How could I live with myself if I abandoned her to you three?"

"No one's here to hurt her," said Bodine.

"I certainly hope not. Still, considering how Shuey now stands close enough to kiss me, even though we all know that's the furthest thing from his mind, you'll understand that I'm skeptical about that assurance."

"We're just here to talk!" barked Persky.

"Good, then you won't mind if I sit in while you have your talk."

"It's a private matter."

"I'm sure it is, but since there are three on your side, it seems only reasonable that she has at least one with her."

Persky stepped toward Michael, pushing Shuey back as he did. "You're getting involved in something that's none of your business. If you make it your business, it could have consequences. *Serious* consequences."

"I'll take the risk. Any gentleman would."

Persky glared into Michael's eyes.

Michael winked. "Shall we go into the doctor's office?"

Michael led the way, taking great care to make it seem he was in serious need of his cane.

Marilena still sat on the couch, clutching a tissue in one hand. She did not stand.

"Doctor, these gentlemen would like to talk with you." Michael turned and pointed to each man as he recited their names. He walked to the couch and sat to Marilena's left.

Marilena cleared her throat. "Gentlemen, find your own chairs and sit wherever you're comfortable."

They chose to sit in a semi-circle, Bodine on an armchair to Michael's left, Persky on a matching chair to Marilena's right, Shuey on a straight-back wooden chair that he spun around so his massive forearms could rest atop its back. He sat directly across from Marilena, his eyes locked on hers.

"So," said Marilena, "who would like to begin?"

"Before we start," said Persky, "it seems unwise to have your patient, Michael, participate in this conversation."

"If he's willing to participate, I welcome his counsel. He's a very wise man, experienced in matters over which I'm totally ignorant."

"Yeah? What sort of matters?"

Michael spoke up. "Let's just say that having Shuey sit as close as he is to the doctor, is a method of captive intimidation I stopped using forty years ago."

Persky sat back in his chair and looked at Marilena. "Do you know who I am?"

"From your name, yes. Your late wife was my patient."

"I only recently learned that, but I assume that means you know a lot about me."

"I cannot divulge client confidences."

"Well, I'll just assume you do."

Marilena nodded. "She was my patient through very difficult times in her life."

"Here's my problem. I'm sure my wife robbed me of something of great value. Something irreplaceable. I've been looking for it since she passed away. It's also recently come to my attention that your brother has it." Persky leaned in toward her. "And you know that he does. Just give it back to me and we walk away with no hard feelings."

"What sort of thing?" asked Marilena.

Persky jerked his head from side to side. "There's no need to describe it. It's my property and that's all you need to know."

"I only asked because how would I know if my brother has it if I don't know what it is?"

"Where is your brother?" said Bodine.

"I don't know, have you tried him at home?"

"He's not there," said Persky.

"Why do you think my brother would have what you're looking for?"

"Because he asked me for the name of someone who arranges to sell such things," said Bodine.

"Excuse me," said Michael. "Are you talking about a fence?"

Bodine nodded.

"Did her brother describe what it was he wanted to sell?"

"No. He said he was asking on behalf of a patient. An obvious cover story."

"Thank you," said Michael, leaning back on the couch. "Sorry for interrupting."

"When did he come to you?" Marilena asked Bodine.

"A couple of days ago."

She turned to Persky. "But your wife died nearly two weeks ago. If she'd given what you're looking for to my brother, why would he wait so long before asking Mr. Bodine for a, uh . . ."

"Fence," Michael supplied.

"Because he already had the name of a fence," said Bodine. "I'd given it to him months before, when I was his patient."

"If he already had the name of a fence, why would he be asking you for the name of another fence two days ago?"

"Because the one I'd recommended back then went out of business *four* days ago."

"OK, but why would my brother have been interested in that other fence way back then, so long before Mr. Persky's property disappeared?"

"He wasn't. I just happened to mention the man's name and what he did in the course of one of our sessions."

She stared at Bodine. "You *volunteered* the name of a fence to my brother several months ago, and from that you concluded my brother was somehow involved with your fence . . . But now you're saying he's looking to hook up with another fence to dispose of something that Mr. Persky's wife may or may not have taken from Mr. Persky." She shook her head. "This is way too confusing. Why don't the three of you simply find the fence who recently went out of business and ask him whether he ever had anything at all to do with my brother. That seems the easiest way to get to the bottom of this."

"We can't," said Bodine.

"Why not?"

"Because he's dead."

"How convenient."

She's a natural at this, thought Michael, suppressing a smile.

Persky stared at Marilena. "My wife gave you a package. Why don't you admit to it, turn it over, and be done with this charade?"

She shrugged. "Because she didn't."

"Then who has it?"

"How in the world am I supposed to know?"

"Because as I see it, you and your brother are the only logical suspects. And in my world, you're guilty until proven innocent."

She glared at Bodine. "And what's your angle in all this, loyal patient of my brother's? Surely, you're not claiming to be a good Samaritan simply trying to help this poor man recover his irreplaceable treasure. What's your real agenda?"

Bodine glared and pointed around Michael at Marilena's face. "I don't like your tone, lady."

Michael hooked the crook of his cane over Bodine's wrist and gently pulled it down. "No need to get aggressive, Mr. Bodine. After all, it does strike me as a fair question."

Bodine swung around to face Michael as he twisted his arm away from the cane. "I know who you are. You're the one they call their savior. Well, you're not my savior, so stay out of my way."

"That's very complimentary to hear, but I prefer being called Michael." He smiled at Bodine. "What *is* your role here?"

"Bodine's an old friend," said Persky. "We've done business together for years, and he knew I'd been going through a difficult divorce. After Brackett Fielding came to him two days ago looking for a fence, he made inquiries, and learned that my wife was his sister's patient. When we spoke earlier today, he mentioned those facts to me. They led me to an obvious conclusion. My wife gave my property to her doctor, who told her brother, and now he's trying to sell it."

Michael cleared his throat. "That's a very interesting theory, but there's another scenario, one that doesn't require us to assume that two naive doctors would dare screw around with any property of yours, Mr. Persky. After all, considering all the time she and your wife spent talking about the intimate details of your *difficult* divorce, I think it's safe to say the doctor knew perfectly well that you weren't someone to cross, let alone steal from."

"What are you implying?" snarled Persky.

"This isn't about you," said Michael, "it's about him." He poked his cane in Bodine's direction. "Let's look at this from a different perspective. Bodine, how well did you know your friend's wife?"

"What's that supposed to mean?" bristled Persky.

"Just what it sounded like."

"We never met. We didn't know each other at all."

Michael pointed at Marilena as he addressed Persky. "Your wife was a long-time patient of hers, and Bodine is a long-time patient of her brother. It's a small waiting room. He's a charming guy, she's a lonely woman. He may or may not have known who she was when they first spoke, but one day he does realize she's your wife. He decides to play dumb, cultivate the relationship, not tell her he knows you. Perhaps she'll tell him something he can pass along to you as your old friend, to help you with your divorce."

Michael cleared his throat. "Then one day he receives a call from your wife, or bumps into her in this very office, and she confides in him that she has something valuable to conceal from you, but she doesn't know who to trust. That's when charming Bodine presents himself front and center as her trustworthy Rock of Gibraltar. He agrees to safeguard it for her, fully intending at that moment to turn it over to you."

Michael paused, giving Bodine's obviously rising anger more time to build. "But then something unexpected happens, your wife dies. And absolutely no one on earth knows that he has your property. This could be the biggest score of his life."

Persky glanced at Bodine.

Michael continued. "Enter the fence. Someone known for maintaining strict client confidentiality. But there's one potential risk. The fence would know Bodine was the seller, or if Bodine had prudently used an insulating representative, he'd know that person's identity. Should you, Mr. Persky, ever learn that your treasure was sold through that fence, do you have any doubt of your and Shuey's ability to convince him to reveal Bodine's name? Or the name of Bodine's representative—another person who'd surely fold when pressed by you?"

Michael leaned forward, gripping the shaft of his cane tightly in both hands. "But guess what? That fence is now dead. All links to Bodine are gone. Still, to be on the safe side, and to keep you from pressing ahead out of sheer rage on a crusade after who ripped you off, he presents you with a fall guy to vent your anger on. And not just any fall guy, but one neatly gift-wrapped in a conspiracy among Bodine's doctor, your wife's doctor, and the dead fence. Ah, yes, who can resist a good conspiracy theory, even one based on fairy-tale facts?"

"You miserable son of a bitch, making up lies about me in front of my friend." Bodine leaped up from his chair and swung his left fist at Michael's face. Michael met his fist with a hard, thrusting two-hand parry of the cane's shaft against a bony part of Bodine's forearm.

Bodine screamed in pain. "Fuck! You could have broken my arm."

"Yes, I could have. I suggest you learn to control your temper."

Persky stared at Marilena, then at Bodine.

"Victor, you know me," Bodine pleaded. "I'd never steal from you. He's selling a bullshit story. I had no idea your wife was a patient here until yesterday, after their receptionist told me about a patient who'd died in a hit-and-run."

Marilena shook her finger at Bodine. "That explains it."

"Explains what?" asked Persky.

"My secretary told me today that Bodine stopped by the office yesterday morning unexpectedly, with no appointment and no message for my brother. 'Just to say hello,' you told her. You even brought her a huge box of chocolates." She looked at Persky, "The box is still out there on her desk if you want to check. At least part of it is."

She turned back to Bodine. "She thinks you're so charming. She even complimented you on being concerned over how the office must have reacted upon learning of the death of our patient."

"Nice try, Mr. Bodine," said Michael. "Stop by the doctor's office for no apparent reason—other than to steer the conversation around to the death of Mr. Persky's wife in an effort to make it falsely seem that's when you first learned she was a patient here."

By now Bodine was sweating profusely, biting at his lip, and still holding his forearm. "These are all lies. Your brother knows the truth."

"What truth?" said Michael. "That you told her brother the name of a fence in one of your psychiatric sessions, a fence you claim her brother reached out to, and who's now conveniently dead? Are you suggesting it's her brother who killed your fence? Or that they're a brother–sister team of cold-blooded killers? And how much further are you going to push your add-on story that her brother's now asking you for the name of another fence? Do you really expect him to admit that? Although, come to think of it, if you use someone like Shuey to help you with the interrogation, you can get him to admit to anything."

Michael turned to Shuey. "What do you think about that?"

Shuey sat stone-faced, still focused on Marilena.

Persky gave an abrupt snap of his fingers and a quick point in Bodine's direction. Shuey immediately swung his chair around and fixed his stare on Bodine.

Michael sighed. "Frankly, gentlemen, I think this is a time for the two of you to reflect upon your relationship. But the good doctor here is *not* the right person to assist you in that endeavor."

"I want it back," he growled at Bodine. "And I want it back *now*."

"Uh, gentlemen, may I suggest that you have this conversation in a private setting. This is not the part of the meeting I signed on to attend."

Persky turned to Michael. "I can see why she wanted you here." He stood up and walked out of the room without saying another word.

Bodine sat shaking in his chair, his eyes blinking wildly. "This is complete bullshit." He looked at Marilena. "You *know* it's all lies."

She looked away.

Shuey stood and waved for Bodine to come with him. The stricken criminal staggered more than followed Shuey out the door.

The instant they left, Marilena started to speak, but Michael cut her off. He waited until he heard the front door open and close, then went to be sure that they'd left. He returned with a big smile on his face.

"You were terrific. You played our storyline perfectly."

"You mean your storyline." She seemed about to cry. "I feel so sorry for that poor man."

"You mean the poor man who tried to set you and your brother up to be killed, or the poor man who likely had his wife killed and would do the same to you in a heartbeat?"

She dropped her head. "I need another pill."

"Save them. It's only the first act. The rest of the play is still to come, and it's time you met the other performers."

SIXTEEN

Before leaving Marilena's office, Michael called Gabriel and invited him to meet them at his home as soon as possible after his dinner rush had passed. Then he called Mrs. Baker to tell her Marilena would be joining them for dinner. She asked how the meeting went, and Michael said, "For the moment, we're still kicking."

Angel met them at the front door and showed them into the parlor. "Mrs. Baker is cooking dinner and said to tell you it will be ready in ten minutes. Is there anything I can get either of you?"

"Marilena, this is my colleague, Angel. Angel, this is the distinguished doctor, Marilena Fielding Sinclair. Perhaps you've heard me speak of her?"

"Yes, sir, I have." Angel extended her hand. "An honor to meet you, Doctor."

Marilena smiled as they shook hands. "And to meet you, young lady."

"If you'll excuse me, unless I can get you something, I should help Mrs. Baker."

Michael nodded. "Hurry along, we'll be fine." He turned to Marilena. "Would you like a drink?"

"Absolutely. Scotch, neat, if you have it."

"How's Laphroaig?"

"Perfect. After what we've just been through, I could use a jolt of that."

"On top of those pills?"

"Worst-case scenario, I'll gain a first-hand understanding of what my patients go through on one of their drugs and booze binges."

Michael smiled. "Let's compromise on a small one." He poured a measure into two cut-crystal glasses and handed one to Marilena. "Take it easy, it's a forty-year-aged treasure."

"Wow, the good stuff."

"You deserve it after your performance. You hit every note perfectly."

She shut her eyes. "I can't escape the vision of Bodine's eyes pleading for me to tell the truth."

"We've already covered that. You had no choice."

She opened her eyes and took a large sip of the scotch. "I still feel horrible. What do you think will happen to him?"

"For the moment, not much. Persky still wants his treasure back, and Bodine is going to continue denying he knows anything about it. He might get roughed up a bit, but for sure he's been through that before. Besides, they've been doing business together for years, so if as I expect, Bodine continues claiming he's innocent, and Persky isn't convinced Bodine betrayed him, they'll likely work this out through some sort of financial arrangement."

"But if Persky doesn't think Bodine was behind it, doesn't that mean my brother and I are still at risk?"

Michael nodded. "From both Persky and now Bodine. That's why I said your performance this evening was only act one. We gave Persky an alternative, and a more believable storyline than the one Bodine was telling, but all that could change in a heartbeat if we don't tidy up a lot of loose ends."

Marilena's hand holding her glass began to tremble. "How do we do that?"

"We'll discuss all that after dinner, but for the moment I have only one suggestion."

She waited for Michael to finish his thought.

He lifted his glass, tipped it to hers, and took a slug. "Drink up your scotch."

Gabriel arrived fifteen minutes after the four had completed their dinner together and before Mrs. Baker and Angel had finished with the dishes.

"I know you," said a startled Marilena as Gabriel walked into the parlor.

"He's a legend in our neighborhood," said Michael.

"But I didn't know *you* knew him."

"You picked his diner to meet in, I didn't."

"But why is he here now?"

"Because his presence has a most definite bearing on where we go from here. That is, if we want to have any chance of keeping Persky satisfied with your story."

"Persky?" said Gabriel. "And what story?"

"You missed my play-by-play of what happened this afternoon at Dr. Fielding's office. Come, find a seat and I'll give you the quick version."

Michael finished recapping as Mrs. Baker and Angel walked into the parlor with silver trays bearing tea and coffee service. They set them down on the table in front of the others and pulled chairs up for themselves.

"So, what's the plan?" asked Gabriel.

Concern flashed across Marilena's face.

"Is everything OK?" asked Michael.

"Uh, perhaps it's just my doctor–patient confidentiality mindset, but is it prudent to have this discussion in front of everyone?"

Michael smiled. "I assume you're referring to Mrs. Baker, who prepared our meal, and Angel who served it. I should have explained that in my tight-knit household everyone has multiple duties, but each plays a vital role in shaping my strategies for matters like this. They are not domestics, but colleagues."

Marilena blushed. "I understand."

"Good. Now on to the plan. First, I think we need to isolate the essential challenge. As I see it, we must convince Persky that Bodine was the source of his wife's introduction to Carlucci, and that the Fieldings had absolutely nothing to do with it." With a nod to Marilena, he added, "And do so in a way that doesn't get Bodine or—" glancing with a sly smile at Gabriel, "anyone else eliminated by Persky."

"Excuse me," said Gabriel, "but aren't we missing someone at this Mad Hatter tea party?"

"You mean my brother?" said Marilena, biting her lip.

Gabriel nodded. "What's up with him, and why isn't he here?"

She wrung her hands. "I don't know what to say. I haven't seen or heard from him since he told me he'd reached out to Bodine. Which is what convinced me to call Michael."

"Michael," said Gabriel, "how can we go ahead with any plan if her brother isn't on board with it? He could blow us all out of the water."

Michael turned to Marilena. "He makes a good point. Do you have any idea where he might be?"

"No."

"Not even a message at your office?"

"No, none."

"*Message*? Oh, my, I must be losing my mind," said Mrs. Baker. "You have a message from your answering service. It came through along with a faxed photograph. I left them both in an envelope on your desk. Angel, be a dear, and run up and get it for Mr. Michael, please."

Angel raced off.

"So, what do we do about my brother once we find him?"

Michael looked her straight in the eye. "Convince him to listen and follow our plan."

"And if he won't listen?"

Michael shrugged. "To be blunt, as far as Persky and Bodine are concerned, I'm an innocent third party, brought on board in an advisory capacity to help you out of a dilemma in no way of my making. The only person likely at risk of going down with your brother is you."

Marilena's eyes began blinking.

Michael leaned over and patted her hand. "At some point you may have to consider how best to protect yourself should your brother refuse to listen to reason. But that moment's not here yet. Let's locate him and see where his head's at, and whether we can get him to work with us on a plan for going forward."

Marilena stood, her eyes tearing up. "May I please use the bathroom?"

"Certainly, dear," said Mrs. Baker. "It's under the main staircase."

Angel came into the room, passing Marilena on her way out and handed Michael an envelope.

"What do we have here?" He carefully opened the envelope and pulled out two sheets of paper. He picked up the cover sheet and read it aloud. "Dear Mr. Rudolph, As a courtesy to a good friend of my detective buddy in homicide, I've checked our proprietary databases for potential location information on your grandson, Daniel aka David Rudolph. I've located what may be a match in a decorated war hero who's currently serving as an

EMT at an area hospital. Below is the information on the hospital. I found no current address or telephone number for this individual. Hoping that he is your grandson, I'm attaching a photograph of him from the official EMT credentials for Daniel Rudolph. I'm sorry for your loss."

Michael looked over at Gabriel. "What a sweet note, and such prompt attention. Please thank your friend for me."

"May I see the photograph?" said Gabriel. "Just to see if it's the right guy."

Michael handed the fax to Gabriel.

Gabriel nodded. "Yes, that's him. The only thing missing is his big black dog."

As he handed the photograph back across the table to Michael, Angel moaned, "Oh God."

"What's wrong?" asked Michael.

"I know him! It was the last time I went back to the apartment. The late afternoon I found Carlucci's body. As I was coming up the steps from the street to the front door of the building, he came barging out with a big black dog."

"Are you sure?" said Mrs. Baker.

"Yes. I'll never forget him."

"Why's that?" said Gabriel

"Because he's the first person who called me Angel, and my entire life's changed since that moment."

Michael began rubbing his brow. "Mine too."

Michael bit at his lower lip. Poor Marilena. She had all the right instincts but the wrong brother. By the time she'd left, her nerves had frayed to the breaking point. He didn't know how she'd survive a confrontation with her brother. But neither was Michael prepared to risk anyone else's life if he wouldn't do as he's told. Michael was not her brother's keeper.

Then there's the late Maria's brother. A different sort of brother, a hero in war and peace. His sister died of an overdose in the same apartment as Carlucci was murdered, but her body was hauled to a dumpster, while Carlucci's was left in place. You'd think a murdered body would be the one more likely to end up in a dumpster, far from the scene of the crime.

Strange, too, is why her brother went into hiding *before*

Carlucci's murder. Michael needed those answers before he could plan. Too many were at risk for him to proceed on conjecture—starting with Angel, who replaced the dead Maria both in her apartment and role as Carlucci's courier.

He knew where to find his answers. But that must wait until tomorrow. Now was time to sleep, though he suspected he should glimpse into the Park. He'd been woefully neglectful in that regard these past few days. He supposed it accurate what is said about how living one's true life tends to get in the way of the imagined.

At least for the sane.

Michael arrived at the emergency room of Benevolent Angel Hospital promptly at 5:30 a.m., thirty minutes before the scheduled start of Daniel Rudolph's twelve-hour shift. At least that's what Mrs. Baker had been told by the kindly ER nurse she spoke to last night hoping to find "that wonderful young man Daniel" to thank for being so helpful to her husband.

He found his way to the paramedic unit, asked the security aide in the lobby to see Daniel Rudolph, and was told he generally arrived fifteen minutes before his shift.

Michael found a seat close by the exterior glass door and waited. Ten minutes later a uniformed EMT walked through the door. He stood about the same height as Michael, but had the sort of fully functioning athletic build that Michael had not possessed in many decades. He was also a dead match for the faxed photo.

"Sir," said Michael, pressing down hard on his cane as he struggled to his feet.

The EMT hurried over. "Let me help you up." He gripped Michael under his free arm.

"Thank you, Mr. Rudolph."

"You're welcome, sir." He paused. "How do you know my name?"

Michael pointed at the badge on his uniform. "I could say it's that."

Rudolph smiled sheepishly. "Right."

Michael shook his head. "But it's not."

Rudolph looked puzzled.

"Is there a place we can talk in private?"

Rudolph's tone turned tougher. "What's this about?"

"Your sister."

His jaw clenched. "Who *are* you?"

"I'm not a cop. Anything else I have to say I can assure you you'll want to hear in private."

Rudolph turned to the security aid. "I'm going to be in Room 3 if anyone's looking for me." He turned to Michael. "Follow me."

They went through a pair of swing doors into a beige linoleum lined hallway packed with equipment along the walls, past rows of curtained treatment areas, toward a door marked with a "3."

Daniel opened the door and motioned for Michael to go inside. "This will give us some privacy."

Once inside he gestured for Michael to sit on a straight-back metal chair and dropped on to a rolling stool.

"OK, so what's this all about?" His voice remained calm and measured, as Michael would expect of someone used to making life-and-death decisions on a daily basis.

"First of all, my sympathies to you on the loss of your sister."

Daniel nodded but said nothing.

"I'm particularly sympathetic to the circumstances of her passing."

"What do you know about that?" His voice still even.

Michael shifted in his chair. "That she died of an overdose in a hellhole of an apartment and was tossed like garbage into a dumpster, ending up as a Jane Doe in the morgue."

Michael detected an increase in Daniel's respiration, but not enough to alarm him over what he might do next.

"All of that is public record. Along, of course, with the fact you identified her in the morgue and claimed her personal effects but did not claim her body." He leaned forward. "What's not public record is your behavior after you left the morgue."

Daniel did not move. "You said you're not a cop. How do you know all this and, more importantly, why are you interested? Are you some sort of private detective?"

"Fair questions. I know what I know because I know who to ask for answers, but I'm not a private detective. I'm interested because friends of mine are now in jeopardy tied to your sister's former employment."

"What employment?"

Michael fixed his eyes on Rudolph's. "Her services as a courier in the late Dante Carlucci's auction business." He detected a slight flinch.

"I see."

"That's all you have to say?"

Daniel shrugged. "Why would I have anything to say?"

"The military trained you well. But it also trained me. I suggest you consider the benefits of a tactical retreat in order to live to fight another day."

He bristled slightly. "What's that supposed to mean?"

"It's not a threat. Take it more as a suggestion on how to avoid what's on the verge of exploding into a full-scale police investigation and media coverage. A situation that will undoubtedly lead the authorities to the same conclusion I've reached."

"Which is?"

"Why did you kill Carlucci? Though I think I know the answer."

"Uh, I think you're crazy."

"That's certainly possible, but on this point I'm not. Let's back up and see what we *can* agree upon. Carlucci's death is directly linked to him arranging for your sister to kill herself with an overdose."

Daniel said nothing.

"No opinion on that?"

More silence.

"My, you're a tough nut to crack. Some might think it's because you don't care how she died or why. That she was just another junkie like the many you pick up off the streets every day. Death is inevitable, so why mourn her loss?"

"Think what you wish," Daniel said.

"Oh, but I don't think that. Not at all. You were a loving, caring brother, one who had lunch with your sister every Sunday like clockwork." Michael detected a slight look of surprise. "You spent that time pleading with her to change her ways, to find a better life. No, you were the furthest thing from an uncaring brother. You were a deeply caring, and now still a deeply grieving, brother."

Daniel drooped his head. "On that I won't disagree. I miss her terribly. She was the last bit of family remaining in my life." He looked up. "Anything else you want to say?"

"As a matter of fact, there is. I know how you got to Carlucci. You knew from your sister that every afternoon he stopped by the apartment to verify his courier's pickups for the day. But he was a security freak, and there was no way you could get into that apartment without a key. You found what you needed in your sister's personal effects at the morgue. I'll leave to the imagination what happened when he walked into the apartment and found you and your dog waiting for him." Michael shook his head. "What perplexes me is why Carlucci killed your sister. If I knew that, perhaps I could help you in a way the police can't or won't. After all, they're not going to be interested in why Carlucci was killed, only in who pulled the trigger."

Daniel spoke in steely, hard-edged tones, staring directly at Michael. "What did you do when you left the military? Were you greeted by brass bands and a good-paying job? Did you get that gimpy leg in war? If so, did the government help you get the care you needed, or were you rich enough to afford it on your own?"

Michael bit at his lip.

"Well, let me tell you what I went through. I came back to nothing. The only job I could get was this," he yanked at his shirt, "paying me barely more than the minimum wage and requiring me to hold down two other jobs just to survive. God forbid I get sick and miss a paycheck. Worse still, I couldn't afford to help my sister get her life back on track. I had no money to get her the help she needed. I tried. Lord knows I tried, but drug dealers kept waiting like vampires to suck her back in."

He exhaled and paused. "Then she got that job as a courier. It actually straightened her up a bit, and she'd go on and on, talking about how it worked. She was smart, had figured it all out, and even come up with ideas on how to make his operation work more efficiently. One Sunday, I suggested we start up our own business."

He looked away. "I know it was criminal, but it wasn't like drugs or prostitution. To me it was a way to get her off the streets, give her something to look forward to doing each day that was better than drugs and would make us some decent money." He looked back at Michael. "But she was scared to death of Carlucci and didn't want to risk it."

He shut his eyes. "I told her not to worry. I'd protect her."

"How did he find out about your plans to compete with him?" asked Michael.

Daniel opened his eyes and shook his head. "I don't know. Maria may have told him or said something to one of her roommates, who told him. Junkies have confessional moments. Does it matter? It was all my fault for pushing her to do something she feared. And it turned out she was right to be afraid."

"Quite a burden to carry," said Michael, softly.

Daniel cleared his throat. "I'm certain he killed her. Her roommate told me no one but she and her other roommate knew Maria was dead, yet people showed up to haul away her body. Carlucci had to know she was going to die from bad drugs and arranged in advance for her body to be hauled away."

"So, that's why he's dead? Revenge?"

"Not really." Rudolph stared at the wall behind Michael. "I'm as much at fault as he was. Maybe more so. But he was a vengeful bastard, and I knew he'd come looking for me. That's why I moved and changed my phone number, hoping that would allow enough time for his temper to calm and things to blow over. But when I went to the morgue to identify Maria's body, I realized he was on the hunt for me, and wasn't about to stop."

"You learned that at the morgue?"

"One of the morgue attendants told me she was on duty the day someone else had stopped by looking for Maria's body. It was a man who said he expected her brother to stop by to make the formal identification; he said he'd like to speak to the brother. He gave the attendant a hundred in cash and a phone number and said he'd appreciate her giving him a call with my contact details once she had them. He said he'd give her another hundred when she had the information for him. She assumed he was an insurance investigator, but the guy made her uneasy, and she didn't want to pass along my information unless I said it was OK. I figured she could use the additional hundred, so I told her to make the call, but gave her my old information."

He shrugged. "Even with Carlucci dead, I still can't risk having a funeral for my sister, because I've no idea who else might be out there looking for me."

"What made you think the guy at the morgue was Carlucci?"

"In order to get into the morgue, you must show a photo ID,

and they keep a record of it. I convinced the attendant to let me see who wanted my information, and the ID read Dante Carlucci."

"I guess that was your him-or-me moment."

"You got that right." He drew in and let out a deep breath. "I called Carlucci at the number he'd given the morgue attendant and said we should meet to end this blood feud. He was surprised to hear from me, but came across as all friendly and chatty, even suggesting we could work together. He said we should meet at the apartment the next day at five. He'd make sure we'd be alone, so I should just knock on the apartment door and he'd let me in."

He exhaled. "I knew I'd be dead the moment that door opened, so I got there at four, and used my sister's keys to get in."

"It sounds like a difficult self-defense pitch to a jury."

Daniel threw up his hands. "I know. My life's fucked. Again."

"Don't be so negative, Daniel. All's not lost. At least not yet. There may still be a way to work this out to everyone's benefit."

"What do you have in mind?"

"Not quite sure yet. But for the moment, I need only one thing from you."

"What's that?"

"A real phone number."

SEVENTEEN

Marilena had barely slept and was wide awake by dawn. But she didn't want to be awake, because her conscious thoughts kept mining her darkest memories for an explanation as to why she'd ended up with such a miserable life. She kept telling herself what she would have told any anxiety-ridden patient: There was no rule requiring her to wallow in the depths of her mind; all she needed to spring back to her old self was focus on the many good things in her life.

But that only made her more depressed, for she could only think of property: her apartment, her car, her jewelry, her clothes. Not a single valued relationship came to mind.

She found a bottle of old scotch, not as good as Michael's, but good enough for her purposes. She sat by her window, looking out at the pond, drinking and reflecting on her life.

And her horrid brother.

So many of her patients came to her steeped in unhealthy relationships. She had no trouble dispensing advice to them, for she could look at each situation dispassionately, applying her professional tools and rational analysis to plot the best course for each patient to follow.

But she could not seem to do that for herself. Not last night, not at dawn, and not now.

She gulped down the rest of the scotch and looked at the bottle. More than half gone. It had started out full.

She poured another small shot of scotch.

There was no need to dwell on how her brother had ruined her life. She'd come to accept that, and that she'd allowed it to happen. The question she could not bring herself to face was how far was she willing to go to prevent him from getting her killed?

It was a reality she must face, and the stakes couldn't be higher: If he didn't listen to Michael, her brother would die. And she along with him.

If I turn on him, I live.

If she didn't make the choice, she knew it would be made for her. But if she betrayed her brother to save herself, how could she live with the consequences?

She swigged down the scotch and reached for the bottle.

Ring, ring.

Where's that coming from? she asked herself.

Ring, ring.

Ah, it's the door. "Who is it?" she shouted.

"FedEx, with a package delivery for Doctor Marilena Sinclair."

"Who's it from?"

"Doctor Brackett Fielding."

Marilena's face lit up. *Could it be that my brother has finally come to his senses and entrusted me with his precious treasure? Of course he has. How could I have so misjudged him as to even considered turning on him. I'm so ashamed.*

"Just a moment. I'll be right there," she called out.

Seconds later Marilena opened the door.

Brackett Fielding arrived at the hospital to find Michael sitting by his unconscious sister's bedside.

"What are you doing here?" Brackett asked.

"Keep your voice down and drop that tone."

"Don't tell me what to do."

"Every day, I admire your sister more and more for her patience. You're a hard man to like."

"Get out of here before I call the police. You've no right to be here."

"I doubt the police will see it that way." Michael looked at Marilena. "After all, I found her on her living room floor shaved of every bit of hair and beaten unconscious, I called for the ambulance that saved her life, and I left the message on your phone telling you where she was and what had happened to her." He looked at his watch. "More than eight hours ago."

Brackett bristled. "You're the reason she's in here. I told her to ignore your phony scare tactics, but she wouldn't listen."

Michael softly, but distinctly, counted to ten. "You certainly do know how to test a rational being's patience." He sighed. "I'll put it to you straight. If my housekeeper hadn't kept calling your sister this morning to see if she'd arrived home safely from our dinner last night; and if, when she couldn't reach her, she hadn't insisted I stop by her apartment on my way back from a meeting to make sure she was OK; and if, when her doorman said she was in but wouldn't answer the intercom, I hadn't insisted he bang on her door; and if, when she didn't respond to the racket he made, I hadn't pressed him to use his passkey, you'd likely be visiting Marilena in the morgue."

Fielding glared. "You're just an old windbag who loves to spin out dramatic scenarios."

"You see your sister's beating as 'spin'? Maybe it's better that you do call the police. There's no more I can do for *you*, but perhaps I can do something for your sister if she tells the police about the mess you've gotten yourselves into."

Brackett smirked, "She'd never turn against me."

Michael sighed again. "You're probably right, so think of it from the perspective of your personal well-being. If you go to the police, you still might be able to save yourself from getting whacked by some very bad guys who have you in their sights."

"There you go again with the drama, trying to scare me as if I'm a child who believes in the boogeyman. It may work on my sister, but not on me. She is obviously the victim of a horrific sexual assault having nothing to do with anything directed at me."

"Have it your way. I think it's time for me to leave." Michael stood. "A parting word of caution, though. I wouldn't reach out to Anthony Bodine until you've had the chance to speak with your sister. Unless, of course, you're looking to confront an even worse fate than your sister's."

Brackett's face tightened. "What do you have to do with Bodine?"

"Me? Nothing. At your sister's invitation, I stopped by her office yesterday for a chat, and, lo and behold, who should appear uninvited but Bodine, Victor Persky, and a third, gigantic man, all looking for you."

Brackett had no response for that, but an eye began to twitch.

"What did you expect? You went to Bodine shopping for a fence, making him curious why you wanted one, and he went looking for a reason. That's when he came up with your sister's connection to Persky's wife. He ran that possible explanation past his long-time associate, Persky, who immediately jumped to the obvious conclusion." Michael deliberately left out the receptionist's role in the chain of events. "You have what Persky's been tearing the world apart to find."

Brackett started rubbing hard at his chin with his fingertips. "What did you tell them?"

"Persky's very angry, but your sister and I were able to move him toward thinking the bad guy in the story was Bodine, not you."

Brackett's expression brightened. "Then everything's OK?"

"Sounds a bit delusional to me, *doctor*, but as Bodine was your patient, I'll defer to you on that. Just keep in mind, the success your sister and I had yesterday redirecting the focus of Persky's anger from you to Bodine will undoubtedly cause Bodine to do whatever he can for as long as he's still breathing to put you back in Persky's crosshairs."

Brackett smirked. "Convenient, isn't it, how you happened to be in my sister's office when they showed up?"

"Actually, she called me in panic, pleading for me to meet with her immediately. She feared she could no longer trust you, that you'd get her killed. Then, right on cue, in walked three men prepared to do just that. You alone are responsible for this," he said, nodding toward Marilena's bed.

"I know my sister. She trusts me implicitly. I have everything under control."

"You've said that all before." Michael pulled a sheet of paper out of his inside jacket pocket and began reading.

"Dear Dr. Fielding,

"This is what happens to those who won't listen to reason. Either return at once what is not yours or you will be next. But we shall not shave you before you die. We shall cut you, piece by piece.

"The time for talk is over."

Brackett began trembling. "Where—?"

"Beside your sister's body. I picked it up before the police and ambulance arrived."

"I don't believe any of this."

Michael started toward the door. "Doesn't matter to me whether you do or not. That's something for you and your sister to work out." He paused in front of Brackett. "Who knows, with your inimitable style, you might just convince her to welcome death as a sign of love for you." He slapped the note hard against Brackett's chest. "Keep it, it's a copy. I have the original. Just in case."

Brackett clutched the note. "In case of what?"

"In case the police want to know why pieces of you are turning up all over Greater New York."

"But this can't be my fault, I'm—"

Michael thrust the crown of his cane up to Brackett's face. "*Stop.* No more words from your mouth."

Michael held his breath. He let it out slowly, lowered his cane, and continued toward the door. "Or I might just kill you myself."

Michael couldn't believe he'd lost his temper to that grating fool.

No matter how self-absorbed, arrogant, and doomed he was his sister knew all that, and yet allowed him to manipulate her to the point of being nearly beaten to death to serve his vanity.

Two fools.

There was nothing he could do to change them. Or save them. They had consigned themselves to their fates.

The moment Michael walked through his front door Mrs. Baker yelled to him from the kitchen.

"Come in here and have something to eat. You probably haven't eaten all day."

He walked toward her voice. She stood in the kitchen by the pale green AGA range, a wooden spoon in her hand.

"You aren't young anymore. You've got to learn to take better care of yourself."

Michael dropped down onto a chair next to the kitchen table. "Thank you for reminding me of that." He pointed at the range. "I'll have a little of whatever you're cooking."

"It's not ready yet." She reached for a plate of biscuits and scones and put them down in front of him. "These should hold you until dinner's ready. I assume you'll also want tea."

Michael nodded and drooped his head.

Mrs. Baker put her hand on his shoulder. "Are you OK? Today had to be extraordinarily stressful for you. Should I call a doctor?"

"No, I'm not ill, just tired. And worried that a past I'd thought long buried has come roaring back to claim me."

He paused, waiting for her to say something, but she went to fiddle with his tea.

"I'd made an oath to isolate myself here, away from a world filled with evil motives dressed up as hallowed values, subtly poisoning us all." He shook his head. "In time, I actually came to believe I'd cleansed myself of my past. That I was a redacted man."

He lifted his head. "But I was wrong. I should never have ventured away from my seat by the window. I cannot help anyone. I'm convinced I only do harm."

"The only thing you're convincing me of with talk like that is you're overtired." She set a cup of tea in front of Michael and sat with another cup in the chair beside him.

"It's not that." He picked up his tea and took a sip. "Less than an hour ago I threatened to kill a man over words. Words spoken by a clearly distraught man as we stood in his sister's hospital room."

"He probably deserved the fright."

"That's beside the point. I didn't say them to frighten him. I spoke them because I *meant* them."

"So, you lost your temper. Who hasn't?"

"This was different. I felt . . . urges, impulses, that I left behind when I stopped serving our country. Back then, I was sure the world had brought evil into my life, but I now realize I had it backwards. The world is not the source of evil. I am."

She shook her head. "Now I'm certain you're overtired."

"That's not it. My anger is toxic. It brings death."

"Did you kill him?"

"Of course not."

"Great. You've changed." She picked up a biscuit for herself. "Your past is long gone. You're nothing like the man you were when you worked for those devils. Your heart has always been in the right place. They just knew how to manipulate you into doing their bidding. That's all in the past."

"Have you heard anything I just said?"

"Every word. Now it's time for you to listen to me." She sat up straight, biscuit in hand. "You've never stopped blaming yourself for the death of Gabriel's father, even though you weren't responsible. You were the target they were ordered to protect from capture by the enemy. He and the others died trying to protect you, and if fate hadn't intervened, you'd have been slowly butchered alive by the enemy for information they knew you possessed."

"I could have killed myself and spared them all."

"That would not have saved a single soul. You forget there was a traitor among you, who could not risk survivors. It's only because you *did* survive that he was ultimately exposed." She dipped her biscuit in her tea. "I have zero doubt that Gabriel's father is in heaven right now, smiling down on you for staying alive to nail that bastard."

He smiled faintly at that. "You sound like a recruiter."

"And you sound like an idiot." She took a bite of her biscuit.

Michael's head jerked back at that.

"Look at all you've done for Gabriel despite his mother's anger at you," she pointed out.

"Anger? At me? Why would she be angry at me? I never told her what happened to her husband. She had no idea we were even together the day he died."

"Her anger had nothing to do with what happened that day. It was driven by the simple fact you survived and her husband hadn't. She could never bring herself to move on with her life. She gave up on living long before she died, absolutely sure that the world was a cruel and unwelcoming nightmare that you *endure*, not enjoy. She carried that with her to her grave, sadly indoctrinating her son with much of that same attitude."

Michael sighed. "I tried to do what I could for the boy. I wanted to tell him about his father, but she'd never let me mention a word about him to Gabriel."

"The memories were too painful for her. She probably thought it would be the same for her son and wanted to spare him her anguish. Whatever her reason, she didn't want Gabriel exposed to memories of his father. But that denied him the very thing children most hunger for from parents they barely knew."

"She wasn't a bad woman."

"No, she wasn't, and you weren't—*aren't*—a bad man. You did what you could for Gabriel, and still do. In fact, you do more for him now than ever."

"Buying meals we don't eat is hardly great help."

She shook her head. "I'm not talking about financial help. Haven't you noticed the change that's come over him since he's been seeing you? He's exhibiting the same sort of courage you so often talked about in his father. Traits of the father are beginning to emerge in the son, all thanks to you."

"What have I done?"

She took another bite of the biscuit. "I guess you could say Angel gets some credit too, but it was your decision to intervene in her life that's changed Gabriel. And for that matter, changed you too."

"Angel?"

"She's changed because of the two of you, just like you have because of her. Dare you imagine what her life would be like had you not stepped away from your window and intervened?"

Michael took a sip of tea. "I—"

"Hello," said Angel from out in the foyer. "Is someone calling for me?"

"In here, dear," Mrs. Baker shouted back, whispering to Michael, "that's what I call perfect timing."

Once Angel joined them at the kitchen table, Michael stopped musing over the state of his life, and told them about his day in Marilena's hospital room, culminating in his confrontation with her brother.

"The brother seems like a horrible man," said Mrs. Baker.

"You'll get no argument from me on that," said Michael.

Angel sat silently, nibbling on a scone.

"What do you think?" Michael asked her.

"I don't know him."

"He's an arrogant narcissist who nearly got his sister beaten to death and shows no signs of remorse."

Angel took another bite of the scone, chewed it, and bit at her lower lip. "I can't believe he's a truly bad person."

Michael did a double-take at that.

"What makes you think that?" said Mrs. Baker.

"He's spent his life as a doctor helping others steer their lives through difficult times. That requires great empathy. And though he took something that belonged to Mr. Persky, and he's being stupid about it, well . . . that doesn't make him a killer like Mr. Persky."

"But by not returning Persky's property, and thereby putting his sister's life at risk, I'd say that makes him closer to a killer than not," said Michael.

She shrugged. "You know people better than I do, but to me he sounds like a lost soul who talks tough but is afraid to confront his own fears and insecurities."

Michael stared at Angel for a few seconds. "Would you mind telling me how, at your young age, you manage to come up with such nuanced opinions on human behavior?"

"It's a matter of survival, I guess. I've spent half my life making decisions that could cost me my life if I misjudged the intentions and character of strangers."

"You're a remarkable young lady." He sighed. "Perhaps you're right about him, but it's not up to me to straighten him out. I've tried to, with no success. He'll need to find another savior."

"Maybe he'll save himself?" said Mrs. Baker.

"His own voice might be the only one he'll listen to."

"I'll pray for him," said Angel.

"That's just what he needs," smiled Mrs. Baker. "A guardian angel."

"More like a flock of them," said Michael.

Angel spread her arms wide. "Well, here we are."

EIGHTEEN

Brackett hadn't left his sister's hospital room. He'd sat for hours, mulling over the many ways he could get back at Michael for the things he'd said. How dare he claim that Brackett didn't care whether his sister lived or died? He'd spent his *life* protecting her. She was the be-all and end-all of his existence.

Had it not been for Michael, she'd have ended up just like . . .

His mind shut down. The thought would not finish. He wouldn't allow it.

Instead, he concentrated on the many things he'd done for his sister. Guarding her, guiding her, growing their meager inheritance into enough to educate them both.

I raised her. I made her what she is today.

He looked at her asleep in the hospital bed and blinked.

Did I make her what she is today?

"I'm not at fault," he mumbled to himself. "If anyone is—" The thought came back, and again he stifled it.

He leaned back in the chair, shut his eyes, and reminisced of their days together as children. Deep into sleep, he saw a twelve-year-old boy and his five-year-old sister in a big, white house on a broad, green lawn. The sister idolized her brother. He could do no wrong in her eyes. He was her protector and interpreter of the world around them.

Their parents appeared in the dream arguing over money, and the boy explained to his sister that was just their way of planning a better life for the family. When the argument grew more heated, he assured her that the intensity of the quarrel only showed how committed they were to doing better for the family.

And she believed him.

Brackett began to twitch, and as a white garage appeared in the dream, with the boy and his sister peering inside through a side window, the twitch turned into a tremble. When the sister asked the brother, "What are Mommy and Daddy doing in there?" Brackett shook himself awake.

He jumped out of his chair with his heart racing and his shirt soaked in sweat. Instinct told him to leave. He looked at his watch. Nearly four a.m. He looked over at his sister sleeping like a baby. A baby hooked up to a bevy of tubes, wires, and monitors.

No, I can't leave. He dropped back into the chair.

Nor did he dare fall back to sleep.

At least awake, I can keep deceiving myself.

Brackett wasn't sure if the dawn sunlight upon her face, the clatter of the breakfast service in the hallway, or simply the normal progress of recovery had Marilena stirring. Whatever the reason, it was the most he'd seen her move all night. He called for the nurse and stayed out of everyone's way until given the all-clear to speak with her.

Once the others left, he pulled a chair up beside her bedside and reached out to pat her hand. "You gave us quite a scare."

She turned her wrist to take his hand. "I'm so sorry . . . so sorry . . ."

He squeezed her hand. "I'm the one who should be apologizing, not you."

"What I did is inexcusable. I should never have blindly opened my door to a stranger."

"I've done a lot of inexcusable things myself, so I think you can stop blaming yourself."

She closed her eyes for a moment, "I'm still tired." Then opened them and squeezed his hand back. "Please, don't go." She squeezed harder. "Thank God you found me. How did you know to come to my apartment?"

"I didn't find you."

"Then how did I get here?"

Brackett looked up at the ceiling and drew in a breath. "Mr. Michael found you. He also called the ambulance and sat with you here until I finally arrived . . . eight hours after he'd left a message for me that you were hospitalized."

"Michael?"

"Yes. His housekeeper worried when you didn't answer your phone, and so he stopped by to check on you."

She shut her eyes again. "How could I have been so stupid as to have opened that door."

He leaned toward her. "Actually, I've been the stupid one in this relationship."

She opened her eyes and fixed on his. "I don't understand."

"I spent much of last night thinking about us, and concluded if either of us is to blame for what happened to you, I'm the one at fault."

"But, Brackett, I—"

He put his finger to his lips. "Please. Let me finish what I have to say before I lose my courage to tell the truth." He bent over to kiss Marilena's hand. "For as long as I can remember, I've been deceiving myself into believing that my anxieties were the product of the conduct of others, and not in any way my responsibility to address. Perhaps that's why I became a psychiatrist. It allowed me to tinker with other people's lives, dispensing advice as to how *they* should live. Advice I've never followed in my own life . . . but could experience through them."

He sat back in his chair. "But what I feared most was you losing faith in me as your protector. It's what drove me to steer you into sharing my professional life, rather than encourage you to pursue what you wanted, and why I destroyed every relationship you valued. I feared that if I let you live life separate from mine, I wouldn't be there to protect you at the moment you needed me most."

He sighed and withdrew his hand. "Last night, all my fears were realized. You were almost killed when I wasn't there to protect you. And then the one person on earth who had been challenging your faith in my judgment rescued you." He paused. "Last night, it struck me why I didn't rush to be with you the moment I received Mr. Michael's message. I wasn't strong enough to confront the reality of what had just happened. For so long I'd survived by deceiving myself into believing my purpose in life was to be your protector, that I'd completely lost track of the truth behind my behavior."

"What truth?"

"That my meddling in your life was my way of using you as *my* protector, to help keep deeply repressed memories from coming back to haunt me."

"Uh, I'm not awake enough to follow you. You'll have to be more direct."

He sighed again. "Do you remember the day mother and father died?"

"I remember you screaming for me to go into the house and to tell the maid to call the police."

"What else do you remember about that day?"

"Police, ambulances, firemen, neighbors. It was quite a neighborhood event. A double suicide."

He shut his eyes. "Do you remember asking me what mother and father were doing sitting in our car in the garage?"

"No, but I remember seeing them through the garage window."

"After you went into the house, I broke that window with a rock and crawled inside. They'd left the car windows open just enough to let the fumes in, but not enough for me to reach in and unlock a door. I screamed for them to open the doors, but they made no effort. I saw a faint smile on Mom's face just before she shut her eyes. I picked up the rock and started banging on father's window, but the carbon monoxide was so thick I could hardly breathe, and I didn't have the strength to shatter it. Dad never budged. He may have already passed on. Still, I kept pounding away at the window. I was woozy when the maid got to me, but I screamed and fought with her as she dragged me out of the garage. By the time the police arrived, they were dead."

He looked down at his hands resting prayerfully on the edge of her bed. "I blamed myself for not being able to save them. I guess that launched me on a crusade to spare you the sort of unhappy life our parents led. Which I did by interfering so completely in your life."

Brackett cleared his throat. "Our parents killed themselves because they thought they didn't have enough money to live the life they wanted. Since that day in the garage, I worried that might happen to us, too. When Persky's treasure fell into our laps, I saw it as the answer to my prayers. With it, we'd never have to worry about facing our parents' fate. I then convinced myself that whatever I had to do to convert Persky's treasure into financial security for us was justified, because it was all to protect you. When I couldn't get you to appreciate what I saw as our good fortune, I grew angry with you and did things I never should have done. Like lie to you and endanger your life."

Tears welled up in his eyes as he reached out to cradle his sister's fingers in his hands. "You have no blame in any of this. It's all on me. I did what I did for the same selfish reason I've done everything. To protect myself from confronting my deepest fear." He shut his eyes. "That you'd leave me. And I'd be alone."

For a moment, the only sound was the ping of a monitor.

"I don't know what to say," whispered Marilena, trying to find her voice. "I'm not sure which emotion raging through me is the truest indicator of how I feel. My sadness and grief at how tortured a life you've led in secret, not trusting even to confide in me. Or sense of betrayal at how you've screwed with my life."

Brackett's eyes remained closed. "I understand."

"Why should I believe you now?"

He opened his eyes. "You shouldn't."

Marilena stared at him. "What do you expect me to say to *that*?"

"Nothing. You have no reason to say a thing. Or to trust me. It's on me to earn your trust."

"How do you propose to do that?"

"I'm not sure yet. But I think I know where to start." He drew in and let out a deep breath.

"And where would that be?"

"With a lot of groveling and apologizing."

It was early afternoon when Michael called Marilena's hospital room. Mrs. Baker had been checking regularly with the hospital on her condition, and when informed that it was OK to call through to her room, she suggested Michael do so at once.

When he hesitated, Mrs. Baker convinced him by saying that, having saved Marilena's life, Michael now owed her the opportunity to thank him. If he preferred not to, well, then he should close the books on the Fieldings and "say goodbye to bad rubbish."

"Hello." The voice was soft but strong.

"Dr. Fielding, this is Michael. I'm just calling to see—"

"Michael," her voice jumped an octave. "After speaking to my brother, I never expected to hear from you again."

Michael shifted in his desk chair. He didn't like the unpleasant direction this call seemed headed. "I'm sorry to have bothered you. I wish you and your brother only the best."

"Wait a minute. Aren't you going to give me a chance to thank you for saving my life?"

"No thanks are necessary. Anyone would have done it."

"Look," she said, "from what my brother said about his behavior toward you last night, I get why you'd be upset, even angry, but my brother was the asshole, not me."

"*Was*?" He heard a giggle on the other end of the line, which he found disconcerting. *Medication*? "*Was* suggests something's changed, and based on my experience with your brother, I'd say that's not possible."

"Up until early this morning I'd have agreed with you one hundred percent."

"What changed? More promises and BS?"

"Since you asked, I'll tell you." Marilena related every detail of her conversation with Brackett.

Michael said not a word until she'd finished. "It sounds like your brother had himself an epiphany right there at the foot of your bed."

"So it seems."

"Or upped his hustle to a new level."

"A fair point, but I don't think so."

"Why?"

"Because he plans on seeing Bodine and Persky to make a clean breast of things."

"That could prove interesting. Most likely fatal, too."

"I knew you'd say that."

"It's obvious. What's not is why you're telling me this."

"Because I told him to see *you* before doing anything."

"What did he say to that?"

"That I was right, and he should, but he's too embarrassed. I told him embarrassment beats dead, and if he gets himself killed, I'll never forgive him."

Michael had to chuckle at that. "So, what's he going to do?"

"I think he's working up the courage. Eating humble pie and apologizing is something new to him."

"Are you telling me to expect a visit?"

"Probably a call, but he made me promise not to call you. He wants to figure his own way through this. If he contacts you, don't tell him we spoke. The last thirty-six hours have been tough on him. He's in a seriously fragile state. He needs to feel he's rebuilding his confidence on his own. On truth and purpose, this time, not his delusions."

Michael glanced toward his window out onto the Park. *Finally, something in common with the brother. He had his delusions and I had mine, and they're what got us into this mess.* "I hope your brother realizes how blessed he is to have you as a sister."

"We're getting there. We're at the stage where he's saying the words, but he's not yet achieved prayerful, true-believer status." Another giggle.

"Well, his change of heart seems to have done wonders for you. I'm not sure what I can do at this point, but I'll listen if he asks me. Strictly as a favor to you."

"Thank you, you're a saint."

"I prefer my fedora to a halo but thank you anyway. When do you think he'll make his move?"

"Hopefully soon."

"If he doesn't, the next time I see you may be at a funeral."

Her voice cracked a bit. "I know."

"Then pray that he does."

"I am. And thanks again. Bye."

Bye.

"Hi, Gabriel. How are you?"

"Michael?"

"Just checking in to see how you're doing."

Gabriel hesitated. "Just checking in?"

"I hope I'm not interrupting anything."

"We're preparing for the dinner rush."

"Oh, sorry, I'll call you at a better time."

"No, that's OK. Just tell me what's on your mind. I know there must be something, and if you don't tell me, the suspense will drive me nuts."

"Honest, it's nothing important. I was going through old photographs and happened to come across some of your father that I thought you might like to have."

Gabriel's voice came alive. "That's wonderful. I'd love to see them. I hardly have any."

Michael was about to say, "I know," but instead said, "If you'd like, stop by the house any time."

"I will. When's good for you?"

"How's tomorrow after your breakfast rush?"

"That's my sitting-in-the-park time, so it works for me." Gabriel's voice cracked a bit. "Thank you. I don't know if you have any idea how much this means to me,"

"I do." Michael shut his eyes. "It means a lot to me, too."

Gabriel coughed. "Well, thanks again. I'll see you tomorrow. Bye."

"Bye."

In truth, Michael hadn't been looking through old photographs of Gabriel's father. He'd done all that years ago, with every photo neatly arranged in an album. He could have had the album delivered to Gabriel and been done with it, but that didn't seem the right way to do it . . . for either of them.

Mrs. Baker was right. The time was long overdue for him to put his past to rest.

Michael opened his eyes and looked out at the Park. Bits of green dotted branches everywhere with promises of spring, and WET PAINT signs hung on the benches. He noticed a familiar man sitting on one of the benches, as if oblivious to the signs, or simply not caring.

Michael stood and reached for his cane.

A little stroll in the Park might just yield me an answer.

"Well, well, if it isn't the illustrious Dr. Brackett Fielding, out and about the town on this fine, sunny day."

Surprise contorted Brackett's face. "What are you doing here?"

"I might ask you the same question, considering that I live across the street, and this isn't anywhere near your part of town. Then again, you are the sort who likes to live dangerously."

"Dangerously?"

Michael pointed to the wet paint sign.

Brackett chuckled. "Oh, yeah, I checked before I sat. The paint's dry."

"That's good to hear." Michael cleared his throat. "Do you mind if I sit on your bench?"

"No, please do. I was wondering how I could ask you to join me. Thank you for graciously making the moment easier for me."

"If I were truly gracious, I'd say 'What are you talking about?' but since we both know what you meant, I'll pass on that opportunity." He sat.

"Yeah, I was way out of line. So far, in fact, that you could justifiably call it unforgivable. You saved my sister's life and all I could do was carry on like a petulant child."

"That's one way to describe it."

"Raging asshole would be another."

"That's closer to the mark."

Brackett laughed. "Well, I sincerely do apologize."

"If you don't mind, I'd like you to answer that question you just asked of me. What are *you* doing here?"

Brackett sighed. "I was looking for a place to think through what to do next. I've apologized to my sister for the years of harm my selfishness has brought to her life, but I know that's not nearly enough. What I need to do now is somehow safely extricate us from the mess I've created with Persky and Bodine."

"Why did you come here to do your thinking?"

"It's where I came originally, hoping to meet Carlucci's messenger and launch my brilliant plan for lifelong financial security." He shrugged. "I thought returning to where it all began might somehow inspire me to find a way out of it."

"So, have you reached any conclusions?"

"Yes. That I'm utterly lost and in way over my head."

Michael nodded. "I'd say that's a good place for us to start."

Brackett cocked his head. "*Us*? After how badly I've behaved toward you, you're still willing to help?"

"Let's just say you're blessed to have a sister who compensates for your shortcomings."

"No argument there. Just tell me what I have to do."

"What are you prepared to do?"

Brackett's eyes trailed after a squirrel skipping about a nearby tree trunk. "I have no idea where to start. So, I guess the only answer I can give is, *whatever it takes*."

"That'll work, *if* you mean it."

Brackett locked eyes with Michael. "I've never meant anything more sincerely in my life. As long as it saves Marilena."

"That's admirable of you, but I must caution you that *whatever it takes* will involve huge risks. If you take it upon yourself to deviate in the slightest from a plan I come up with, you and your sister will be in *far* worse shape than you are now."

Brackett nodded, clearly catching Michael's meaning. "I'm the one with the most to gain from your help, so I'm tempted to say, 'Sure, no problem.' But since going ahead will put my sister's life in greater danger, too, I'd better ask her before I say yes."

Michael smiled. "That's the best possible answer you could have given. Assuming Marilena agrees, let's you and I plan on getting together at lunchtime tomorrow at my home. It's right over there. Number 221." He pointed with his cane.

"I can meet you earlier."

Michael shook his head. "I have something else to do in the morning."

Brackett extended his hand. "I can't thank you enough."

Michael took it. "You're welcome."

Brackett stood. "Turns out I made the right decision coming to the Park for guidance."

"That remains to be seen, but in light of who might be looking for you, I think it's prudent for you to avoid any more such public appearances. Keep a low profile until we have a plan."

"Understood. Until tomorrow." Brackett turned and strode toward the exit, a man full of purpose.

OK, Park, you worked your magic for him, so how about coming up with a little something for me. Like a plan that won't get us all killed.

NINETEEN

Gabriel arrived around nine, and Angel sent him up to the study, where he found Michael sitting at the leather-top table looking through a photo album.

"Morning, Gabriel. Sorry to have started without you, but I hadn't seen some of these photos in decades, and I just couldn't resist."

Gabriel stood where he could see the album over Michael's shoulder. "Are all of them of my father?"

"Yes. Some include your grandparents and your mother, plus, of course, a few of you."

"I never knew they existed." He grabbed a chair from the other side of the table and pulled it up next to Michael.

"Let's start at the beginning." Michael turned to the first page. It bore a single photograph of two seven-year-old ragamuffin boys, arms around each other's shoulders, showing off matching baby teeth gaps in broad, unposed smiles.

"Is that my father and you?"

"It's my favorite. Innocent times. A different world. Or maybe not. Perhaps it just seemed that way back then." He turned the page. "Here's the earliest photo I have of your father."

Gabriel leaned in. "Is that his baby picture?"

Michael nodded. "Your grandmother gave a copy to my mother. They were close friends."

Gabriel stared at the photo in silence for several minutes before nodding for Michael to go on.

Michael slowly turned through the album, remaining on each page until he'd answered Gabriel's questions, and Gabriel nodded for him to go on.

They spent hours following the journey of two inseparable boys growing into men, one marrying and becoming a father, the other not. Except for one photograph, the final photos were of soldiers. The lone exception was the last one, a photo of Michael standing beside a young Gabriel and his mother at his father's gravesite.

"This one's my second favorite. It shows you at about the same age as your father in the first photo."

"That would be two years after he died."

"I was in the hospital for his funeral, so this was my first opportunity to pay my respects to your family."

Gabriel looked up from the album. "I vaguely remember that day. There were so few opportunities I had to learn anything about him."

Michael said nothing.

Gabriel turned to face him. "Don't you think this is a good time to tell me what happened?"

Michael drew back slightly. "What do you mean?"

"It's obvious that you and my father were best friends, and your families seem to have been just as close, but suddenly *poof. Gone. Vanished.* Not a photograph or sign of you anywhere in my mother's home. She acted like you were just another person in the neighborhood. Something must have happened. Since you've opened the book of my life," he pointed at the album, "don't you owe me an explanation for the missing chapters?"

Michael sighed. "It's how your mother wanted it. She couldn't accept your dad's death. Wanted nothing around her that reminded her of him. Including me."

"And me?"

Michael looked down. "Maybe I shouldn't have done this. I thought it would bring you joy, but—"

"No," Gabriel said. "You can't imagine how good it feels to see who my father really was. I'd imagined all sorts of reasons why my mother pretty much wrote him out of our lives. I thought maybe he was a bad man."

"The opposite. He was the bravest, kindest, most generous man I've ever known."

Michael almost added, *And he gave up his life for mine*, but instinct told him this was not the time. There was plenty on the table for Gabriel to digest already.

"I never understood why my mother isolated herself so much, and rarely smiled. I thought it was my fault she was unhappy. Maybe I reminded her of my father but didn't measure up to him. Was it some dark secret she was hiding? Whatever her real reason was, I created a hundred more in my mind, each worse than the next."

He touched the album cover and smiled. "Now, I see he was a hero, a truly great man, with wonderful friends, and he'd lived a full and rich life. This was a great thing you did for me, Michael. I can see now that my mother was terribly depressed. So much so that she simply couldn't bear to experience joy. I guess that's why she shut Dad away so completely."

"I'm sorry, Gabriel. I truly am. I should have spoken to you about this long ago."

"You bear no blame in this. Nor can I really blame my mom." He paused. "I take that back. I could, but she never meant to harm me. She was so depressed she couldn't even help herself."

Michael patted Gabriel on the shoulder. "I'm pleased to see that forgiveness is in fashion these days."

"What's that supposed to mean?"

"We'll talk about it some other time. This morning is all about you and your family." He picked up the album and handed it to Gabriel. "I want you to have this."

"But they're your memories."

"I have the memories here." Michael pointed at his head. "It's time for you to put them in here." He pointed at Gabriel's heart.

"I don't know what to say."

"You already said it."

Gabriel took the album from Michael and cradled it in his hands.

Michael suddenly looked at his watch. "I'd better get ready for my meeting."

"With whom?"

"Brackett Fielding."

"I thought you'd washed your hands of him."

"It's a long story."

"Ah . . . does it involve the 'forgiveness' theme you mentioned?"

Michael nodded and gave Gabriel a speedy summary of Marilena's attack and all that followed.

"Wow," said Gabriel. "And I thought *my* time growing up was painful. Do you have a plan to get him out of his jam?"

"I'm working on it."

"Care to share?"

Michael looked at his watch again. "He's going to be here any minute."

"And I've got to get back to the diner. So, talk fast."

"You sound more and more like your father." Michael quickly spun out the outline of a plan, and when he'd finished, asked, "What do you think?"

"I'd say that you're crazy, but you've heard that many times before."

"Thank you for being so understanding."

"I have only one suggestion."

"What is it?"

"That you add Gee to your cast of characters. Otherwise—"

The doorbell rang.

Michael rose and signaled for Gabriel to do the same. "That must be Fielding."

"All right, I'm leaving. So, will you use Gee?"

"Not sure yet."

"It's meant to save your life, Michael. Don't be a hero."

His father said much the same to me the day he died. Words that cost his life. Dare I take the same advice from the son?

Brackett had all of last night and much of this morning to reconsider his newly professed dedication to doing right by his sister. Based on their family history, and Michael's own experiences with Brackett, Michael wondered whether the brother would remain gung-ho once he realized what he was being asked to do. Michael's plan for saving Marilena from further harm required her brother's full-throated participation in a tricky gamble that would put his own life at immediate risk.

What made Michael particularly uneasy had less to do with Brackett's sincerity, and more with whether Brackett could muster up a tour de force performance of patience, humility, subtlety, courage, and—most of all—chutzpah that Michael's plan needed in order to succeed. As far as Michael could tell, none of those traits were particularly high on Brackett's original-equipment list.

Michael pulled no punches in laying out to Brackett the importance of him demonstrating all those traits with meaningful conviction, nor in spelling out what would happen if the plan failed. Brackett never blinked, only nodded and said he'd do it.

Brackett accepted everything so calmly that Michael wondered whether he'd been self-medicating.

"When do we start?" asked Brackett, looking at his watch.

"Right now looks good to me."

"So soon?"

Michael nodded. "You're ready to go, and that's the most important consideration."

Brackett slapped his thighs. "OK, let's do it. Where are we headed?"

"Straight into the lion's den."

Brackett raised an eyebrow. "Just us?"

Michael smiled. "I'm happy to see you're concerned. I was beginning to worry about that cool nonchalance."

"I'm in a state of peace, not denial, and as a psychiatrist, I'm all too familiar with how erratic the cornered can behave."

"That's a good thing not to forget."

"So, is someone else coming with us?"

"A proven lion tamer. We'll pick him up on the way over. With him along, we can concentrate on you selling your story. Just keep in mind where you're headed, and that getting there isn't going to follow a predictable route. You've got to stay alert, flexible, and never lose sight of where we want to end up."

"Or else the lion will bite my head off."

Michael grinned. "That would be among the more painless alternatives."

Brackett stretched his arms out wide and yawned, his blue blazer hiking up along his crisp white shirt. "Is that your version of a pep talk?"

"Anxiety is a great motivator."

"Then I can safely say I'm more motivated at this moment than at any other point in my life."

"Wonderful. So, let's get this show on the road."

And may heaven protect us.

Brackett and Michael sat quietly in the back of the limo, each preparing in his own way for what was about to play out.

The limo stopped in front of the diner. Gee was waiting in front. He gave a quick nod to Michael as he jumped in next to the driver.

"That's our protection?" whispered Brackett. "Isn't he the grill man at the diner?"

From Brackett's tone, Michael worried that his initial bravado might be unravelling.

"That's his cover. He knows what he's doing. Trust me on that."

A little lie in aid of reassurance is not a sin, Michael added silently.

"Why do I sense there're more intrigues afoot than I'm aware of?"

"Because there are," said Michael, patting Brackett's knee. "And they're all designed to protect you and your sister in the most inconspicuous ways possible."

Brackett drew in and let out a deep breath. "I guess I have to trust you on that. After all, you're my only game in town."

Michael nodded. "You'll do just fine."

The driver made his way from Manhattan, over the East River via the Willis Avenue Bridge, into Bodine's Mott Haven South Bronx neighborhood. Once there, he kept to the main thoroughfares, and though Michael preferred the back streets to avoid traffic, he understood the driver's reasoning. A limo in the areas they were passing through attracted a lot of attention. Getting boxed in on a narrow backstreet could lead to all sorts of unpleasantness not visited upon those who kept to the main roads.

The limo pulled up in front of a tiny grocery store, its windows plastered in ads for cigarettes, beer, and any number of government-sponsored games of chance. The grocery occupied the street level of a nondescript, three-story brick building, amid a row of similar buildings hosting a pawn shop, two restaurants, a real estate agency, and a storefront church. A solid metal door leading from the street to the building's upper floors looked far sturdier than any other on the block, leaving little doubt that what went on upstairs was of a far more serious nature than in the grocery.

The moment the limo stopped, Gee jumped out and opened the rear door for Michael and Brackett.

As the three men walked toward the metal door, Michael pointed with his cane to a camera mounted on the building's roof. "I guess we won't have to worry about announcing ourselves."

No sooner had they reached the metal door than a buzzer sounded, releasing its lock.

"I wonder if that means we're welcome?" said Brackett.

Michael went through the door first, followed by Brackett and Gee. He'd not yet made it up the narrow first flight of stairs, when Anthony Bodine stepped through a doorway marked OFFICE and on to the second-floor landing. He glared down the stairs, his fists clenched. "What the fuck are you doing here? I should kill you where you stand."

Michael kept climbing. "That would be a serious blunder, since the reason we're here is to save your life."

"Save *my* life? You and your bullshit lies destroyed it."

"Then I'm sure you can appreciate that we're likely in the best position of anyone on earth to resurrect it."

"Fuck you and your fancy talk. Get out before I *do* kill you."

"Now, now Anthony," said Brackett, from two steps behind Michael. "Anger is no way to process your anxiety. You should know that by now."

Bodine didn't budge. "I don't know what you're doing here, but this man and your sister ruined my life."

"Well, to be perfectly honest, Anthony, I think it's fair to say that you tried to do the identical thing to me. Did you expect Marilena to let you set me up to be murdered?"

Bodine gave a quick glance over his shoulder back through the open doorway. "Don't talk about that here."

"We have to talk about it. As your doctor, I get how severe anxiety made you put my life at risk in order to protect your own. I'm here now hoping to find a way for all of us to come through this safely. I'd strongly suggest that you at least listen to what I have to say."

Bodine looked back again into the office. "Follow me." He turned and climbed the stairs to the third floor.

Michael allowed Brackett to pass him on the second-floor landing, giving him a wink as he went by.

The third floor was not at all what Michael had expected. A half-dozen bull-necked men sat in cubicles slogging away on computers, seemingly oblivious to everything going on around them. It looked more like a hedge-fund trading floor than the backroom to a money-laundering operation.

Bodine stomped toward a door behind the cubicles, barking to everyone he passed not to disturb him for "anything." He opened the door to a small room fitted with a serviceable conference table and somewhat matching chairs. He waved the three men into the room, before slamming the door shut behind him, and flicking on two light switches.

Bodine glared at Gee. "Who are you?"

Michael answered. "He's my aide."

Gee pulled out a chair for Michael.

"Thank you," Michael told him as he sat.

Brackett sat next to Michael, across the table from an empty chair in front of Bodine. Gee remained standing.

Brackett motioned toward the empty chair. "Anthony, please sit."

Bodine shifted from one foot to the other several times before sitting. Michael nodded to Gee, who promptly sat at the far end of the table and facing the door, his hands tucked on to his lap.

"You wanted to talk, so talk," said Bodine, crossing his arms tightly over his chest and fixing his eyes on Brackett.

"The problem, as I understand it, is a simple one. Persky claims that his wife took something from him that he wants back. Are we in agreement so far?"

"Go on."

"I'll take that as a yes." Brackett paused. "In fact, Persky wants it back so badly that he's willing to kill to recover it. And if anyone knows how to do that, it's Persky. Agreed?"

"Stop with the psychobabble already and get to your great plan to save us all."

"Bear with me, Anthony. The success of the plan depends upon whether we agree upon the truthful background of our current situation."

Bodine bit at his lip. "Fine, fine, I agree. Just get on with it."

"When you realized that Persky's wife was a patient of my sister in our joint practice, and learned that Persky was turning the world upside down looking for what his wife had taken from him, you panicked. You thought somehow Persky would link you to his wife through our office and blame you for its disappearance. So, you took the easy way out and planted a bug in Persky's ear that his wife had handed over to her doctor."

"That's old news," scowled Bodine.

"Good, then we're still in agreement. So, here's where you screwed up. You were so blinded by fear, that you missed the obvious true explanation for what happened."

Bodine leaned in toward Brackett and grunted for him to continue.

"Mrs. Persky gave it to Carlucci on her own, without any participation by you or me or Marilena."

Bodine sat back and smirked. "How would she even know about Carlucci?"

"I can think of any number of ways but considering our present circumstances—which we're in because of you—let me suggest an alternative explanation to the one you made up for Persky that works with the facts you presented to him."

Bodine clenched his teeth but said nothing.

"Mrs. Persky was an attractive woman, and you're an irrepressible charmer, so it's understandable that, one day, when the two of you happened to be sitting together in my office waiting area, you struck up a conversation with her. She, being in a continuous state of borderline hysteria over a husband who she believed might kill her at any moment, opened up to the kindly gentleman showing an interest in her. You took it as interest in you."

Bodine gave him no reaction whatsoever.

"So," Brackett continued, "this anonymous lady, who you did not know at the time was Mrs. Persky, started in on you with her tale of woe featuring a very rich husband screwing her in a divorce settlement. You, hoping to impress her, offered a simple suggestion, 'Steal something valuable from him and sell it.' Her response was just as simple. 'I could never sell it. No legitimate auction house would ever touch it.'

"That's when you came up with what you saw as a sure-fire response guaranteed to get you into her pants. 'I know a guy who can sell it for you. All you have to do is use my name.' That got her excited, which got you excited, and in the passion of the moment, you slipped her your card, on which you'd written Dante Carlucci's name and number."

"Um, that doesn't strike me as a scenario likely to improve my standing in the eyes of her husband."

"I'm not done yet."

Bodine rubbed his eyes. "OK, what happened next?"

"Nothing. You never heard from her again, and since she never told you her name, you forgot all about her. That is, until the other day, when you realized she was Persky's wife, and she'd been killed by a hit-and-run driver outside my office. That's what set you into a full-scale panic attack."

"Why would I be worried?"

"If your card with Carlucci's name and number *ever* turned up among Mrs. Persky's things, you'd have a lot of explaining to do to Mr. Persky. You needed a story to cover you. Sadly, the tale you told made *me* the fall guy, but it allowed you to say you gave me Carlucci's information, and therefore I must have passed it on to Persky's wife.

"All you actually had to do was admit you'd given Carlucci's name to some anonymous woman you'd met in my office, and you only learned after she'd died that she was Persky's wife. Had you said that, none of us would be a target now.

"I think it's fair to say that's a far more believable explanation than the one you tried to peddle Persky about my sister and I being involved in some grand scam with Carlucci."

"At this point, Persky won't be interested in hearing any of that from me. All he wants to know is who has what his wife took from him."

"With both Mrs. Persky and Carlucci dead, that's close to an impossible question to answer," said Brackett. "We can't even prove that Persky's property ever made it to Carlucci, let alone who has it now."

Michael raised his hand. "Pardon the interruption, gentlemen, but if you're in agreement that this slight revision to what's been told to Persky about how his wife came to know of Carlucci is in the best interests of everyone, including Persky, I may be in a position to substantiate that Mrs. Persky did in fact personally arrange to have her husband's item delivered to Carlucci."

"How the hell would you do that?" said Bodine.

"I have my sources."

Bodine frowned. "If you expect me to tell Persky any of that, let alone convince him, I'll need to know your sources."

"No can do."

"Perhaps some of my friends outside can convince you to share."

Michael smiled. "I *thought* they were a bit burly for computer operators."

"They multitask."

"Frankly, I'm not worried about them."

"You should be."

Without taking his eyes off Bodine, Michael gestured in Gee's direction.

Gee's right hand came up from his lap, gripping a .45.

Michael turned back to Bodine. "Now that we've finished posturing, may I continue?"

"Fuck you." Bodine slammed his hands on to the tabletop. "I've been screaming for days to Persky that you set me up to look like the bad guy in this. Now you expect me to traipse into his office, confess to having put Carlucci's name into his wife's hands, and top it all off by telling him *anonymous sources* say she passed the item on to Carlucci but no one knows where it is now? Persky would whack me on the spot!"

"Quite the contrary," said Michael. "If you explain it to him correctly, you'll be off the hook. We'll all be off the hook. And he'll have a better chance at finding what he's looking for."

"With that fairy tale? Bullshit!"

"Now, now," said Brackett. "It's no more a fairy tale than the one you already told him. Besides, you're not admitting you stole from him, only to falling victim to a panic attack brought on by a realistic fear that he might blame you for something you hadn't done. In desperation, you made up a story to shift blame to someone else."

"Frankly," said Michael, "since he hasn't killed you yet, it should work. Your doctor's explanation shows you in a far more favorable light. I think you'll be far better off once you tell him. Besides, if you'd like, you'll have Dr. Fielding and me along to corroborate your story, and confirm that Carlucci, even dead, offers the best lead for Persky to pursue for finding his missing property."

Bodine drew his elbows up on to the table and dropped his head into his hands. "The only reason he hasn't killed me is I'm paying him every day to stay alive. He's milking me dry."

"Sounds like you should thank us for dropping in on you," said Michael. "This should get him off your teat."

"He's at my throat, and he isn't the sort of vampire who gives up once he's hooked on to a meal ticket."

"Then I suggest you confront him sooner rather than later," said Michael. "Otherwise, get used to wearing Persky around your neck for the rest of your life."

In a sudden change of mood, Bodine slapped his hands lightly on the tabletop. "Gentlemen, thank you for your suggestions. You've given me a lot to think about."

"Just let us know if you want us to join you to meet with Persky," said Brackett.

"Thank you, but don't hold your breath. The last thing I need when I'm begging Persky to give me back my old life is you guys in the room running your game on my time. I haven't forgotten how my last meeting with Persky and you," he pointed at Michael, "turned out for me. If I need you, I'll call you."

Bodine stood, walked to the door, and opened it. "Gentlemen, good day. I'm sure you can find your own way out. You seem good at that sort of thing."

Brackett followed Bodine out of the room, with Michael and Gee trailing behind. Michael paused in the doorway only long enough to turn off the light switches, one at a time.

Just as I thought.

Brackett didn't say a word until the limo had pulled away from the building. "Damn, damn, damn."

"What's bothering you? Everything went well."

"*Well*? How can you say *well*? It's obvious he plans on speaking to Persky without us. Who knows what he'll say?"

"There's no percentage for him in making trouble like that. He's way better off sticking to our storyline."

"Only if Persky buys it. Without us there, how's he going to convince him that you have sources who can prove his wife delivered what he's looking for to Carlucci?"

Michael smiled. "He'll play the part of the recording where I said I did."

"What recording?"

"The one he turned on when we walked into the room. I don't know if you noticed, but he hit two light switches, not one. As we were leaving, I tried them both. One worked the lights, the other something else. My money's on a recorder. That's what guys in his line of business do. They're so used to dealing with liars and double-dealers, they tape everything."

"I wish I'd known going in about the possibility of a recording. I'd have been more careful with what I said."

"That's precisely why I didn't tell you. I didn't want the thought inhibiting you. Obviously, I made the right decision, because you were terrific."

"But if he plays the tape for Persky, won't it show us trying to get Bodine to lie?"

"That's a possibility, but from what I heard you say, the more reasonable conclusion is this was a diplomatic effort on your part to convince your former patient to admit to the truth of what actually happened: he met Persky's wife in your office, he spoke to her, he gave her Carlucci's number."

Michael patted Brackett on the arm. "In fact, if I were Bodine, I'd only play the part for Persky where I say I have sources."

"But what if he plays the whole thing for him, and it fires Persky up to come after us?"

"Persky's primary goal is to recover his property. So, no matter who or what he believes, I don't see him doing anything of a drastic nature until he's learned my sources."

Brackett drew in a deep breath, held it for a moment, and exhaled. "What do we do now?"

"For you, nothing at the moment. I'm going to return home and wait to hear from Persky."

"You think he'll call you?"

"More likely drop in unannounced. That's his style."

"When do you think that'll happen?"

"Once Bodine lets him in on what I said, I'd say as soon after that as Persky can find out where I live."

"Sounds like it could be dangerous."

Michael smiled. "It could be . . . if Persky's not careful."

TWENTY

The front doorbell rang at little after eight that evening.

Mrs. Baker answered through the intercom. "Who's there?"

"Is this where a man called Mr. Michael lives?" said a gruff male voice.

"Oh, you must be Mr. Persky. I'll be right there." Thirty seconds later she opened the front door, and two men stepped inside.

"Where is he?" said Persky.

"And you must be Shuey," she smiled to the second man. "Welcome."

"Lady, I don't have time for this. Where is he?"

She looked at her watch. "Frankly, we were expecting you earlier." She pointed toward the parlor. "He's in there, waiting for you."

Persky stormed off toward the parlor, but Shuey lingered by the door, fixing a steely-eyed glare on Mrs. Baker.

She patted his arm. "Oh, stop flirting with me young man. I'm old enough to be your grandmother."

Shuey blinked.

"Please, be a good boy and run along inside with your friend." She turned and walked into the kitchen.

A puzzled-looking Shuey stood alone in the foyer for an instant, as if deciding what to do next, then did as she'd said.

Michael sat in a wingback chair facing the door, his cane resting between his legs. "Ah, Mr. Persky, please excuse me for not getting up, but it's been a long day."

Persky hovered in front of Michael. "I don't like it when people play games with me."

"That's a trait we share." Michael reached for a teacup and saucer on a small table next to his chair. "So, what can I do for you?" He took a sip of tea. "Please have a seat. We have a lot to talk about, I assume."

"Enough of your bullshit; just tell me where my property is."

Persky slapped his hand across Michael's hands, sending the cup and saucer crashing into the fireplace.

"I take it you don't like tea."

"Listen, wiseass." Persky reached down, grabbed Michael by the collars of his blazer, and jerked him up out of the chair.

As Persky yanked Michael to his feet, Michael gripped the shaft of his cane, and drove the crown up between Persky's open arms hard into his throat. While Persky grasped for breath, Michael stepped to the side, caught Persky around his neck with the crook, and yanked him down into Michael's chair.

Shuey charged for Michael, but not quickly enough. Michael whipped the shaft of the cane around in an arc that caught Shuey on the outside of his knee, sending him crashing to the ground. He tried climbing back to his feet as a sharp downward blow shattered his collarbone.

Michael quickly cocked the cane high above his head and said calmly. "My next strike will be to your head. And we both know what that means."

Persky winced as he struggled to speak through his bruised trachea. "You motherfucker. You're fucking dead."

Without taking his eyes off Persky or Shuey, Michael said, "What do you think of that sort of talk, Mrs. Baker?"

The unmistakable sound of a racking 12-gauge shotgun vibrated through the room, freezing Persky and Shuey in place.

"I think you should step aside, Mr. Michael, so you don't get blood all over your jacket."

"Mr. Persky," said Michael, "would you please remove your gun and toss it on the fireplace hearth?"

Persky hesitated, but Mrs. Baker wrapped her finger around the trigger and leaned in toward him.

"Slowly, please, and grip it by the barrel," said Michael. "I wouldn't want you startling Mrs. Baker."

Persky fumed but did as he was told.

"Now, kindly remove the guns from your colleague, in the same careful way."

Persky lurched out of the chair and pulled a compact sub-machine gun from under Shuey's jacket and flipped it on to the hearth.

"Don't forget the gun strapped to his ankle. And the other one in the small of his back."

Persky removed and tossed two semi-automatics toward the fireplace.

"Quite an arsenal these fellows brought with them for a bit of tea and conversation," said Mrs. Baker.

"I guess you could say it's a sign of the times." He looked at Shuey. "I know you're in pain, young man, but that seems to be part of your business, so you'll excuse me if I don't call an ambulance. As soon as we're done with our business here, I'm sure he'll see to it that you get all the appropriate medical attention." Michael flicked a glance at Persky. "And if you try any more heroics, I'm sure he'll take care of your funeral arrangements."

Michael stepped back and dropped into a chair, facing both men. "So, let's get straight to why you're here. You want me to tell you what I know that might help you locate what you're looking for. What I have is proof that your wife delivered your item to one Dante Carlucci, deceased. As for where your item may be now, or who has it, I've absolutely no idea. That you'll have to figure out on your own."

"Why should I believe a word you're telling me?" Persky growled, rubbing his throat.

"I'm not asking you to, nor did I expect you to believe me." He pointed at the table next to Persky's chair. "Would you please toss me that remote on the table next to you. Whoops, we seemed to have knocked it on to the floor."

Persky looked around, found the remote, and flipped it to Michael.

Michael pressed a button, and a screen next to the fireplace came on with an image of two people sitting on a park bench. Michael and a young woman with long dark hair, wearing a gray cloth coat.

"What's this?" said Persky.

"It's an interview I conducted with Carlucci's courier. As you probably already know, or can easily find out, Carlucci used her to carry messages to him from his customers. She had a regular route through the Park, and customers would stick whatever they had for Carlucci in her coat pocket for later delivery by another courier."

"I can't make out her face. It's all blurry."

"It's supposed to be blurry. It's the only way I could convince her to talk. But I'll give you a copy of the video, and I'm sure any of your colleagues who dealt with her will vouch that the person on the video was Carlucci's courier."

"How did you find her?"

"It wasn't difficult. This house is across the street from the Park where Carlucci did his business. I'd seen her there many times, and when the police put out a drawing of who they were looking for, I knew it had to be her. I hadn't seen her for a while; then the other day she showed up in the Park. Sort of a lost soul, it seemed. I introduced myself as a documentary filmmaker interested in hearing her story. At first, she said no, but I offered to pay her. Not much, but enough to get her to believe I was serious. Funny how turning on a camera gets otherwise quiet people to open up and tell their secrets."

"Enough with the psychology. Just play your movie."

Michael pressed play, and the video opened with Michael asking her how she'd met Carlucci, where she lived, and when she started working for him. Then he asked her to explain precisely what she did for him. She talked about her morning route through the Park collecting written messages for Carlucci in her coat pocket, her daily trip to a "shop," where she'd hang up her coat in a specific place, and how when she went to put her coat back on, the pocket would be empty.

When he asked if she'd ever delivered anything directly to Carlucci, she said "No."

"Where did she hang her coat?" asked Persky.

"I'll get to that later on in the film. The part of greatest interest to you is coming up next."

The video showed Michael handing the woman a photograph and asking whether she'd ever seen that person before. She answered, "Yes, twice. Once when she gave me a letter, and a few days later when she gave me a package."

Michael asked her to hold up the image for the camera: it was a photo of Mrs. Persky.

"How big was the package?"

"About the size of a book."

"Why do you remember her?"

"Because she's the only person who ever gave me a package,

and she had difficulty stuffing it into my coat pocket. I told her I couldn't accept packages, only envelopes, and she told me not to worry, because Carlucci told her to give it to me."

"And what did you do next?"

"I followed my normal routine, hung up my coat on the hook, and when I came back, the pocket was empty."

"Do you have any idea who took the package or where it ended up?"

"No."

Michael then thanked the woman, and the screen went blank.

"That's it?" asked Persky.

"Not quite."

Another image came up on the screen. An obviously nervous young man, in a full jet-black beard and matching dreadlocks, sitting on the same park bench with Michael.

Michael asked him how he came to know Carlucci, and what he did for him. He said he worked as a delivery guy for a neighborhood company, and that every day Carlucci would phone in an order to his boss, who'd then have him deliver it to whatever address Carlucci had given for that day's delivery. Each morning he'd empty out the girl's coat pocket and deliver what he'd found along with Carlucci's order for the day. His boss knew nothing about his side deal with Carlucci. It was just a way to make some extra money. Everything he found in her coat pocket was always sealed, and he never had any idea what was inside.

Michael asked him whether he remembered ever delivering a book-size package to Carlucci.

"Yes."

When asked why he remembered, he said the same thing as the courier. In all the time he'd been working for Carlucci, that was the only *package* he'd ever delivered. But there was also another reason he remembered. The address Carlucci gave for that delivery was different from any address he'd used before. All the other addresses repeated every so often.

Michael asked him for the address, and he said, "I don't remember it, but it was the apartment where the police found Carlucci's body."

Michael asked if he knew who'd sent the package, and he said no. The only person in the chain that he'd ever seen was the courier, and, of course, whoever happened to be at the address where he made the deliveries.

Michael asked who was at the place where he delivered the package.

He gave a one-word answer. “Carlucci.”

The video ended there.

“This sounds like made-up bullshit,” smirked Persky.

“You have the right to your opinion, but if you’re looking for what happened to your treasure, you now have two low-level operatives in Carlucci’s network without an axe to grind tying your wife and a package directly to Carlucci.”

“You could have paid them to lie.”

“I could have. But why would I?” Michael adjusted himself in his chair. “Let’s take a longer view of the situation. *IF*, and I emphasize *if*, I am lying to you and made all of this up, you know where I live. And our earlier tiff aside, you can surely come back and take me out for misleading you. I have no reason to lie to you. I’m only involved because you and Mr. Bodine drew me in. And whatever pain I caused you this evening, you brought upon yourselves.”

Persky struggled to keep his cool. “How did you know about the delivery guy?”

“I didn’t. But once I figured out where the courier was leaving her coat, it wasn’t all that difficult to figure out who had the most likely access to it every day. And, bingo, I guessed right. He opened right up when I told him it was either me or the police.”

“I assume you won’t tell me where the delivery guy works.”

“I’m sure you can figure it out if you want to, but it’ll be a waste of time because he told me everything he knew. Still, if you want to chase after him rather than your precious package, be my guest.”

Persky rubbed again at this throat. “You said I could have a copy of the video.”

“So I did.” Michael reached into his jacket pocket, pulled out a thumb drive and tossed it to him.

Persky stood, still rubbing at his throat. “I’ll be back if this is bullshit.”

“I expect that you will. But it isn’t. I assume you’ll forgive Mrs. Baker and me if we can’t assist you in getting Shuey to the door, but our hands are rather full at the moment.”

Michael lifted his cane and Mrs. Baker gestured for them to go with the shotgun's barrel.

Persky squinted but said nothing as he struggled to help Shuey to his feet. Together they limped to the front door and out of the house, pausing only long enough for Persky to slam it behind him.

Mrs. Baker lowered the gun and sighed, "I need a brandy."

"You did very well."

"I'm too old for this."

"We both are. But don't worry, what's yet to come will keep us young."

"If it's anything like tonight, the question is, will it keep us breathing?"

"Let's hope so."

"Excuse me, Mr. Michael," came a tentative voice from the doorway.

"Angel, I told you to stay in your room until I came for you, and not to leave it no matter what you heard going on up here," scolded Mrs. Baker.

"I know, but I saw two men staggering down the stairs into a car, so I figured it was safe to come up."

"Did anyone see you looking out the window?" asked Michael.

"No, my lights were out and the curtains drawn. I just peeked out between them."

"That was a very foolish risk you took," said Michael, shaking his head. "We've gone to a lot of trouble to keep your identity hidden."

"I'm sorry." She bit at her lip. "I just wanted to know how the video worked."

"You were terrific, dear," said Mrs. Baker.

Angel smiled. "Good! I was worried that when I lied my face might show I wasn't telling the truth."

"Deception in aid of overcoming treachery is a virtue."

"Who ever said that?" said Mrs. Baker.

"I just did," said Michael, smiling. He looked at Angel. "It's good that you're uncomfortable with lying, but since I'd blurred your face on the video, they wouldn't have been able to tell."

"Why didn't you hide Gabriel's busboy's identity, too?"

"Because if I had, there'd be no way for Persky to independently verify he was who he said. You were well-known as Carlucci's courier—he literally advertised your description—so many people could confirm that's you in the video. But Carlucci kept the busboy's identity secret, so I needed to give Persky something to chase, in order for him to have any faith in the busboy's story."

"But why would the busboy take the risk of becoming the target of a guy like Persky?"

"He felt he owed it to Gabriel for not firing him over his side deal with Carlucci."

"But if Persky tracks him down, do you think he'll stick with his made-up story about delivering that package to Carlucci?"

"We share that same concern, which is why he's off with his family on a two-week paid vacation, courtesy of Dr. Brackett Fielding."

"But what if someone recognizes him from the video?"

"If you noticed, in the video he wore a shirt with a tiny logo on his chest. It's for a major delivery operation based on the other side of town. Hopefully, that bit of misdirection will keep Persky busy for a while looking there."

"But he has such a distinctive look . . ."

"Not anymore. The dreadlocks and beard are gone. He shaved them off right after our interview." Michael yawned. "If everything goes as planned, we'll have a lot more action to look forward to tomorrow, and within two weeks this will have all blown over."

"Or blown up."

"Such optimism, Mrs. B."

"In my experience, whenever I'm told to prepare for guests by having a loaded shotgun at the ready rather than tea, I'd say the future is a bit iffy."

Michael rose up from his chair. "On that bit of wisdom, I say good night," he limped for the doorway, "and continued good luck to us all."

Early the next morning, Michael set off from his house for the diner. Last night his instincts had kicked in and done the job he'd long ago trained for them to do. Yet, as he was getting ready for bed, common sense and a slight twinge in his back combined to remind him that confrontations of that sort were more of a younger man's game. Still, there was no denying that his encounter with Persky and Shuey had once again brought a decided spring to his step.

Gabriel was in the throes of his morning-rush madness but had saved a stool for Michael close by the cash register. From there they could talk over the din of the dishes and the diners.

"Did Maria's brother stop by?" asked Michael.

"He was waiting outside before we opened."

"And?"

"He picked up the package that you had Mrs. B leave for him with me last night and said to tell you he'd take care of it."

"Did he happen to mention what he was going to do with it?"

"It's your package. Don't you know?"

"Did he or didn't he tell you?"

"No, he didn't. And while we're on the subject, would you mind telling me why you had him pick it up here rather than at your house?"

"After last night's little excitement, which I'm sure Mrs. B shared with you, it seemed wise to limit the number of visitors coming to the house. No telling who'd be surveilling the place."

"Mrs. B also passed along a warning for Gee and me to be prepared for Persky to figure out that the busboy in the video worked here."

"Did you tell her that I wouldn't have gone forward with the video if you and Gee hadn't signed off on that risk?"

"No, it was more fun listening to her tell how the two of you whipped the bad guys' asses. I didn't want to step on her story."

Michael laughed. "OK, I get it." He glanced toward the door as a group of four men walked in, waving hello to Gabriel and heading straight for an empty booth in the rear.

"The tall one's my detective buddy. The others are also detectives. They generally have lunch here together a couple of times a week. Today it's for breakfast."

"Do you think he can be trusted?"

"If you mean, is he the sort who would go for putting Persky's money in his pocket over a departmental feather in his cap, I wouldn't know."

"That makes him a bad choice for our betting so much on his cooperation."

"I haven't asked him yet."

"But we'll have to soon. Or come up with another way to wrap this up."

"I wonder what was in the package?"

"It's no secret. I had to get rid of the guns I took off Persky and his muscle. No telling the number of crimes they'd been used in. With all the players involved in this game of murderous musical chairs, I didn't want them ending up in my possession when the music stopped. So, I asked Daniel to get rid of them. He owed me a favor."

"That's all very interesting, but I was talking about the package the Fieldings are holding."

Michael chuckled. "Shows you where my head's at. I don't want to know anything about that package. I sense it's one of those curious-cat situations where the satisfaction of knowing doesn't bring the poor kitty back to life."

"On a totally different subject, what can I get you for breakfast?"

"Surprise me."

"That seems to be the story of your life these days."

"Tell me about it."

Persky hadn't been this angry in years. Except at his wife, and he'd taken care of that situation the same as he would this one.

For his wife's hit-and-run, he hadn't dared risk even the hint of a direct tie-back to him, so he used out-of-town talent. This, time, though, he'd do that asshole Michael personally, along with that old woman who lived with him. He'd make it look like a murder-suicide. Both of them are as good as dead.

I'll use the bitch's own shotgun.

He clenched and unclenched his fists. Once he recovered his package, the Fieldings were equally dead. They knew too much. Bodine would get a pass, at least for as long as he kept paying.

It was too early in the morning for the people-of-the-night residents of the building to be awake. The two men saw no one on their way up the flights of stairs leading to the top floor. They paused at the beginning of a hallway running between two parallel rows of doors.

"You're sure it's the last one on the left?" whispered Persky.

"That's what I was told by someone who knew Carlucci well."

"You'd better be right," he warned Bodine.

"Well, if this is the building where that guy in the video said he delivered a package to Carlucci, then that's the apartment." Bodine pointed down the hallway.

"Any idea who's in there now?"

"Last my source knew, it was only girls."

Persky shook his head. "I wish Shuey were here to handle this."

"Yeah, I was wondering where he is."

"He's in the hospital getting his busted collarbone fixed."

"What happened?"

"He slipped in the shower."

Bodine thought better than to question that.

When they stopped outside the apartment, Bodine pointed at the door and whispered. "Even a healthy Shuey couldn't kick this one in."

"On to plan B." Persky shrugged and knocked on the door.

No answer.

He knocked harder. Still no answer.

On his third and harder knock, he heard a female voice from deep inside the apartment, "Who the fuck is it knocking on my door at this hour of the morning?"

"Sorry, to disturb you, ma'am, but I have a package to deliver."

"Leave it outside the door." The voice was closer.

"I can't. It's from a bank and I need a signature."

"A bank?" The voice was on the other side of the door now.

"Yes, ma'am."

"There must be a mistake. I don't have a bank."

"I'm sorry, but is this the residence of Dante Carlucci?"

A long pause, then a tentative, "Yes."

"Well then, this package is for him. I just need a signature and I'll be on my way."

Persky smiled at the peep hole, certain the woman on the other side was studying him. He heard the deadbolts move and the door swung open just wide enough to pass a package through the doorway.

Persky dropped his shoulder and rammed it bull-like into the door, slamming it hard into a dazed blonde girl wearing only a sleeper size tee-shirt. Persky slapped her twice across the face, grabbed her by the throat and drove her past the kitchen into a living room made up as a bedroom. She started to scream, and he punched her in the solar plexus, dropping her to the floor, gasping for breath.

"Where is it?" he asked calmly.

She didn't answer.

He smacked her hard across the face.

"Where is it?"

She still said nothing.

"I don't think she can breathe yet," said Bodine.

He hit her again. "Shut the fuck up and tear that kitchen apart. It could be in there."

He hit her again. "Where is it?"

"I don't know what you're talking about!" she cried.

"The package that was delivered here for Carlucci."

"I don't have any packages for him."

He grabbed her by her hair, yanked back her head, pulled a snub-nose revolver out of his jacket pocket, and stuck it snug against her eye.

"Where is the package?"

She screamed, "*GUN.*"

Persky paused, not sure what to make of her reaction. That's when he heard someone moving behind a door he'd not noticed on the far side of the room.

"Who's in there?"

"It's my roommate's room."

"Bitch." He pulled the gun away from her eye and cracked it across her skull, knocking her unconscious.

"We've got more company to deal with," he barked to Bodine.

Persky stepped toward the closed door, gun in hand. He turned the knob, but it was locked. Unlike the metal front door, this was a simple hollow-core door, easily opened by a quick kick just below the doorknob.

"Open up, sweetie. It's your turn to answer questions."

Persky lifted his foot and kicked, sending the door crashing open with a loud CRACK . . . immediately followed by a rapid series of higher-pitched cracks coming at him from the room.

Seconds later came the boom of a slamming front door as Bodine fled the apartment—and whoever had just ended Persky's quest for his treasure.

TWENTY-ONE

"Mr. Michael, it's Gabriel calling for you," came through on the intercom at Michael's desk.

"Thank you, Mrs. Baker."

Michael picked up the phone. "It's a bit of a surprise hearing from you so late in the day. Did I forget something at the diner this morning?"

"No, but you missed the excitement."

"Gee cooked up a new national dish?"

"Remember those detectives who came in for breakfast?"

"Yeah. What about them?"

"They hung around for quite a while after you left, then all of a sudden jumped up and ran off. My detective friend came back later and apologized for running out without paying. He said a murder had just gone down in the neighborhood, and they were closest to the scene."

"Did he tell you who got killed?"

"A criminal bigshot, and that had the Mayor worried about a gang war. He said it's been all-hands-on deck since the call came in." Gabriel paused.

"Why do I sense you want me to ask who the victim was?"

"Victor Persky."

"Why am I not surprised?"

"It gets better. He was killed in Carlucci's apartment. The place where Maria and Angel lived."

"How did he die?"

"Someone emptied an automatic into him."

"Traditional."

"What's not is the gun. It was registered to Persky."

"You mean he was killed with his own gun?"

"Two guns registered to him were involved in the shooting. One in his hand and another found near his body. The second gun is what did him in, wiped clean of fingerprints. Three other guns were found in the apartment, all unregistered and unfired."

"A regular armory."

"Not surprisingly, neighbors claim to have seen nothing and have no idea who lived in the apartment. By the time the cops arrived, anyone who did live there had packed up and fled."

"I can't blame them, what with the number of corpses turning up in that apartment of late."

"That's sort of what my buddy had to say."

"So, he doesn't see them as suspects?"

"Correct."

"That must be a downer for him: bodies keep turning up in the same apartment and zero suspects."

"To the contrary, he sees what happened in the apartment today as solving both the Persky and Carlucci murders."

"How's he figure that?"

"From what he learned from another friend of yours. Anthony Bodine."

"What's Bodine got to do with this?"

"The crime lab treated this as priority one, and they picked up his fingerprints all over the apartment's kitchen."

"What was Bodine doing there?"

"He told the cops that Persky asked him to come along to pick up a package that belonged to him, but he never told Bodine what was in the package. When they got to the apartment, a blonde woman opened the door to let them in, and Persky told Bodine to search the kitchen for the package. He never went beyond the kitchen and was in there when he heard the shots. As soon as he did, he ran out of the apartment and had no idea what had happened to Persky."

"Sounds like Persky picked the wrong guy to back him up. I'm surprised your buddy isn't looking at Bodine as a prime suspect."

"As I said, he thinks he's already solved everything, and Bodine's not the killer. He's convinced that the package Persky was after contained drugs. He figures Carlucci was killed by someone looking to steal drugs he'd been holding for Persky, but the killer never found them. When Persky went to the apartment looking for his package, he didn't expect anyone to be there. That's why he brought Bodine along—to help him search for his package. Instead of his usual muscle."

"Interesting logic, but I wonder if his bodyguard will support that story."

"He's nowhere to be found. He'd been in a hospital, but when word reached him that his boss had been killed, he checked himself out and took off for parts unknown."

"That rats-leaving-a-sinking-ship touch adds to the drama. What does your friend make of the missing woman from the apartment?"

"Nothing. He thinks Bodine made up that part in order to avoid a burglary charge. There was no blonde woman."

"Then how did they get inside the apartment?"

Gabriel cleared his throat. "With the keys they found in Persky's pants pocket."

"With the *what?*"

"You heard me. *Keys*. With all the guns in the place, the police are writing it off as a dispute among drug dealers, and the only victims being combatants, not innocents, no one cares who died or who killed them. The Mayor and everyone in the department are happy, especially my buddy. He gets to clear two high-profile murders off his desk in one day and may even get a promotion. Their only worry is that more gang violence could follow."

"Amazing how the detecting mind works."

"I think *amazing* pretty much describes everything that's gone on over the past twenty-four hours." Gabriel paused. "Now, why don't you tell me what really happened."

"What do you mean?"

"Remember that package you mentioned to me this morning? Well I—"

"Ah yes, I remember. Why don't you stop by later so we can discuss it."

"Fine, I'll see you in a bit."

"Looking forward to it," said Michael.

"I'm sure."

Mrs. Baker opened the front door and stared at Gabriel. "I'm starting to long for the good old days when all Mr. Michael did was sit in his study and stare out at the Park."

"What has you in such a good mood?" said Gabriel, stepping inside.

"Back then, a person could get to sleep at a decent hour in this house."

"Huh?"

"Look at the hour . . . and the evening's just getting started." She waved him toward the parlor. "Just go on in."

Gabriel heard two voices coming from the parlor.

"Ah, perfect timing," said Michael, motioning for Gabriel to sit in a chair beside him. Across from them sat a young man on a sofa. "I believe you know Daniel Rudolph."

"Of course," said Gabriel, his face showing obvious surprise.

"I invited Daniel to join us, because I thought he'd be the best person to answer the questions you raised in our conversation earlier this evening. At least I hope he'll be able to do that."

Daniel bit at his lower lip.

"Before you arrived, I was telling Daniel he could trust your discretion completely, and not to hold back on anything he might want to say." Michael cleared his throat. "So . . . I got Daniel involved as soon as I realized the two girls living in his sister's old apartment would soon be in grave danger from Persky. I asked Daniel to go there, convince them they were in danger, get them to move out immediately, and give them some money from me to relocate."

Mrs. Baker stuck her head in the doorway. "Would anyone like something to drink? Coffee or tea?"

"No, thank you," said Michael. "Daniel, why don't you pick up from there."

"The brunette recognized me, and I was able to convince her to leave right away. But the blonde wouldn't listen. She was a prisoner to her drug addiction, too afraid to change her routine, even for the money." He looked down at his hands. "She reminded me of Maria. I couldn't leave her alone. Not while knowing someone might kill her if I did. Like they did to my sister. I told her I'd be crashing in the brunette's room for a couple of days. She said she didn't care as long as I didn't bother her."

He leaned forward on the sofa. "When you called me last night to get rid of the guns and told me you thought a break-in by bad guys could happen at any moment, I told her not to let anyone into the apartment. But I didn't have a lot of faith in her remembering that. So, I also told her that if she ever felt her life was in danger to yell out, *Gun!* I figured that was simple enough for her to handle."

Daniel stretched his neck from side to side. "First thing this morning I left the apartment, picked up your package at the diner, and came straight back to the apartment. She was out cold, so I went back to my room and locked the door—just in case she woke up while I was asleep and decided to snoop around my room . . . I didn't want her finding the package."

"Go on," Michael said.

Daniel exhaled deeply. "I woke up when I heard her yelling, but she yelled a lot, so I wasn't startled. Then I heard her scream *Gun!* and I jumped out of bed and grabbed a gun from the package. Next thing I know, some guy with a gun in his hand kicks in the bedroom door, and so I shot him."

"A wise decision," said Michael.

Daniel gave a half-hearted nod. "After I brought the girl around from a nasty crack on her head, I told her to grab her things; she no longer had the option of staying there. I gave her your money, took her to the bus station, and sent her back to her hometown."

"With everything happening so quickly, I'm surprised you remembered to wipe your fingerprints off the gun and leave it next to the body," said Michael.

"I didn't wipe the gun."

"Then why weren't there any prints on it?" said Gabriel.

Daniel gave a slight smile. "I wore nitrile gloves the whole time I was in the apartment. I figured if anything went wrong, I didn't want my prints hanging around."

"What about the other guns in the package you picked up from Gabriel?"

"I'd never touched them, and since you'd told me they were clean, I left them there but took the packaging with me."

Gabriel smiled. "You're one savvy guy."

"For sure," said Michael. "And I'm willing to bet your savviest move was the one you made with the keys. It was you, wasn't it, who put them in Persky's pants pocket?"

Daniel shrugged. "I figured it might confuse the police if they thought he had keys to the apartment. So, I gave him the ones I'd found in my sister's personal effects. I had no further use for them."

"Your gamble seems to have paid off," said Gabriel. "The police are calling it a battle over drugs and have no interest in taking it any further."

Daniel shut his eyes and leaned back against the sofa. "That's a relief. I couldn't take much more of this drama." He opened his eyes. "I can't wait to get back to the predictably chaotic life of an EMT."

Michael smiled as he reached into his jacket pocket and pulled out an envelope. "Here, this is for you. To help ease you back into that life and make up for the shifts you missed."

"You don't need to do that," said Daniel.

"I know I don't *need* to, but I want to. Now take it and head on home. You need some rest."

Daniel stood and shook Michael's hand. "Thank you, sir. For everything."

"You're welcome." As Daniel walked toward the front door Michael yelled, "And stay in touch."

"Nice kid," said Gabriel

"He is." Michael looked over at Gabriel. "So, have all your questions been answered?"

"No."

"OK, what are they?"

"Did you know when Persky showed up at the apartment, Daniel would be there to kill him?"

"Absolutely not. The plan was for Daniel to get the girls out of the apartment long before Persky ever got close to it. I wanted Persky to ransack the place to his heart's content. That way, when an anonymous tip later came into your detective buddy that Carlucci had hidden away something of immense value in the basement of his apartment building, Persky would only have himself to blame for not finding it."

"And how were you planning on obtaining that treasure?"

Michael looked at his watch. "From the pair due here just about now."

Right on cue, the doorbell rang.

"I've about had it with this parade of midnight visitors," mumbled Mrs. Baker, heading through the foyer toward the front door.

She opened the door. "Why, Doctors Fielding, how nice of you to stop by. Please, the rest of the crew's waiting for you in the parlor."

Brackett and Marilena exchanged puzzled glances but smiled at Mrs. Baker and walked toward the parlor.

"Please don't mind Mrs. B," said Michael. "It's been a long day for us all. Come, please sit on the sofa." Michael waited until they sat. "First things first. How are you feeling, Marilena?"

"Still a bit shaken up, but the wig and the judicious use of an eyebrow pencil make me feel more presentable to the world."

Michael smiled, "To me you look great, and I think what we have to tell you will make you feel even better. It's very good news."

"Well, that's a relief," said Brackett. "When you called and told us to be here at midnight, we didn't know what to think."

"Well, things didn't work out quite as we expected, but I think it's fair to say they ended up even better for you than I hoped."

Marilena reached across the sofa to squeeze her brother's hand. "See, I told you to trust him."

Brackett nodded. "Yes, you did."

"I'll put it to you straight. Earlier today, Persky was shot and killed in a manner the police believe closes out both his murder and that of Carlucci."

Brackett jerked forward on the sofa. "Are you serious?"

"I know it's a surprise, but yes. It's all true."

"Then we're in the clear," said Brackett, turning with a big smile toward Marilena.

Marilena smiled back and sank back in the couch with relief.

"And now no one alive but us knows what we have," said Brackett.

Marilena's smile faded. "What are you saying?"

"I'm saying we can sell it without worrying about Persky any longer."

"But it still doesn't belong to us."

"We still can sell it."

"I thought we'd agreed that the item would be returned to its rightful owner," said Michael brusquely.

"No one knows who that is," said Brackett. "For millennia, its ownership has been determined solely by the level of guile and brutality a possessor was willing to use to keep it. With Persky out of the picture, we can sell it openly and be rich beyond our wildest dreams."

Three stunned faces stared back at him.

"Don't misunderstand me, folks. I don't mean just Marilena and me. I mean the four of us. Equal shares. After all, we wouldn't be here without what you've done for us."

Michael relaxed. "Well, I'm pleased to see that you haven't had a complete reversion to your previous style of thinking. But I'm sorry to say I cannot accept your kind offer. Temptation comes in many forms, and I prefer to pass on this one. That's not to be judgmental, I'm speaking only for myself, and I leave it to you all to decide how to handle it."

"I'm not interested either," said Gabriel.

Marilena stared at her brother. "I have a suggestion. Allow me to dispose of it as I see fit. I can assure you I will not do so cavalierly and will take into account all your fantasies of how life might be if you profited from its sale."

"Are all of you crazy," asked Brackett. "Do you realize the amount of money you're walking away from? It's insane."

Marilena looked him straight in the eye and did not blink. "Brother, I think it's long past the time you began to trust me."

Brackett looked away, then down to his clasped hands. In a much calmer voice he said, "Crazy, absolutely crazy." He shut his eyes and dropped his head back against the sofa. "OK . . . if you say so."

"I promise you won't be disappointed." She leaned over and kissed her brother on the cheek.

"And so, the saga continues," mused Michael.

How quickly spring and summer passed. The leaves had served their time and now waited to drop, to gather in swirls among their fallen mates at the feet of the benches. Perhaps a passing breeze would scatter them to another place never seen or imagined.

Michael liked that thought. A bit overdone perhaps, but it summed up his feelings as he stood by his study window looking out upon the Park, pondering what will bloom there next, and what shall be their fate.

I'm not a gardener, so I shan't interfere.

That thought rang familiar to him: a vow not to get involved with what he saw seeking nurture in the Park. He'd ignored that covenant once and four lives had changed, perhaps twice that number . . . or even more.

Michael glanced at a newspaper headline atop his desk and wondered how Marilena and Brackett would fare on the heady course they'd charted for themselves; one that had captured the curiosity of the world.

Who Are the Fieldings?

(Reuters)—That's a question everyone seems to be asking these days. This brother and sister duo blazed on to the worldwide cultural scene with their Brackett and Marilena Fielding Endowment for the Arts Foundation. It is among the largest foundations of its sort in the world, annually awarding one hundred percent of its net income toward the betterment of art, music, theatre, and literature. Their generosity has instantaneously elevated the pair into the upper echelon of international powers and influencers in the arts.

The Fieldings have also sent the popular press into overdrive, seeking to tease out the story behind their sudden wealth. All that is known is that the Fieldings funded their foundation with the proceeds from a record-breaking private auction price obtained for a yet to be publicly revealed near-mythical treasure believed lost to the world millennia ago, on terms that left them blameless to the buyer for any competing claims to its rightful ownership.

Up until now, the Fieldings have refused to discuss what they know of the provenance of the treasure other than in a brief statement from Marilena Fielding: "The treasure upon which our foundation is built is steeped in tales of pain and misfortune befalling those who possessed or sought to possess it. It is our hope that the price paid by its current owner will enable our Foundation to redeem the treasure's rightful historical position as a new source of joy, hope, and betterment for our world."

Today, the Fieldings announced they will appear this evening on public television to identify to the world what has come to be called the Fielding Treasure.

Michael had to admit Marilena had come up with a brilliant strategy for bringing glory to the Fielding name and gaining her brother the recognition he craved. He only hoped the two of them could live with all else that comes with great fame.

As for the others, so far so good.

At Marilena's urging, Angel was awarded the initial Fielding Foundation Student Fellowship, putting her firmly on the road toward achieving the better life her parents had promised would someday be hers.

Brackett surprised everyone in naming Gabriel's diner as the official caterer for all Foundation local events. The new business had Gabriel going crazy gearing up to handle it, but Michael had no doubt he'd make it happen. After all, he was his father's son . . . and Michael's godson.

Those four souls, whose imagined lives Michael had followed from his window, gained newfound hope and direction through Michael's real-life interventions. But such meddling was never his intention. He wanted no more reality and cared not to know what the Fielding Treasure might be.

He'd long considered his window an impenetrable barrier between the imagined and reality. One that allowed him to see life as he wanted it to be, not as it had become. To imagine life left him free to be fearless and forever hopeful. Facing reality meant confrontation, sacrifice, and risk to all he held dear.

But his window had failed him.

Before it did so again, he should shutter it.

Perhaps tomorrow.